ODE TO LATA

GHALIB SHIRAZ DHALLA

A NOVEL

10th ANNIVERSARY EDITION

FWB

Final Word Books
Los Angeles, CA

Library of Congress cataloging-In-Publication Data available.

First Trade Paperback Edition 2012

Cover by: Chris Rucker, www.createruckus.com
Photo by: Ghalib Shiraz Dhalla

ISBN: 978-0615702759

Printed in the United States of America.

Bonus short story, *A* follows at the end of this book.

FOR PARVIZ

ACKNOWLEDGEMENTS

Special thanks to Victor Riobo,
Israel Velasquez, Deborah Ritchken and Nina Wiener;
and, of course, to Lata for the inspiration.

Gone, inner and outer,
no moon, no ground or sky.
Don't hand me another glass of wine.
Pour it in my mouth.
I've lost the way to it.

–RUMI

CHAPTER 1

THE SNAKE

There are only two things in life worth living for; passion and truth. Passion came to me in plenty, but the truth it seems, eludes me still.

I'm driving down the Los Angeles snake, this creature upon whose curvature our lives have been unwittingly trapped, trudging along at twenty miles per hour in a sea of cars. It's 7:59 and I'm afraid that I will miss the first half of *Melrose Place*. That is all that concerns me at this moment. That my auxiliary family of vixens, faithless men and a token gay man, will move on and deprive me of the vicarious pleasure of their lives, leaving me mired in my own.

The night before had been the search for the bed of yet another stranger's bed to wake in; the morning the start of another mechanically meaningless day and my insatiable hunger for Richard.

On the radio the news reports of another drive-by shooting, and then of the massacre of two young men – a possible hate crime. I switch the station to some dance music and revert to modern man's shield against the tyranny of the city: apathy. Too depressing. It doesn't concern me. It's not my problem. I have my own to worry about. Reality has grown so harsh, so unforgiving, that paradoxically, only the mundane, the absolutely frivolous is able to elicit any concern anymore. I don't want to know how the disgruntled, bi-polar man managed to buy a gun, or why he stormed the offices and sprayed his now disowned family of ex-co-workers with bullets; I only want to know if Amanda will get promoted at the agency and if that psychotic Sidney will manage to seduce the young buck dating her sister.

I gaze at the American flag hoisted up the pole of a building just off the freeway as I grudgingly bring the car to a standstill again. The image of the Kenyan flag with its brilliant red and green colors flashes through my mind and the traces of a smile tease the premature gauntness of my face. I think about all that the American flag in front of me has meant to people everywhere. What it had meant to me. Its impregnable promise of benevolence.

It occurs to me that this flag was very much like those three-dimensional prints that everybody gazes at in the malls these days. Squinting, waiting, hoping for a vision to appear. It was only when the tentativeness gave way and you were pulled into its panoramic window that your heart began to sink, and the mesmerizing specks of color integrate to reveal an unexpected aftermath.

I remember first seeing that flag up-close eight years ago. I must have been on the fifteenth floor of a building in Kenya that housed the American embassy, applying for my visas. My mother sat close to me, half dreading the impending departure of her only son – barely a man, still her boy – and I, quite insensitive in my exhilaration, sat transfixed at the sight from a window in the lobby. It flapped authoritatively in the wind, imbuing me with such hope that I felt as if I were already there.

It was a moment my entire life had been leading up to. The beginning of a new life of adventure and possibility that Kenya could never offer me. A place with people I had never met, far away from those whom I had known. The excitement of forging an identity independent of them overruled any trace of sentimentality. I would miss them all, but who cares, right? Soon they'd all talk about me. The one who got away. Someone would undoubtedly start a rumor about how I'd become this big star living in a flashy apartment and driving an expensive car in L.A. and boy, would they roll those two initials when speaking! EEI-LAY! With a thrust of the hand, that gesture that looks like a pigeon released into the air, a sign of deep mysteries and awe. Of course they would never know for sure, but the touristic postcards I would send home – and the Indian capacity for exaggeration – would assure my fame and glamour. It was all waiting there for me, this unconfined life, and the door was about to open and let me in.

I look at that flag now, and suddenly it's not all so simple. Hollywood Boulevard is not adorned with stars as much as it is littered by hookers and pushers who contrast the memorable sidewalks with their own agitated lives. Beverly Hills serves as little more than a foil to the barrios of East L.A. Downtown looks pretty only from a distance at night, engulfed by the darkness that cloaks its destitute, the lights of office buildings gaping like empty, hollow eyes at marveling tourists. The Los Angeles of Jackie Collins novels, which I had devoured as rudimentary to my introduction to the city, is nowhere to be found but in the pockets of a privileged few.

Now, I'm no longer a spectator gazing at the print. I've leapt into its dimension and I'm one of those little colored specks that constitute the big picture. It stands there, stealing some of the light from the bright Arco gas station sign behind it, brandishing itself petulantly in the wind, flapping and employing its most critical acting talent to appear immaculate in the putrid L.A. smog.

Hell, in this city everyone needs a good publicist.

CHAPTER 2

IMMACULATE CONCEPTION

Whenever she had the choice, my mother preferred taking the train over the arduous six-hour bus ride, or even the elite hour-long commuter flight from Mombasa to the capital city of Nairobi.

The East Africa Railway, engineered by the British in 1896 and largely built by immigrant Indians, was responsible for the exodus that brought my ancestors to Kenya. It represents, even now, the romanticism of colonialism – a different type of mechanical snake, one that undulated through the verdant land its creators once tried, albeit in vain, to tame. As the seductive plains opened like thighs, Africa enveloped us in her limbs. Years from then, in another corner of the world, even a faint smell, a flash of sight, a distant sound would send a chill of nostalgia up some part of my body, and for a split second, standing in a crowded mall or in the elevator of some skyscraper, I felt as if I was back there; that it had somehow, miraculously, projected itself onto my realm.

I had found freedom in geography only to be forever captured by the memories of the home I left behind. In my dreams, I still ride the railway. Listen to all the sounds and senses that are Kenya: Swahili songs from village women clad in colorful and light cotton batiks, delicately balancing baskets of fruits and vegetables on their heads; urchins and villagers who keep pace with the train, awaiting the arrival of fresh customers at stations to buy their hardboiled eggs, biscuits and roasted maize pressed with lemons and chilies; at dawn, the animals of the land respond to our exhilaration with pure indifference; and upon arrival, the chaotic sounds of reunions, departures and coolies who compete to ferry our luggage to the car. And always that smell, that distinct perfume of Kenya, a smell of salt as the breeze comes off the ocean, of food cooking on wood fires and mingling with diesel smoke, of the sweat of hard labor everywhere.

As we chugged along such a journey, my mother could always be counted on to tell me two things. That it was on such a ride one balmy evening, albeit in the reverse direction, that I had been conceived, a story that increased in detail and waned in credibility with each rendition.

"You know," she said, her eyes widening and one hand flipping up to express amazement. "We never even had, you know, proper intercourse!"

She maintained that on that life-altering night simple peripheral contact had impregnated her, lending an almost mythic prowess to my parents' virility and a sense of destiny to my close-to-immaculate conception.

"Your father and I – all we had to do was touch each other and I would become pregnant!"

Contrary to expectation, such details never made me feel even faintly uncomfortable. Rather, they served to inspire me in finding such a marvelous love story of my own.

Perhaps the memory of their lovemaking that night is why melancholy would unfailingly seize her at certain points of the journey and she could be found staring out the window at the fleeting land, her tongue struck silent in her mouth; as if she was, years after my father's demise, reliving that very experience in the same compartment. It was the same look that came upon her when, listening to an old cassette of *filmi* music on what we called an impressive three-in-one (radio, tape and record player), a song that my father had loved would unexpectedly play. At these moments, it was enough just to look at her and know that so much of her innocence, her idealism of love, her zeal for life (a part of herself) had also died with him. At these moments, she was completely lost to the world that had carried on without his existence, and she could not fathom why.

The other thing she liked to tell me, which only worked when I was a child, was that if I didn't obey her by finishing everything on my plate, the two legendary man-eating lions that had killed over a hundred people during the construction of the great railway would tear in through the compartment's formidable window and gobble me up instead. I was a scrawny child, and she blamed me for making her look bad since all her in-laws had to do was take one look at me and accuse her of starvation. "There," she said, one hand hoisted up to my mouth with a hillock of rice and the other pointing out to the impenetrable darkness beyond the window, "I think I see them right now."

CHAPTER 3

DANCE OF THE BLIND

Heaven dispels its hordes of drunken angels.

Outside West Hollywood's trendy nightclub, buff bodies and their devotees spill out onto the street like wingless creatures, disoriented from the closure of these pearly gates. Indignant cries rise up to the heavens. No one, no matter how long they've lived in this city, can get used to the fact that the elixirs of rum and vodka stop flowing at 2 A.M. At this hour, even the city's ardent loyalists threaten to move to its nemesis, New York. Others throw nettled glances at the lamenters, their hands confirming little plastic bags, vials, bullets – alternative inspiration – in their jean pockets. They negotiate urgently through the crowd to the next destination, filled with something akin to a patronizing sympathy for the poor souls who haven't progressed to ecstasy or GHB or Special K or some other animal tranquilizer delivering nightclub nirvana.

Adrian's arm is hooked into mine and we don't so much walk as sway out in the tide of men. He asks me how I'm feeling.

"Just like Dorothy Parker, darling," I drawl. "Just like Mrs. Parker."

Pleased with my metamorphosis, Adrian guides my hand to a bulge in his leather jacket and throws me a conspiratorial look. He's smuggled out a bottle of booze. I hope it's Bacardi with that regal bat, posed spread-eagled – quite the way one feels after a few – on the label. He probably hung around inconspicuously while the bartender boxed up his supplies and nabbed whatever he could reach. We laugh and Salman, now hanging heavily on our shoulders and propelling us dangerously into the crowd, asks us what the hell is going on and then without waiting for an answer, bursts into a Hindi film song –

something campy that a vamp like Helen or Bindu would have enacted in some B-grade Bollywood film, nothing quite as tragic as the stuff that would appeal to me. Not something by Lata. Now, one thing about Salman is that he has no voice, a fault only made worse by his disregard for his limitations and insistence on volume. We ask him to shut up but he's annoyed I won't sing along.

"Come on, sing *na?* Forget those melancholy Lata songs, *yaar*," he says. "It's time for some – '*Dam maro dam, mit jaye gaam...*'"

We affix ourselves into a spot where we can stand still while others mill around us. In the flurry of activity, a strange calm, one not unlikely between kindred spirits, pervades Adrian and me. I have found some reprieve even if I haven't managed to find Richard tonight. Adrian, one hand still holding the bottle securely under his leather jacket, pulls me down to him with the other, and I rest my head on his shoulder while Salman unleashes a medley of other *filmi* hits. He has turned his back to us and is now assaulting the poor Mexican man selling hot dogs on the boulevard with his impromptu performance. As the vendor tosses links and sautés peppers and onions on his mobile grill (the mélange creating a strangely repugnant yet appetite inducing aroma) he looks somewhat bewildered at being singled out for Salman's attentions. This could be keeping customers away.

I can't hear Salman anymore, and I'm quite sure Adrian can't either. Dusky horns blow in my mind. And Lata, that ethereal voice from every Hindi film I've beheld as a child, chimes in. I am content in this state if not happy. With my body slumped against Adrian's, we must look like lovers. The kind that through years of reinvention, long after the rush of new love has quelled, have found an almost platonic way to stay together, something made visible by a shared sense of style and demeanor. Many have even asked us if we are a couple, but Adrian always relegates the answer to me, like someone uncertain of the mood-driven response – usually "no, just friends" or, at times when we're feeling more mischievous, "yes, but only on rainy nights." We look like the best of lovers precisely because we aren't. Romantic love is savage, vengeful, demanding, rarely the foundation for the kind of calm one mistakes for a lover's relationship.

With Adrian's heartbeat in my ear, I envision Richard's painfully beautiful face during the siesta where I synchronized my breath with his so that our bodies would rise and dip with graceful alternation, our hearts beating in unison. The frenzy that flared in me only hours earlier, one which sent me goring through the club with no regard for my friends or potential lovers, has been sedated by the administrations of my favorite bartender and Adrian's pacifying breast.

An argument erupts behind us. We turn around to find Salman being hollered at by an Asian queen in conspicuous, black latex pants. His intoxication coupled with the incommodious surroundings has caused him to step one too many times on her highness' toes, and she's not having any more of it! Far be it from Salman to apologize to her. After a few drinks forced down his throat, he turns into the nemesis of his former, typical sober personality – the perennially apologetic, martyred son of an ultra-conservative Ismaili family. Salman tells her that is *she* who should apologize for subjecting the rest of us to the hideous Hefty trash bag she has the audacity to parade herself in!

"Listen, you bitch," hisses the queen, hands on hips. "These pants cost five hundred dollars, more money than you've probably ever seen in your pathetic little drunk life!" Her faithful coterie of handmaidens nod vehemently, especially the tall, sassy black one with braided hair who attitudinizes by tossing her head around and garnishes him with a "Yeah, you go sista.' You tell her!"

But Salman is already laughing uncontrollably at his next line and asks, "What? All of your life savings so your ass can look more like your face?"

I yank Salman back, irritated for being beckoned out of my languorous spell. "Okay, break it up. Salman, come on, we don't need this right now."

"Yeah, you'd better take that trash away before she gets hurt," says the queen.

I raise a preemptive hand up to her, asking her to hold back while wedging myself between them but Salman peers over me. "Honey, even trash gets picked up once a week. What's your excuse? You've even dressed the part!"

The growling queen lunges forward and her body collides against mine as I try to hold her back. Her talons claw the air, reaching for Salman who is being expedited through the crowd by a reprimanding Adrian, still unable to suppress Salman's hysteria.

"Just let it go, let it go, man," I say. "He's drunk, don't pay any attention to him."

She backs down grudgingly, still spitting out threats, encircled by her entourage. The ritual display of witty comebacks and catty remarks checked; fully clawed catfight adverted.

I start to walk away when I hear her cackle, "Fucking Ghandhis. Who let them out of the 7-Elevens tonight?"

I stop dead in my tracks and slowly turn back around. "What did you say?" I ask her.

"You talkin' to me?" she says. "You talkin' to me?" She glances back at her friends for quick endorsements, and they 'ooh' and 'aah' supportively. "I *know* you ain't talkin' to *me*."

"You wanna repeat what you said? Huh?"

"Just fucking get lost, okay?" She turns her back, dismissing me.

I want to thrash her face and I tense up. The adrenaline pumps through my veins like a drug and I am shaking so hard, it makes me feel strangely weak. "You stupid little cunt," I say. "Who the hell do think you are? We may own all the convenience stores in the city but at least we're not out on the rice paddies like your peasant family and eating dogs for dinner!"

"Just get out of my fucking face, okay, Apu? Go whip up a Slurpee or something."

She's done it. Two things you should never mention around me – or any Indian for that matter – 7-Elevens and "a large Slurpee, please!"

I grab her by the slinky top she's wearing – something she no doubt designed herself – and yank her up to me. But I should have guessed the bitch had mastered some form of martial art because no sooner have I opened my mouth to deliver some threat than I'm being hurled back and end up landing on some horrified bystanders. There's blood dripping off my chin and I don't know where it's coming from. Salman and Adrian, who apparently haven't managed to get far enough, rush back to help me to my feet.

"Oh, my God! What the hell has she done?!" Adrian says, whipping his shirt off and dabbing my chin. "Are you alright?"

"I'm so sorry...I'm so sorry," Salman says, sobering up.

People are holding the queen back and *she's* wailing! Imagine! I'm the one bleeding but *she's* the one rapt in a relentless dirge.

Adrian and Salman have located the cut on my brow and dab the bleeding. And when they least expect it, I break away and lunge back at towards the queen, managing to penetrate through her army of friends to deliver what is possibly the most degrading blow to someone of her persuasion: I've yanked out a handful of her hair, and she shrieks like her peasant family has just been massacred outside of Heaven.

"Oh God, my hair! My hair!"

Adrian picks me up off the floor and starts to drag me away just as the security guard appears, like a delayed superhero. He pauses to inspect my face quickly, lifting it up by the chin while Adrian props me up like a pole. The guard has become a kind of parental figure since the first time I tried to enter Heaven with a fake ID years ago; he has given me the kind but disapproving *you're up to no good, as usual* look ever since.

"Get him outta here," he says and moves on to the queen who has collapsed on the ground and is swearing "war."

We drive to the supermarket around the block, and now I'm victimized by two nurses whose true callings were never realized. Hydrogen Peroxide, cotton balls and Band-Aids galore. It's as if my head has been split open by an axe with all this fuss being made about it.

"Maybe he needs stitches!"

"Stitches?" I say. "Are you crazy!"

"Stitches," agrees Adrian. "Yeah, you may be right, Salman."

"No, I don't need any fucking stitches! I need sex! Just let me go! It's two in the morning. I should have my legs up in the air instead of being fussed over by you two!"

We settle for the Band-Aid, and now Salman starts in with the guilt. He blames himself for drinking in the first place and progresses into a fest about everything from overeating to dancing with some stranger he ended up kissing to ever having known the joys of gay sex. What all this has to do with his fixation on that queen's plastic pants a little while ago beats me.

But it is always that way with him. Never enjoy yourself too much without feeling remorseful about it right after. Penance was always an important part of the pleasure partaken. A true Indian, after all. What was a responsible boy like him, one from such a renowned and respectable Ismaili family doing drinking, dancing and kissing some black man in West Hollywood instead of pursuing some nice Ismaili girl around the mosque compound?

"Oh shut up, Salman," I say. "What we need is to get laid." Going home is no longer an option. Was it ever? We head for a sex club up by Highland to salvage the night.

It's three in the morning – that midwife between what could still possibly turn out to be a night of passion from chance meetings and the frustration of not being able to drink anymore. This is the hour during which, if you weren't prudent enough to carry a bottle of Bacardi in the trunk or sophisticated enough to be high on X, you are entertaining the idea of stealing a bottle from the grocery store. And you're still drunk enough to believe you can pull it off too. Unless someone's arms embrace you soon, unless flesh finds itself welded with flesh – or at least another drop of liquor smoldered its way down your throat – you feel as if your world will come crashing down.

The line to get into The Vortex is going out the door. New members are taking so long to get registered, you're turning from a nymphomaniac into a psychotic. *Come on, come on! Hurry up, for Chrissake!* Although you want desperately to push past them, you inhale deeply and try to calm yourself.

As always, there is *that* someone who's forgotten his membership card and another whose membership has expired and is wondering how that can be possible and if he can pay by MasterCard (all the while pulling out these little promotional fliers from his pocket). As I wait, I watch others leave. They look sinister and unappealing, unlike how most of them look inside. Is that a trick of the light? Or, rather, the lack of it? Perhaps these are just the worms wriggling their way home. Your man may still be in there, and the sound of the creaking floorboards over your head may be his footsteps pacing from room to room until you find him.

The dexterity with which you swipe your card through the scanner tells you you've been there much too often, as if the familiar faces of the check-in clerks don't. There was this old, stocky, no-nonsense dyke who used to work the door, clad in a Budweiser T-shirt, and you wonder what happened to her. The last time you saw her, this drunk queen was throwing a tantrum because she wouldn't let him in without his I.D. In resignation he had walked out, pinching his nose and saying, "Stupid old rotten fish. Why don't you go back to the pond you came from?"

Once inside, you are immediately struck by the number of people anticipating new arrivals through the door. You want to go to the bathroom, but there are a million people waiting in line and someone is already grumbling about what the hell might be going on in there.

"One person at a time! Don't they read?" You hear a man complain to someone standing behind who simply shrugs, clearly embarrassed by the theatrics.

You decide to come back after a walk, so you join the dance of the whirling dervishes around the dark rooms and corners, which have ceased to be a mystery anymore.

Frantic at first, you calm down after making a few rounds. Oddly enough, you hear the strains of a Hindi film song in your mind as you walk. Some song that film star Rekha sang as a courtesan in *Umrao Jaan*. *Yeh kya jage hain, doston. Yeh kaun sa dayaar hain*...Christ, of all the things that should be going through your mind! Strange phenomenon, but even Salman has admitted to singing some classic *filmi* songs to himself while wandering through the labyrinth on his own. You wonder if this is a South Asian thing. A way of steadying yourself, as you swagger through this lair of carnality. You want to hold on to something culturally rooted as you stumble your way through the uncertainties of rampant salacity. Or maybe you're just feeling tragic again. Aware with much regret that despite all of your apparent potential, you are still here in *this* place. Dateless. Nothing but an empty bed waiting for you at home. Apparently all the blessings and prayers from Mummy have come to no avail.

Up the staircase you go. Into a musty room. Doing this dance of the blind. Not quite able to see. Not really wanting to either. Only touching and feeling. Limbs. Hair. Mouths. Tongues. Fingers. Cocks.

Someone brushes your hand rudely off them. You feel momentarily startled. As if you've just been slapped across your face. Broken from the erotic spell you were in.

He has just reminded you that even here, away from the nightclubs and mushrooming coffeehouses, rejection awaits.

How dare he? How fucking dare he? Can't he see that he cannot do this? Not *here!* This is the "blind" room tonight. The darkest one of them all. The room that most revert to when the dimly lit rooms downstairs fail to reap any interest. No picky-choosy behavior here. Press up. Feel up. Leave your selective behavior at the door. Or at the nightclub you came from. Here we are only to yield and derive pleasures. Indiscriminately. Unflinchingly.

This kind of behavior is unacceptable here. Just a little squeeze on the probing fingers. A pat on the hand before gently pushing your hand aside would be sufficient. Anybody who persisted after *that* deserved what they got. But not *before* that, you asshole. Not before that. Why be so rude?

Your expulsion agitates you enough to want to find the manager and get the s.o.b. kicked out. *You know, some asshole up there is being really obnoxious! I mean, he's just like, rudely pushing people away and I think he's going to start some trouble...*Paint him up to be some repressed homosexual that's slipped in just to get ugly with others.

Maybe you could tell them you felt him trying to pick your pocket. That would really do it. Sounds less like some rejected queen. More like a conscientious faggot. That's always a problem here. Every few hours that announcement. *Watch your pockets! Pickpocket in the house!*

You just decide to let it go. There is no more alcohol, and the last thing you need is to get overexcited and blow the little high you are riding on. The next time you see him though, you vow to push him down this flight of stairs. For now you call him an asshole under your breath and go back down and into another room.

Downstairs there is a little more light, and you recognize some people from the last club. There, they had been acting conceited and too self-absorbed to entertain just anyone's advances, posing like art pieces you may look at but better not touch. Here, they are panting around like dogs in a pound, all gropes and grinds.

You attempt to walk all the way to the back of the room, gently, yet persistently pushing your way through warmth and sweat. There is a strong odor here. A stench of urine, semen, stale cologne, poppers and perspiration all mingling into one. But it's not so bad. You've smelt worse. Without even thinking, you stifle your breath and inhale spasmodically until you've gotten through the throng of people.

At the end of the room, you allow your hands to carelessly wander over the chest of someone standing against the wall. He doesn't move or seem to mind so you move closer and then up against him. Your lips search him out, and he responds with the same urgency. Although you can't see his face in the dark, you like the way his body feels. Strong and reciprocating. He will do just fine.

You ask him if he wants to fuck you.

"What?" He asks.

"Do you want to fuck me?"

"Yeah," he says. "Sure."

Even as the words left your lips, you are aware of how cold and vulgar they sound. But what you know more assuredly is that because your behavior is devoid of any bullshit, it is quite apropos. These are the only words that have been spoken with any genuineness tonight. Here, in this place, everyone has been reduced to a cock and a butt hole. Trading pleasantries is not only impractical, it's unnecessary. In the cold light of day, nothing else that two people will have confessed or revealed through the course of the night will matter.

A week down the line, when the two of them run into each other at an ATM somewhere in West Hollywood, less will be remembered. The chance that either one of them will even want to recognize each other is still more questionable.

As they say in Hindi, *Raat gayi, Baat gayi*...The night is gone, the affair is over. So you might as well get the show on the road.

You don't get to go to the bathroom, where the line is still long. The man you saw having a fit earlier is at his wit's end and is now talking to someone who works at the club, gesticulating dramatically.

You bump into Adrian and tell him that you must both leave right away. Adrian eyes the guy standing beside you and doesn't question your decision. He knows better. Salman, even in his drunken stupor, had insisted on driving separately so you don't even bother looking

for him. Besides, it would be a feat to find him buried
under someone's legs in the dark. You've considered
yourself pretty good at hunting down your friends down
at the Vortex, but Salman has challenged this gift
repeatedly.

Within minutes, you have walked out of the club
and are racing in Adrian's black Acura down Wilshire
Boulevard and into the heart of Santa Monica. On the
way, you don't look back to make sure he's following but
ask Adrian frequently if he can still see him from the
rearview mirror.

"He's keeping up, baby," Adrian assures you more
than once, his voice tinged with excitement. "He's right
behind us."

After sex, I lit up a cigarette and lay on his bare chest. I
didn't generally smoke, but at times like these it felt
glamorous and appropriate. The amber glow illuminated
his beautiful young face, and for a moment I felt caught
up in a film-noir moment. Everything was black and
white.

"You're *so* passionate," he said. "So intense!
God, what were you on?"

"Don't you mean, what *am* I on? I could still be
on it, you know."

"Oh yeah, I know," he laughed nervously.

"Well, I'm not on anything," I hissed. "Why do I
have to be on anything?"

I realized my inflection was tinged with hostility.
That the wonder in his face and the naiveté in his eyes
came from what he had been accustomed to all his life.
What most Americans knew as sex – the orgasm oriented,
routine, blow-me, jack me off, "you got some poppers?"
kind of sex. A means to an end. Not the kind of sex
where people simply fed off of one another's bodies for
hours without ever satiating the hunger that brought
them together.

Then again, did anybody else have a need for that kind of sex? Was there any point to it but to foolishly extend the torment of unfulfilled urges?

He told me that the incense that was burning reminded him of Paris, and that he loved the "classical" music playing on the stereo.

"It's a film score," I told him, suppressing the "for Chrissake" part.

"Oh, it is?"

"Yeah." I exhaled. *"Bugsy."*

"I think I saw that movie."

"Mmm," I responded, unimpressed. "So you've been to Paris?"

"Yeah, a couple of years before I joined the military."

"Did they know about you there?"

"Where? In Paris?"

Oh, God, please don't let me roll my eyes around. "In the military, of course."

"What, are you kidding?" He laughed. *"We won't ask and you don't have to tell,* remember?"

Clinton's face went through my mind. And then, absurdly, Barbra Streisand at the inaugural.

"Where are you from?" he asked.

I tensed up. *That* question again. I was unsure if he was asking me this because he was so taken with my passion or because he was just unfamiliar with South Asian men in general.

I stubbed the cigarette out on the silver condom wrapper lying at the edge of the bed and he seemed more concerned about the safety in doing so than I was. The image of him savagely tearing it open with his teeth as he mounted me flashed through my mind, and I felt a stirring in the pit of my belly again.

I could feel his eyes on me, still waiting for my reply.

Where are you from? Who are you? Where have you been?

Such a little mystery I'd become to him. Maybe he was trying to make sense of what had just transpired between us. Of how I had compelled him to give up so much of his control and inhibition.

But I remained silent. Evasive. I didn't want to answer him. Maybe it's because I didn't think it should have mattered *what* I was or *where* the hell I've come from. None of his damn business.

But maybe it's because *what* I am mattered too much to me. South Asian. Indian.

I decided to leave him unanswered. To spare myself from my shame. I rolled off him and allowed Adrian to have his turn.

In the morning we had sex again. The kind when you're drifting out of sleep and where the man you're with could easily be imagined as anybody else. Even Richard.

This time he fucked me vehemently. He was brutal in his charged determination to reclaim some of the power he had relinquished to me in the night. He cast himself over me like a punishment. For making him feel so bare while barring his understanding of me.

I felt as if I might have been drawing blood from my lower lip as I bit into it, but I didn't care because my whole body was convulsing with pain.

I looked over my shoulder to see his face over me, beads of sweat collecting on his forehead and his eyes closed in concentration. At that moment there was nothing in the world that mattered more to him than being inside me. I knew this. And nothing mattered more to me than to know that I could command this from him. It made all the pain worthwhile.

Suddenly he paused and looked down at me. "Are you alright? Jesus! I'm so sorry...I..."

I realized he'd noticed just a little bit of blood from my lips on the pillow. I shook my head as best I could. "No, no, go on. I'm alright."

"But you're bleeding..."

"Please," I implored. "Just go on. I'm fine."

"Okay. Just tell me if you want me to stop."

I rested my face back in the pillow, resenting his concern. I didn't want him to stop or to be gentle or even care if my lip was bleeding. Didn't want him to stop even if I asked. Why couldn't he just shut up and stop being so damn nice? Force me down and take whatever it is he needed to fulfill himself.

Slowly he started to move again and pressed his lips against the nape of my neck. I felt his kiss. It felt tender and suddenly I wanted to cry. *Shit! It's the last thing I want. I know I shouldn't let myself feel this way. Too dangerous. Still too soon. This is meant to be nothing more than pure, uncomplicated sex with no room for emotions or heart.* Then he started to pick up the pace, his body rhythmically slapping up against mine, the physical pain enveloping me again and me disappearing into it. The surging in my heart started to quiet down. I was shrinking into a ball. Barbed but tightly woven. Retreating as if into a womb where nothing else existed. Into profound safety. Emotional silence.

You see, this pain was so familiar. It would not disappoint. It was the only constant, in bed with him and once he was gone. I knew that when this was all over, it would be waiting for me like an unshakable friend, grimacing at my futile attempts to momentarily alienate it. But for a few moments, I had decided to embrace the pain because of its perseverance in tracking me down.

No man had tried that hard to find me. And I wondered if any man ever would.

I lay on my stomach, entwined in the soiled and crumpled sheets as he walked back into the room after taking a shower. He hovered awkwardly around my bed – just a mattress thrown over a box spring. I could sense that he was nervous and didn't quite know what to do or say because I was making no effort to turn around. I just lay there. Not looking at him. And more importantly, not letting him see me.

He mumbled something about having to drive back to Anaheim and thanked me for everything. I was curt to the point of being cruel. Adrian said something about it being a long drive. He offered his number.

"Adrian, can you just take care of it?" I slurred.

They left the room and I started to feel relieved. I knew that I had been insensitive and had probably made him feel like trash. But what was I supposed to have done? We had met in some dark corner at a sex club where he could barely have made out *what* I was. I might have even seemed Latino to him at some point. But now, with daylight intruding through the blinds, and him showered and satiated, he might have seen me for the South Asian I was. And that would have been embarrassing, wouldn't it?

All those images of 7-Eleven salesmen and heavily accented, singsong dialects would have come flooding into his mind and maybe he would have cringed. He'd realize his exotic passion flower was just the basis for a *Simpsons* character. Seen my typical South Asian features and realize that I looked nothing like him. Large, dark eyes. That long bumpy nose, thanks to a deviated septum. Skin, dark not from tanning on the beach, but from birth. And then what if he had felt cheated? Defiled?

And what about my body? How, in this culture of gym-bodies would he have felt about having had sex with someone whose body didn't look like he spent at least two hours daily in a gym. The thought that he probably didn't care about all this or that he already had a pretty good idea about it after fucking me all night hadn't even entered my mind. It was the visual that worried me.

Swathed in my sheets, now that neither the night nor his lust could have obscured me, I found solace in being ironically passionless and cold to him. Turning into a typical, cold queen just to keep him – after all this – from rejecting me first.

Was this not the curse of every South Asian whose standards of beauty were in conflict with his own appearance?

No, no, he couldn't see all this. I couldn't have let him see that I was Indian.

CHAPTER 4

THE LADDER

I can't seem to remember exactly when it all started. This shame. All I know is that it must have happened a long time ago. Long before I knew what was happening or had any control over it. Perhaps it's the result of being born in the shadows of colonialism.

Imagine growing up in a country where being white automatically meant that you were entitled to the privileges that everyone else had to struggle for.

Even the South Asians and the Africans who warred against each other with class and economic prejudices cast everything aside to act as subservient as they could when the *goras* or *dhorias* came into view. There were many of them, the white people, some of them expatriates who had had to unwillingly relinquish the luxuries of colonial, pre-independence Kenya, but had decided to stay on, others who had come back with the hope of educing anything reminiscent of their golden era.

I remember how excited my mother was at the prospect of taking me to see a *dhorio* doctor by the name of Dr. Jewel, who had his office in another very tall building in Mombasa island, all fifteen stories of it. He was by no means inexpensive and had expatriated from England, so naturally he *had* to be the best around. He would perform virtual miracles on me since his knowledge of medicine had to be superior to any colored doctor. The women in her community circle would raise their brows and drop their jaws because they would be so impressed that Parin had taken her son to none other than *the* Dr. Jewel.

"He looks *just* like our *Hazar Imam*," she would enthuse, referring to the spiritual leader of our community, and inexplicably feel more comforted by the resemblance to his accent and Caucasian appearance. Ironic as it was, even the spiritual leader believed to be the direct descendant of the Holy Prophet, the very man who most in my community regarded to be God's very incarnation on earth, looked nothing like his followers and more like the intimidating white man that commanded such awe-inspiring respect.

It was no wonder then that by the time we had ridden the elevator up those fifteen floors for me to stand in front of Dr. Jewel in my underwear with a thermometer in my mouth, both my mother and I felt as if we were standing in the presence of God himself. Moses had found the burning bush. We had found Dr. Jewel.

As *muindis* we learnt to live by certain principles. Imported was always better than local. Ready-made was always better than tailor-made because it came from abroad. A four-week vacation in London or Canada (always pronounced *Cay-nay-da*), two of the most popular travel destinations, was enough justification to come back with a ridiculously self-imposed accent so that we sounded more like them and less like ourselves. The ruling principle was, of course, that a fair complexion was always more desirable than a dark one. That was obvious from the class structure that had based itself through centuries on how light or dark-skinned you were. Even religious conversion into the Muslim faith could not completely eradicate the traces of this predominantly Hindu belief.

Remember Shehnaz, who lived in the same flats as your family? Everyone always referred to her as *masoto* or dirt-rag? Your grandmother had often mentioned to you that her family had descended from a sect of "untouchables," a lower-class people in India subjugated to serve the others. *Shehnaz masoto* they had called her. The snooty women in the community would often grimace behind her back when considering her eligibility as a daughter-in-law; but to her face, they would give one of those superficial smiles. No teeth. Just upturned lips stretched thin in an effort to be civil.

It was no wonder that mothers were constantly urging their daughters not to stay out too long in the sun from fear of turning dark. *Who will marry you if you turn as dark as coal, stupid girl?* There's a reason why Fair & Lovely and Pond's Vanishing Cream –
and not suntan lotions – were Asian bestsellers.

But most important of all, despite the alarming similarities in both races, we learnt that we were always better than the *golas* or blacks. The darker the *masoto*, the lower your class.

No question about it. Simple law of nature. An apparent hierarchy of pigmentation had been a fact of life difficult to miss. The *dhorias* were the top rung of the ladder. The *muindis* the middle. And the *golas* right at the bottom like the dirt they resembled.

CHAPTER 5

CUT THE CORD

My mother called me from Kenya. There was an echo in the connection, and she acted like she was stuck in my answering machine and was trying desperately to get out. The notion that the machine was on because I would not or could not come to the phone never entered her mind. So she continued to call out dramatically, pleading to be recognized.

"Ali, are you there? It's Mummy. If you are there, Ali, can you please pick up the phone? Ali! It's Parin! It's mummy! Ali? Ali? Are you there?"

This went on for a couple of expensive minutes until she resigned herself to the purpose of her call.

I continued to lie in bed, recuperating from a terrible hangover. I didn't feel like talking to her. Hardly ever did these days. She and all the rest of my family possessed the unique talent of driving me up the wall by repeating everything they had to say until I wanted to shut my ears and scream, *I heard you! You've said if fifty times already! Just stop bloody nagging me!*

Then naturally I'd hurt their feeling and they'd claimed I didn't give a shit about them anymore and perhaps they shouldn't have bothered to call to begin with. Enter guilt and feeling like crap.

Groaning, I covered my face with a pillow and turned away, trying to block her out. "Oh, just shut the fuck up already!"

It was as if she was able to detect this; she began to speak even more loudly so that her voice took on a surround-sound quality. I thought about yanking the telephone cord out but then she would have called back and started all over again.

She confirmed the dates for her upcoming trip to Los Angeles. As I listened, I wasn't sure that I wanted

her to come. Apprehension filled me. I just didn't think
I could deal with her. Once that voice had meant so
much to me that I had broken down crying every time we
spoke. That was when I had first come here. How
miserable it had made me feel to be away from her. All I
wanted to do was run back home and be rescued from
the demons of this city. Lay my head in her lap and be
calmed by the familiar scent of her White Linen perfume.
But that was so long ago. Before I developed this love-
hate relationship with L.A. Before I had allowed the
city's material abundance to spoil me, to let the freedom
of lifestyle make me fear returning. So I had learnt to
detach myself from that need. One tends to do that after
missing someone terribly, and after all those years, I had
finally extricated myself from the umbilical cord. Framed
it between my own teeth and gnashed until it was cut.

Now here she was, making plans to come and see
me. Trying, albeit in futility, to tangle me back into
dependency. How could I accommodate her in my life as
it precariously stood? Where in between Richard and
drinking would she stand?

Where was there any room, any need, for yet
another to identify myself with?

CHAPTER 6

SISSY

In thinking of Richard, I think about all the other men who have drifted through my life. All created from the same mold it seems. Having successfully auditioned to be the able benefactors to a hungry dysfunction, they had somewhere along the line ceased to be individuals and had become the sludge of a distinct personality instead.

It was different with Richard only because, in exorcising his own ghosts, he had decided to stay. Most had been in too much of a hurry to stick around long enough to burst the bubble themselves.

Maddeningly unstructured, it was within the pockets of such precariousness that we found the fuel for everything that attracted and eventually repelled us from each other.

Passion thrives on many annihilating emotions. It's fueled by catalysts so fickle, so fleeting – the promise of lasting love is never one of them. Richard's affection for me bore such fugitive traits. Unpredictable. Capricious. Ephemeral. It swallowed me alive.

Little in my life has come close to being as passionate as this indefinable relationship.

Except perhaps my relationship to my father or his with my mother.

Who knows what experiences in early life form the indelible scars that sear in the years to come? Propel us into recreating the familiar scenes that have an uncanny ability to convince us that this time we would have control in manipulating the outcome? Often we start out with almost mythical bravado and end up as pawns instead.

My earliest memory of being in kindergarten is not of childhood bliss on the playground or of finger painting. It is one of deep yearning. It's of myself running behind some five year old, calling him, inexplicably, by the same nickname my mom had for my father, *Shila.* That's what she called him. Why I was calling Munir or Sandeep (both confounded at being expected to respond to another name) by this nickname as I chased one or the other relentlessly around slides and seesaws would have given any psychotherapist a multiple orgasm.

It seems there was always someone I was trying to keep from leaving. Always someone without whom it just didn't feel right. On the playground. In the classroom. At home. In life. Somebody should have seen it then. But my mother was too busy making a living and smothering me during the little time she could spare, and my father too busy being unfaithful to her and countering her affections with his wrath. *Don't treat him like a girl, for God's sake! He's a boy, can't you see that? You are bringing him up to be a bloody sissy! No son of mine is going to grow up to be a bloody sissy!*

My grandmother, *mama kuba,* tried even harder to make up for the anomaly of both her own life and the absence of my feuding parents, only to exacerbate the belligerent convictions of an only child in the most tempestuous of surroundings. In her later years she often told me of how, as a child, I had never crawled on account of her fear of me bruising my knees. I had gone straight from her arms to learning how to walk, my hands carefully held up by her own.

She told me about the ordeal she had to undergo whenever it was time for me to bathe. Having spent the afternoon playing tea party – I wouldn't have been caught dead jostling through a soccer field with the boys – I convinced all my neighborhood girlfriends to escort me home. There, as my grandmother bucketed warm water over my head, I stood in all my naked bliss, a six year-old exhibitionist in all his splendor. I simply refused to take one unless they gathered and watched. She would laugh and say that I had needed an audience even then. Adrian says that I might have been too afraid to let them out of my sight lest they disappeared and didn't come back.

It was no surprise, therefore, that when my father left to end matters with his mistress in Nairobi and promised to come back but wound up being stabbed, his blood splattered all over her room instead, I was determined that nobody would ever leave me again. The consummation between father and child that comes from spending intimate moments that last more than a couple of hours every few weeks never came. Teaching me how to water paint as I sat in his lap and then disappearing for months at a time suddenly became a mercifully acceptable notion compared to not being able to see him again.

No, it would not happen to me again. This abrupt and unjust abandonment. Perhaps if I hadn't failed him in some way. Disappointed him. Held on to him tighter. Appeased him by comprehending signs that he surely must have emitted.

No, never again. I would love him as nobody ever had. He would never have to look elsewhere. I would manipulate any circumstance. Experience as an only child had taught me how to manipulate situations. Offer any sacrifice. Grant any kind of freedom. Keep him by my side. Never find myself in a situation that required reclaiming him. He would be the father that had been slain. The mother who had worked too hard. He would make everything alright.

Enter Richard.

CHAPTER 7

LOVE STORY

Let me tell you about Richard Lopez. About this 22-year-old boy who has me in the grips of an obsession. Richard is the perfect boy. The object of everyone's desire. He has the kind of muscled body that everyone gawks at and spends hours in the gym trying to chisel into. When he lays on top of me, his weight pinning me to the bed, a trembling creeps over my whole body. My wit and cynicism disappear, my tongue struck silent in my mouth. I feel then like Sappho's ode to man from 600 B.C.: "Greener than grass, at such times, I seem to be no more than a step away from death."

Richard is the boy upon which the fantasies of dark, lonely nights formulate themselves. He is aesthetic perfection removed from the realm of art and thrust into the flesh. His eyes, dark and deep-set, slay hearts from under his heavy brows. When he smiles, as he does when I've pleased him, he lifts the darkest of my despairs. But when displeased, his face contorts into a scowl that condemns me infernally.

Often friends come to me with reasons to leave him. They coax me with their compassion and then, frustrated, badger me with rhetoric. *Can't you see he's just using you? You're just his security blanket when things don't work out. Don't you care that he sleeps around town but he doesn't want you? That slut!*

They ask me exactly how he managed to conquer my most rational and independent spirit. They want to know how an immature boy like Richard – too caught in up in a world of hip-hop clubs and random sex to even pursue an education or hold a substantial job – can bring a hardworking banker like myself to such degradation.

Using wit where common sense would not dare thrive, I tell them perhaps it's because we're born in degradation that some of us still remember to have a penchant for it. In the primordial filth of blood and piss and shit. Then they roll their eyes because they know I'm full of shit, determine that I revel in torture, and resolve never to hear another word about Richard.

Who can explain why I long for Richard? For a man who pours his declaration of platonic love in my ears and his seed into the bowels of other men? Who would believe the desperation, the madness, even the love that I feel for this boy who climbs into my bed at three in the morning but refuses to touch me in the way I want to be ravaged? Only someone who has felt such fire. Someone who, instead of recoiling from the burn, is enchanted by the crackling of flames.

The problem – and what I can't explain to my dear friends – is that Richard has been unable to disenchant me. Yes, I've been seduced by the lure of his random beckon. But I've also been kindled by the cruelty of his rejection. Richard can do without me. Walk away without so much as a backward glance. To him, I'm dispensable, and this I cannot accept. I was unable to change this about my father. Perhaps I can change that in him.

Sometimes it all seems possible, and I become optimistic. Drawing fresh inspiration from self-help books by Williamson and Chopra, I'm able to envision the very moment when the jousting will end and a mutually impassioned loving will begin. I pilfer through these aids ravenously, underlining everything that puts me in command of my desires, with Richard at the very top of that list. My faith is then restored and like a fool I believe we're making strides toward some destined consummation. But this was not one of those moments.

That night, as I sat holding my tear-stained face in my hands, waiting for the phone to ring, for Richard to call, I was in complete acceptance of his power over me, his fascist role as both panacea for and provider of my pain. That night, as I sat there, checking again and again to see if the phone was resting properly in its cradle – because it wouldn't ring – that is just how I felt. Condemned.

Right then every New Age guru and their motivational psychobabble had perished, along with all my fantasies of a blissful tomorrow. All this because an hour before I had been expecting him to show, Richard reneged on our plans to see a movie together. Changed his mind. Didn't feel like it anymore. Wasn't up to it. Not in the mood.

It should have been quite simple. People changed their minds all the time. It's their prerogative. So one took a rain check, stifled his disappointment and tried to articulate an understanding, "Oh, no problem, Richard. I was feeling a little pooped myself. I'm disappointed but we can do it next week. No big deal...."

But not for me. For me, it suddenly became a matter of life and death. I was a starved refugee who had been promised a banquet, even permitted to smell the redolence as it cooked, only to discover a change of heart had tossed everything into a dumpcart. All I could see then was his face and think the unacceptable – that I almost had him there within my reach, and then I didn't.

How could Richard be expected to understand my ceremonies for that evening? To understand that every time I'd felt dismayed with life, I had shaken the bleakness off with the promise of our evening together. The reverie of him next to me and smelling him and feeling his touch sustained me as my fingers mechanically punched away to open a savings account for someone. God, just listening to his laugh....That full-bodied, robust laugh like he could grasp life and just swallow it whole. How can he have known such longing?

"Listen," he said, without even a hint of remorse. "I have to do something else. I have to go and see this guy."

"What guy?"

"Oh, just some guy, you don't know him, okay?"

"Well, tell me about him! Who is he?"

"What difference does it make?"

"Just tell me," I pleaded, as if knowledge of the lucky person would assuage my own misfortune. "I want to know."

"His name is Louis, okay? Happy? Now can I get off the phone?"

It crushed me to think that our time together meant so little to him and my very salvation. Oh, the horrible things I wanted to do when I thought of where he would be going and what he would he would be doing. From meat cleavers above his cock to razors upon my wrist.

I've been told that two people can never love each other the same amount, at the same time. Often when one's suffering ends, the other person's begins. Problem was that not only could I not imagine Richard suffering for me, I didn't think he was even capable of it.

I would have done anything for him to keep his promise, to make him change his mind, and God knows, I tried. At first, I made bargains that were impossible to keep. *Please, Richard, just this time, don't cancel on me. We don't have to see a movie again for as long as you wish. But just this time...I just need to see you so badly this time...*When that didn't work, I tried to cajole him with humor, to remind him of how witty and funny I could be. I then shifted to emotional blackmail by recalling his promise. And finally, stripped of any dignity, I capitulated to the most basic of human techniques – crying. None of it made any difference.

Instead Richard told me he needed to get off the phone because now he definitely didn't feel like being

around me in this desperate and needy state. So I began
to pray, as I have night after night, for a boon. Bent
down on my knees, I looked up at the framed picture of
our Imam – who among many things had inspired my
mother's choice of doctors – and with teary eyes I
bargained petulantly with his spiritual worth.

Why would you deny me this? What's wrong with wanting
Richard? That, after all, isn't materialistic. It's not like I'm
praying for a car or money or anything. All I want is for Richard
to love me back. For him to want me. How can you just stand
there in that damn picture, smiling down at me, and do nothing to
answer my prayers? Give him to me! You must give him to me!

It didn't occur to me then that I'd performed this
little scene more than once in my life. At about thirteen,
I had stood unshakable by a *taqat,* a coin depository in the
mosque where the followers supplicated in idolatrous
fashion at a life-sized picture of the Imam, and poured in
all the change I had to my name. I had joined my hands
in prayer, the rosary twining through my fingers, and
lodged a desperate plea to make my best friend fall in love
with me. I'd learnt early in life that the commodity that
proves scarce in the world and could make grown men
grovel was love.

Oh, God, let me have Richard. Richard, Richard,
Richard. I blubbered and convulsed on the floor, calling
God's name and Richard's as if they were one and the
same.

Until then, having exhausted both – myself and
the dear Imam – with a paroxysm of threats and tears, I
sat by the phone, hoping for a miracle. My head was
pounding, the tears had run dry and I felt weak and
admonished. I'd been turned to ash. After another
fifteen minutes, I knew I had no other choice. I picked
up the receiver with much apprehension, and dialed his
number. All the time, a part of myself, the part that I felt
was standing outside of me, was saying, *What are you doing?*
You can't go on like this. This must stop.

The answering machine came on.   I panicked. *He's avoiding me.   Surely he's standing right there with his arms folded across his chest, and his face contorted with disgust.   He'll never pick up the phone again, and I'll be shut out of his life forever.* I felt my insides, with every beep that gave way to a message, contracting into little knots.

Oh God, what have I done?   Why couldn't I just let him go to whoever and been understanding about it?   Pretended to be nonchalant.   Maybe then he would've taken me out tomorrow.   Or some other time.   Now he's punishing me.   I'd rather die...

But I had no other choice.   Delayed gratification had never been part of my training as an only child.   I had always wanted it *now* and I had always gotten it *now*. Never had to wait.   All I had to do was fling myself onto the ground and start kicking and throwing my fists around and whatever my heart desired would be provided.   Toyshops would be re-opened, and ice cream would come by the gallons if I had so desired.   If required, I could cry until it became difficult to breathe and I started to hiccup and compel them with my trauma.   Not that one time though.   No, it certainly wasn't working this time....

I opened my mouth to speak but there were no words.   That's when Richard unexpectedly intercepted the call.   "Yes?"

"It's me," I said carefully.   As if he hadn't known that.   As if he hadn't known that unless he picked up the phone, I would have been driven to incessantly calling and hanging up.   I was only grateful that he'd spared me from that portion of my sickness.   He remained silent, and I was afraid I was making this worse.   "I just wanted to say that I'm sorry...I know, I know, I've said that before, but I *really* am, Richard.   Oh, God, I love you, please don't be angry with me...."

I heard him sigh with exasperation.   *He thinks I'm pathetic.   I think I'm pathetic.*

"It's just that, it's been a whole week since I last saw you, and I was really looking forward to tonight, you know? I mean, I was all ready and everything, and then you call me—"

"I really don't want to talk right now. Didn't I tell you that?"

"I know, I'm sorry. Look, let's just forget about it, okay? Maybe another time. It's fine. Just go ahead with your plans. I just...I guess I just over-reacted...."

"*Again!* You over-reacted *again!* You *always* fucking do this, Ali. I'm tired of this shit! I don't want to put up with this any more. Who the fuck do you think you are, giving me shit?"

"Richard, please, I love you. Work with me on this...Please, show me how. I didn't mean for it to get this way. I know I'll change." There. I repented. Repented for him letting me down. Repented for him wanting to go fuck some other guy. Repented for crying. For questioning. For my very existence. One more chance was all I was asking for. I'd discipline myself not to act needy or give him a hard time about other men or for flaking out on me at the last moment to accommodate someone else.

Somehow, he must have felt sorry for me because he said, "Look, what time is it?"

"Uh-I think about seven..."

"Well," he paused for a moment. "We can still make the eight o'clock show."

I started to cry again, uncontrollably so, only this time it was out of gratitude. I'd been forgiven. Redeemed from myself. It was as if somebody had his finger primed on the nuclear button, a little red one as is popularly imagined, and had decided to postpone the meltdown so he could enjoy a last cigarette.

You see, you fool, he does love you. He's coming back to spend time with you, and everything will go back to normal.

"Don't cry, it's okay. I'll be there soon," he said, his voice resounding with a tenderness that I feared I had killed.

Wiping the tears from my eyes, I began to smile. Everything would be alright. He had said so himself.

Thank you...Thank you...

The Richard who showed up at my doorstep was different.

I'm not quite sure what I'd been expecting. Maybe a Richard that was ingratiated and expected me to feel indebted to his mercy. The Richard that had made me suffer. Resentful. Unyielding. Begrudging. But this Richard looked down at me tenderly when I opened the door. I threw my arms around him and tried hard not to cry. *I must act composed. Everything has to appear normal. Must make it fun for him to be here with me. Regain some of my integrity so that I don't appear completely worthless to him....*

Here came the calm after the storm. The best few hours we would share. The ones that would comprise our most intimate memories in the future. We had paid dearly for these moments. Lacerated each other. Now, as had been anticipated, came the sweet rewards to revel in.

What had just happened here?

What had we been trying to do to each other?

Questions raced through my mind unanswered.

Nothing seemed to make any sense anymore. I'm not sure if we even wanted to make any sense of it. The important thing was that we had reached such moments of kindness after we had wounded each other. Neither one of us, it seemed, knew of any other way to get to this place.

During the movie he held my hand. And when we walked back to his car, he held me close to him without a care as to who might have been watching in Westwood village. I felt like a baby that had been pacified by his parent. His solace came from the knowledge that he had hurt me and successfully managed to reclaim my devotion by taking the pain away.

When we lay in my bed, with only the moonlight illuminating us, he started to cry and I was confounded. I asked him what was wrong. He kept saying that he loved me and promised to treat me better. "You'll see," he said, sliding his arms possessively under me and kissing my forehead gently. "You'll see how different it's going to be."

Can't say that I really believed him. But at that moment, with his surrender so complete and his eagerness in such garish contrast to his earlier mood, I would have accepted any promise, heard any confession, absolved any sin. There was such an innocence about him, he became like a rebellious child who had realized his belligerence and returned to the comforting bosom of his parent. Our roles were constantly being turned inside out and backward.

We held each other so tightly that it hurt. I found it difficult to breathe, his body compressed against mine, my rib cage encased by his strong arms. It was in the fervor of this embrace that I sought my hope and sensed his apology. Here was the completion, the consummation that went far beyond that of sex. We were mending each other, dressing the wounds we had been condemned to inherit by those who had borne us, and the ones we had inflicted upon each other.

Yes, we had injured each other as carelessly as our parents had one another, but we would make up for it more quickly than they had and make promises that would prove true only to the moment. Never to inflict such injuries, cause such pain. He would make up where our fathers had left off – abandoning, betraying and being absent. I would make up where both our mothers had tried – forgiving, enduring and perhaps even preventing him from straying again.

The fact that we never went any further than making glorious promises and holding and kissing each other started to matter less to me as time went by. I never stopped wanting him, though. Craving him inside me. In fact, it was the image of him hungrily taking from others what he refused me that would play in my mind when, after moments of such close physical contact, I would be left alone to find myself helplessly masturbating. It was the scent of his deodorant as I stood sniffing at the counter of some supermarket that evoked sensations and liquefied my stomach.

*I don't want to jeopardize our friendship...It's just not what I want from you, Ali....*And I would be left to contend with intimate brushes against his body and caresses that titillated but never quenched.

That was just the "Ali-Richard" relationship. There was no changing it. Too much time had gone by and there was no chance of crossing that line. We had become "snuggle buddies." A kind of relationship, we both discovered later, that was not uncommon in the gay culture. You fucked around with everyone and to them you gave your body and your cock. And sometimes you had that one person to whom you gave your sweet moments and your grief, not much else. Often two people, driven by different emotional needs, found themselves dependent on each other for the kind of loving that, for at least one half of the pair, precluded any kind of sexual compulsion. I told myself that there were ties more binding, and more lasting than those built around sex. And this, I was determined to believe, was one of them.

When Richard broke away from our embrace an hour later and smiled sheepishly for pardon, I composed myself, still glowing from his touch. In years to come, the memory of accepting such charity would repulse me. But not that night. That night I had gotten more than I had dreamt possible. Injected with my favorite drug, I knew I could confidently bear whatever came my way until the shakes came again. I could go to sleep now, safe in the knowledge that I had not been shunned. That I was still loved. That nothing I had done had alienated or driven him away from me.

Soon he would be gone, and I knew I would have to employ the memory of that hour we had spent together to satiate myself. But that mattered very little now. With a satisfied smile on my face, and a glow emanating from inside me, I kept telling myself over and over again that sex was such a trivial omission from our relationship. Who needed it when there was so much sincerity, such genuine caring? You can't have everything and this is so much more substantial than *that*.

Richard ran his hand through his tousled black hair as he stood at the foot of the bed, looking down at me. He buttoned up his shirt and tucked it back into his pants and said that he had been glad to be able to spend that very special evening with me. "I love you," he said again. "And don't you ever forget it."

"Don't you ever let me," I said, smiling.

He glanced at the wristwatch I had given him for his birthday and shook his head at the time like it was late. It was 11:30, and luckily he wouldn't have to drive too far from my apartment.

Louis lived only a few streets up and had promised to wait up until at least midnight.

CHAPTER 8

ROPE OR RAT POISON?

Beware of the "*bankra* committee!" Once your name ends up on their shriveled lips, even the world's best selling tabloid cannot accomplish what a clump of tongue-wagging, trudging-along-with-a-walker matriarchal types can.

Growing up in the equatorial heat of Mombasa island, in the bosom of the Ismaili community, it has always been evident to me what a woman's role is. Most of my knowledge on this subject was derived from the Hindi films that dominated our Sundays – and every day, religiously after the popularization of VCRs – and from the chatter of the women from the "*bankra* committee." The rest of it came from observing my mother.

Bankras are the benches that skirt the mosque grounds. Most of these women were ailing from arthritis or old age and were unable to climb the flight of stairs leading up to the mosque. The impending elevator that had been talked about for the last few years had yet to be installed. So they just sat around on the *bankras* and pretended to observe the prayers that were being cast out over the P.A. system while avidly discussing the state of community affairs. Their bodies had given up on them a long time ago. But their faces were like operas. Completely animated. Eyes squinting. Frowning. Brows arched up in exaggerated shock. Mouth gasping away. And their hands, that was another thing, they were always in motion. Like they were creating, molding in the air. Gesticulating. Slapping their foreheads. Jabbing and pointing. It was as if their bodies were the instruments giving song to their words. They sat there, on the *bankras*, conducting each other with exaggerated gestures in a symphony of infamy and ruination.

It was through them that I learned of the tragic circumstances of Gulzar aunty's death. She was of no relation to me, but in a small community every older woman was your aunty and every older man your uncle. Hence Gulzar aunty. After arthritis rendered my grandmother incapable of climbing the stairs to the mosque, she unwittingly became inducted into the committee and, although reluctant at first, trotted home with a fresh installment of the daily *panchaat* for us.

A close friend of my mother, Gulzar aunty – the same one that had given me that beautiful blue tote bag from KLM where she worked – had hung herself. Depression is what they'd called it at first. Just some hormonal imbalance that aging women go through and doctors can't remedy. All those valiums that she constantly devoured. But some time later the rumors surfaced through the committee. *He had been seeing some Arabi woman, that husband of hers! Chii! Chii! They had been fighting all the time! Bechari, no wonder she couldn't bear it any longer!* remarked the women in the community during their ritual gossiping. In a town like Mombasa, talk about "other women" spread like wildfire.

And now, what about their poor eleven-year-old daughter? What will become of her? Men! They are such dogs, I tell you! She should have left him a long time ago, the bastard, but instead what does she do? Hang herself!

And Shainoor? *Yah, Khudda! Alnoor and her had been high school sweethearts, imagine that! Do you remember how beautiful that girl was? That long black hair all the way down to here! Tsk, tsk, tsk....beautiful fair complexion....And that magnificent voice when she sang at all the music parties! And such a bhagat! She attended mosque daily! Such a pleasant girl! Truly, she was the pride of the community...*Rat poison! That was her response to his infidelity. Not a separation. Not a divorce. Not to wager him with her own affair. But to drink up poison. Rat poison, no less!

I wonder if any of them had had a choice, really, being in love and bound to their traditional notions of love as they were. What could have been expected of them? To endure faithlessness from their husbands would have meant to have hope. A light at the end of the tunnel. These women had been driven to the point where both entrance and exit appeared barricaded. To have an affair? Every woman who had rebelled and indulged in an extra-marital affair, regardless of what had driven them to it, had ended up dubbed as the community whore. Soon, everyone's husbands called with lucrative offers to spend a night at some beach hotel. Many even gave in, unable to ever absolve themselves from such a reputation, a kind of death in itself.

I've known, much to my dismay, that in situations both turbulent and trivial, I've always played the role of the victim, the heroine in plight. It's what has kept me from telling Richard to fuck off, turning around and walking away *first* for a change. I've listened to the ramblings of the "*bankara* committee" and I've avidly watched the melodrama unfold in Hindi cinema through my youth. Mourned with the community over the suicide of some beautiful irremediable woman and jumped on top of my seat to jubilate the formulaic success of a struggle in love. And now my life has become just that.

Images from these Hindi films often flashed through my mind. As I waited for Richard to satisfy himself with yet another trick and to return to me, spent but just little more tender, I became Jaya Bachhan in *Silsila*, lamenting in song until tall and handsome Amitabh comes back to her from carousing with his mistress...Faces of actresses whose names I knew so well. Scenes from movies, the titles of which are long forgotten...And those songs. Yes, those *filmi* songs with the poignant lyrics that epitomize the suffering of love and which only Lata can sing.

They are all there in their pomp and melodrama. Directing me. Reminding me. Unfurling within me in their systematic chaos. How can I help but heed to their instinctual direction? It's a hopeless situation. Just like scores of Indian women who have learned to identify with the martyred heroines of the Hindi film, I've also learnt to relate to them instead of the independent, free-spirited hero. It's not my role to realize the error of my ways and return to the one I love. Mine is to love unconditionally, shed the perfunctory tears and wait for dawn. It was in waiting patiently as he caroused, in having the opportunity to be there upon his return, to forgive him and take him back in, that I had to find my meaning and validation. Any good, traditional Indian woman knew that.

I don't burst out into song and dance but I've come to believe in this melodrama. That good has to win. Patience is a virtue that always pays back. And that those who love the most, and are willing to suffer for it, always get the object of their affection to realize that they belong together.

Penance is a prerequisite to romantic fulfillment.

Life without the one you love quantified death.

Men could leave. But if you had the misfortune of being a woman – or relating to one – the respectable thing to do, the right thing to do, was staying. How else was love for an Indian homosexual who grew up in a gilded world of cinema – one who related to the psyche of his dramatic Indian mother – meant to be?

CHAPTER 9

THE GIFT

The years have nothing to do with aging. It is the heart that governs that process. It etches out its infliction upon your face like a sketcher dribbling carelessly on unsoiled paper, leaving irrevocable histories of the wars and wounds endured.

I see old people, and I wonder about their wars. I try to read their faces, their lines of countless frowns and laughs – an attempt to extract some wisdom. I am sometimes left wondering if someday my hull will reflect my stories but be accompanied by the placidity I see in these people. That dovish, enlightened quality that only comes late in life, that allows the thought of love to elicit a melancholy smile rather than to crush my heart.

Sitting at my desk, displaced by my need for Richard, such nirvana seemed inconceivable. Although corporeally I may have been perched there, everything that lived in me, every single atom in my body was in that physically inaccessible realm where Richard thrived. I called my machine for the ninth, maybe tenth, time that hour, hoping that Richard had called. There were messages from Salman and Adrian, which I skipped over without even listening to, cutting them off in mid-sentence, but not one word from him. The rest of the time, I just stared into space, reliving every moment from my night with Richard, trying hopelessly to change the ending of a movie I had seen one too many times. I was past caring if the people around me witnessed my dementia.

Love, I reminded myself, didn't just make you blind. It also made you repudiate those who didn't yield to its vertigo.

A voice from somewhere: "Excuse me, young man. Can you help me?"

Startled, I looked up to find an older man with his cane, holding bank brochures in his hand. I would've made some excuse and passed him onto someone else, so that I could have remained in my world, but it was too late. He had already started settling into the chair across from me. After the perfunctory questions had been answered, we began opening an account. I tried to focus on the task I was being paid for but ended up asking about his life. Maybe he would say something, impart some pearl of wisdom, that would bring about an epiphany. The broken-hearted are a desperate breed looking for signs in everything. It turned out Mr. Newman had been to Kenya.

In his thirties, he had taken his late wife on her dream vacation to Tsavo where she could experience the wildlife that she loved so much in their natural habitat. They had even ridden the railway. In his wallet, speckled with the dust that had managed to get under the plastic, was a sepia-toned picture of them together, which he proudly showed me.

"That's my Naomi," he said, smiling down at her with undying love and placing the open wallet in my hands. "She's beautiful!" he said, as if she were waiting for him at home or in the parked car outside.

I was astonished at the metamorphosis. I looked at the picture and then I looked up at him, an old and shriveled reconfiguration of the strong, young man in the picture. But not on the inside. Inside he was still 10.

"If Naomi had her way, she would even outlaw zoos," he said, laughing heartily. "Nobody should live in a prison."

As he slowly and diffidently stretched out of the chair, having made an investment he would probably never live to reap, he lamented about his arthritis; but in his voice was a vigor undefeated by the unjust crippling of his shell. A spirit that felt completely diminished in me.

"Thank you for coming in, Mr. Newman," I said, rising to my feet, and suddenly thinking of my grandmother. "I'm so sorry you're in such pain."

"That's life," he said, smiling warmly. "Enjoy your youth. It will be a long time before you have to worry about such things."

I smiled at him, ingratiated in the reminder of how wonderful it must be to be so young and have a whole lifetime ahead of me. But my face began to ache and my smile, I was convinced, came across as a contrived failure. My heart felt tight and sore. And I found myself suddenly running to seek cover in the bathroom, as I had been doing frequently, where I could perch over the basin and cry.

When curdling, love was a bastard child noxiously debasing from within. So I hunched over and put my arms around myself until tears were pressed out from my eyes. To expel it was the only true remedy. If I could only learn to live with the vacancy ensuing its procrastinated abortion, but I was no longer sure I knew how to be happy alone. Six years had gone by. They told me I was still only a child and yet I felt I was a child only when I had first met him. Not since then. Not ever again.

I felt afraid. Terrified of imagining life without Richard. Without this madness to contend with for everyday of my life what would I do? Who would I be? Ali had become the obsessor of Richard. My every conversation. My every thought. My only ambition. When awake, I spoke of him. About him. As only I could see him. What promises he had made to me. And where he had failed in them.

And in my sleep, he came again. And most of the time we were both silent. He held me close, and nestled within him, I felt safe and assured again.

Sometimes he made love to me. And in rousing myself from bed and discovering my semen marked on the sheets, I would enter into the day consumed by a tumult of arousal and shame.

Take all that away and what would be left of me? It was a death in itself to walk away from the Ali I had so distastefully helped create. And loathe him as I might, it was the only Ali I knew now. How would happiness embrace me after all this time of adulating misery? I didn't know how the door would open up. But I knew I had to get out. Nobody could love their jailor forever.

I looked at my reflection in the mirror above the basin. I didn't see someone in his twenties. I saw a man much, much older. More ravaged than he should be. The skin around my face was still tight. There was only the hint of dark circles around my eyes. My lips were firm and full. My hair dark and thick. But it all felt like shellac filming a decaying core.

Is this why Mummy struggled to raise me? So I could learn such pain? Is this why I was doted upon, bundled from the cold in blankets and kept from grazing my knees on the ground? Force-fed and fussed over? So that I could grow up and in losing my heart, trip and break it into a million fragments?

I felt cracked. Broken. Bits of jagged edges stuck outwards from within me and poked me until I winced. It must have been apparent from my eyes, this bungling collapse of my spirit. The self-loathing. My disappointment in myself. That must be why I meet no one else. Embarrassed by my insufficiency, I averted my eyes from others in fear that they would catch glimpses of my worthlessness. I looked away before they did. Sometimes I may have stumbled upon the hope that maybe someone would be persistent enough to scale the walls that I had cloistered myself in. But in Los Angeles that doesn't quite happen. Apparently, we were all waiting for our saviors.

Instead I stood there and looked into the mirror, freshly doused but unable to eliminate the glassiness in my eyes or the swelling around them. A soul in dire need of absolution from its demons, waiting for an absentee messiah. Nobody was coming anytime soon. I might as well face up to it. I was going to have to wake up and realize the task had to be accomplished on my own.

I splashed cold water on my feverish face, unable even to drink it as it gushed forth from the faucet – not like Kenya, no. The sweet waters that I could cup in the palm of my hands and drink. Straight from the tap. *Oh, God, help me find a way....Lift me out of all this.*

Like so many times before, I took a deep breath, hoping that when I got back out there something would be different, Richard might have called. On my desk, I did find an urgent note waiting for me. But it was a message from Richard's mother, asking me to call her right away.

Something had happened.

I found him at the I.C.U. in a cold, sterile room, the steel efficiently humming away around his sleeping body. Slowly I took the chair next to him, not removing my eyes from him for even a second. Looking down at his face, I felt as if I was looking into my own. That's how much I'd lost myself in him. Nights of forging his features out of the darkness and frantically stitching them together in the absurd hope that he would materialize had left me with no recognition of any other face. *I don't know where you end and I begin.*

There was something else in that face. A subtle quality that I could not quite put my finger on but I recognized as being the same as in my father's pictures. Both had that timelessness about them. The kind that would elicit a soft gasp from a picture that escaped from an old box and skittered to the floor. The topography of handsomeness. Plains and curves in a face that stirred the eyes that looked at them. One could not help but hope when looking at such a face that Nature had been benevolent enough not to stop right there. A face this beautiful had to have been blessed with a disposition just as gratifying. But I knew from experience that Mother Nature never did have a reputation for being quite so generous.

In the waiting room, his mother, surprisingly steeled, had told me that Richard had jaundice. Worry was written all over her face, but if she had cried any tears, no one had been witness to them. Her strength both angered and awed me.

Looking down, I realized that the pallor in his face had done nothing to discredit his looks. And this, much to my guilt, embittered me. Maybe it's because I'd always considered his looks a weapon that he had been able to use against me. He had always been undefeatable there.

Jesus! Just thinking about all those times that I had to stand by him and listen to everyone – from my own friends to other hopefuls – coo about how cute he was, completely glazing over me. And him, immodestly basking in their compliments and brazenly undressing them with his eyes while I had stood right there, right next to him, dissolving within.

Their memory made me want to claw at his face and rip away those features from it like some mask he might have been wearing. To demonically mutilate the attributes in his face that he, and others like him had held up as a mantle over the likes of me.

And then there was that conflicting, simultaneous urge to touch him with every ounce of tenderness I possessed. Always this war within me. Part of me wanting to hit him. And part of me just wanting to cry. Most of the time, it was that later urge that overcame and suppressed me – I was back in for the haul.

I was tempted to run my finger down his stubbled face, to touch his closed eyes and feel the unusually long curl of their lashes against my fingertips. The bridge of his nose and the curves of his lips. But I hesitated for fear of waking him, disrupting the moment. There had been so much chaos. So much anguish. The arguments. The public scenes. I just wanted to stand there with him in front of me and for there to be some peace. No words. No promises. No defenses.

Six years had gone by and I was there still standing at his bedside in some hospital because he just might have literally fucked his life away, while I had spent nights with nothing more than my fantasies of him. Nights when my body had cried out for him, ached, as if every nerve ending had become a gaping mouth. Nights when I had felt something much deeper than a yearning.

Where were all those people he had fucked now? Only I stood there. Devoted. Praying. Stealing a few moments that his mother and siblings had been kind enough to allow me as they waited outside. *Everybody uncertain. Still running tests. Hard to say how long they would have to keep him here.*

What if he tested positive?

I went through the motions, questioning and yet uncertain if I wanted to hear the answers. *How many times have you fucked without a condom? When was the last time you did that? Who was he? Did you even know him? God! What were you thinking? Oh, no, never mind, don't tell me.*

The anger festered within me again. I started to feel sick. In my mind, I could hear his answers and I wanted to drown him out and vociferate. *Fuck you! You did this to yourself! I told you so, and now see what you've gotten yourself into! Should have stuck with me. Let me love you instead of fucking, fucking, fucking every goddamn slut like yourself! You deserve this, and I hope that you suffer just like I have for the past six years. I hope you feel scared, and I hope you cry and regret.*

Yes, regret!   Regret that you have been so unappreciative of me.
Regret that you never wanted to fuck me.   This is your punishment.

But I started to cry instead.   It was I that was
starting to feel scared.   There, lying in front of me, had
been not just Richard but the last six years of my life.
Seeing him like that made mortality shockingly believable.

And I wondered, if Richard never woke up again,
what would all those years have been worth?   Feeling the
way that I still did for him, how could I fathom life
without him?

And all this for what?   What had he given me to
show for those six years?   How, without looking absurd,
would I express my grief over someone who had been
known to boast of my obsession over him? All this over
someone who had not seen fit to give me one day of total
commitment, never mind the lifetimes.

It was then that it started to occur to me that
perhaps this was not about Richard at all. My whole
relationship with him was suddenly being questioned with
a kind of objectivity completely lacking in such turbulent
relationships.

This hospital room, his illness, these were only
props for something much more profound evolving in
our lives now. Perhaps this is all about me. My lesson at
his expense.   A chance for a long-sought redemption.

Maybe after all this was over and Richard had
recuperated, he would go back to his same old ways.   But
not I. Not anymore. I would never be able to go back to
the way it was.   Seeing him there, like that, had invariably
changed the course for me.

This is how I would have normally preferred to
have him – ailing from some cold or infection so that no
one else would have interfered with my devotion to him.
So that he would need me to attend to him. Wouldn't
have the strength to fuck every golden-haired boy in West
Hollywood. And I would have driven the 405 and battled
traffic from Santa Monica to Carson, laden with a freshly

baked peach pie from Polly's and a tub of vanilla ice cream. So much to look forward to. Richard all to myself. Helpless. Unable to get away. Needing attention. Mine, especially. Mummy's coming. Don't you worry, everything will be alright. I will simply love the illness away. And maybe in the process my own too. Snuggle time. Watch a mushy romantic movie for the third time with him. Something with Julia Roberts in it. He always made me feel like Julia fucking Roberts when I was around him. Demure. Pretty. Martyred. I had always wanted him to see this one with me but he had been too busy going out to some new hip club or some private party. Or fucking. Fucking someone new. Someone hot. Someone with a gym-built body and white fucking alabaster skin and golden fucking hair. And, oh, let's not forget the blue or green eyes. But not tonight. Tonight he was my Richard. They would all have to wait while he ailed from fucking too much.

I remembered the times I had, much to my own horror, secretly wished that he would be struck with something like this. Something irrevocable. Something that would last longer than a cold or food poisoning. So that in being cast down from the heights I had helped elevate him to, he would have understood my pain and met my vulnerability with his own. It was only when he was at the lowest points in his life that he needed me in that way. When he was sweet to me. When he baby-talked with me and fluttered his long lashes at me and gobbled up all the pie and ice cream and affection. Well, there he was again in that same way. And the thought that what I had wished for might have come true filled me with dread.

You see, this time, although he would wake to need me, I feared that maybe he wouldn't stay that way. He would wither in front of my eyes. The cheeks would sink in and the muscles on his body would disintegrate so that the flesh would hang around his bones like sagging clothes. Just like those horrifying pictures. His hollow eyes would look at me, vacant and insipid, and this passionate creature would be reduced to a sack of bones and dwindled spirit.

Is that how much I loved him? To want to possess him at any cost? Any price? Any sacrifice? Even his own?

I buried my face in my hands and shook my head. No, this was not how I wanted Richard after all. This was not how I wanted things to end. Not even as punishment for his rampant promiscuity while he remained unavailable to me. Not like this, dear God.

Time for mental bargains with God. That same God that I had hoped at first would help me procure him, I now wished would work in his mysterious ways to free me.

I would walk away from him if he recovered from this. If the tests came out negative. No turning back. Wish him well with whomever he chose and not interfere again. Just please let him live, God. Let him come out from this to be the buoyant, energetic boy that I fell in love with.

And in return, I would do my maker proud. Finally live up to my full potential and exploit every talent I had wasted in pursuit of Richard. But he had to live.

Together, we were both doomed. As long as I felt this way about him, this third entity that we had both created, a relationship that eluded a name, would never allow either one of us to feel any intimacy with anyone else. We would remain together, too weak to sever the ties, still punishing each other for the inadequacies of a strangely mismatched relationship.

He had touched parts of me that perhaps no other man would know. Secret rooms that would have to be barricaded for good. He had done things I didn't have a name for, kept me feeling ecstasy, anguish, doing backflips through my soul. I had loved him the way we love unspeakable perversions, the ones that are unshakable.

But the time had come.

The answer that I had prayed for so fervently had arrived in the disguise of this adversity, and procrastination was suddenly an unaffordable luxury.

Over the years I had given him many gifts. My last gift to him would be my absence.

CHAPTER 10

THE SILVER FLASK

For a while, Adrian dated someone called Jeremy, who was positive. These were the years that we both refer to as the "Jeremy" or "Richard" years, a time we were both mostly out of touch. An unfortunate reality of gay life. When single, friends become a replacement for the absent mate. And Adrian was the kind of friend I had spend Saturday nights with, dancing in the clubs and pounding down drink specials. The one I'd call late Sunday afternoon with a dreadful hangover and who always remembered a little bit more than I would and didn't hesitate to recap my escapades. The one I'd call on Valentine's Day and on public holidays because being with family was either unendurable or geographically impossible. And Mr. Last Night – well, he had zipped his pants up and driven home to the "open relationship" he had clocked a few hours out from. Adrian was the friend that I'd distance myself from when the eligible one came along. I'd claim exhaustion and the inability to sustain any more late nights, disinclined to return any calls. Until, much to my chagrin, the relationship would miscarry and I'd resurface to the barstool I had previously disowned, the loyal friend having reserved it for me, his hand patting it gently, a wry smile masking the relief of my prodigal return, confirming that I was indeed doomed to cruise clubs and parks and sex clubs for the rest of my gradually enervating existence.

While Adrian acquired both sexual and emotional skills in conducting a relationship with someone who had to suddenly base his life on a count of T-Cells, I grappled with my obsession of Richard. And once in a while, in the spirit of those who kept a lifeboat handy in case of disaster, Adrian and I would call each other and quite superficially inquire about one another's lives. Most of the important details got lost under the knowledge that, since we weren't intimate enough to talk regularly, it would be a waste of time to reveal too much.

By the time Jeremy's health began to show its first distressing signs of the disease, he and Adrian had already split up. At first, Adrian had me believe that their separation had been for many reasons, the most important of them being that Adrian had felt stifled in such a committed and routine relationship with a man fifteen years his senior. After quite some time, when Adrian and I had resumed our closeness, when the barstools had been reclaimed, he told me the truth. He had witnessed the ravages of this disease and was terrified of losing yet another person he cared about to it. Flipping through his uncle's record collection of seventies disco, Adrian still felt the horror of acknowledging his family's paralysis against AIDS while his thirty-year-old uncle languished in a hospital room. He never wanted to feel so vulnerable, so helpless, again. He didn't have the strength to endure the putrescence that was inevitable for Jeremy.

"It's just a matter of time, Ali," he said between swigs of the rum that was helping him loosen up. "Another breakthrough, another promising cure and then all of a sudden – whoosh! Nobody hears about it again. The promise vanishes as quickly as it was publicized. Meanwhile, Jeremy is dying. And I just don't have the courage to hold his hand and watch him go through this. I don't!"

"Adrian, we're all dying everyday," I consoled.

"But not like *this*," he objected. "Not like *this*. In his case, he's almost certainly going to go through...hell. I don't know, sometimes I think maybe, maybe they don't want there to be a cure, you know? I mean, there's people out there that stand to lose a lot if a cure's found, don't you think? My God, just imagine! What the hell would the AIDS industry do if a cure's found? They'd all be out of a job!"

Adrian had decided to leave before it got too late. His fear had made it impossible to love the man any longer. By the time Jeremy had started to lose sight in his left eye, their relationship had been reduced to an occasional phone call. From practically "living together" to practically "acquaintances." From the beneficiary of Jeremy's will to the deserter of his affections.

Deeper still lay other phobias. In sabotaging his relationship and having grieving over the loss of his openly promiscuous uncle, Adrian couldn't help but feel paranoid that he hadn't succeeded completely in vanquishing this disease from his fate. It was bound to find him or someone he loved. Somewhere. Somehow.

Then, a couple of years after Jeremy, by which time he was mentioned to us only through mutual acquaintances, Adrian started to date Steve. Steve, who gave Adrian a venereal disease. They'd been the model gay couple that had somehow seeped through the strainer of doomed, transient relationships; Adrian and Steve (our own little Adam and Eve), had hoped to buy a house together and live in domestic bliss. It turned out that between planning futures together and driving the rest of their single friends envious, Steve – unlike Jeremy, who had courageously and rather gallantly revealed his HIV status on the first night – had decided to keep his gonorrhea a secret.

Adrian told me all about the nightmarish Q-tip insertion and, more painfully, his feelings of filthiness about being infected. The fear that something much more formidable was lurking in his fate lanced forth after his brush with gonorrhea. "It was a warning," Adrian said, "of what could have been."

So we both drank. One to assuage the guilt and paranoia; the other to blur the jagged edges of unrequited love, hoping to open up to other men.

Were we alcoholics, Adrian and I? I don't know. We seemed to have our own personal definition of what we considered alcoholics to be. My grandfather had been an alcoholic. One of my spinster aunts, Leila – the one who admonished me for speaking nasally and not like a "proper" man, the one we all suspected had been a lesbian because she wore *kaunda* suits – had been an alcoholic. My last memory of her is of spooning her holy water on her deathbed at the Aga Khan Hospital, a task made difficult for me because she kept turning her head from side to side in a state of dementia. Her flesh had turned pale and urinous, and her eyes had melted into impenetrable orbs of blood, shockingly beyond recognition. If a person was too drunk to go to work the next morning, craved a cocktail every waking day, screwed up his priorities, then it had gone too far. Then he was an alcoholic. I'm sure this isn't necessarily true; in technical terms, we were both alcoholics – weekend ones though we may have been – and anyone who could have witnessed just how much elation we culled from our booze would have sponsored us to a twelve-step program immediately.

It didn't bother us much. Not then, anyway. The emotionally wounded find their balm in various mitigators. A sex club where the flesh can quell the thirst to be touched. Or a convenient little silver flask brimming with spirits to palliate the emptiness and arouse passions that, in the absence of *the* one man, would paralyze the heart forever.

It was on nights in the parked car up on Dick Street, drinking from my little flask and listening to a music score fill the air and heart, that the world finally started to make a little bit of sense. At those moments, reality lost its garishness and cushioned the falls of weeks past and the anxiety of those lying ahead.

The night seemed to douse herself with a mystical perfume that the senses could suddenly register. Like a

fickle mistress, she began to reveal passions and secrets
that she wouldn't have shared with those that had chosen
the path of sobriety. The seduction in everything around
us became exclusively apparent. And age, time,
discrimination and responsibilities came to form the ethos
of an alien race.

Friends had often suggested that we cut down on
the rituals. That, impeccable ironing and long showers
with exotic soaps aside, if we were to cut down on the
compulsion to listen to what they called sad, depressing
music, we just might get into a club in time to find
someone and not go home alone.

But that was unthinkable. That was the part that
we both looked forward to most each week. As the
weekdays dragged and Saturday approached with all its
promise, both Adrian and I anxiously anticipated these
ceremonies that would purge us emotionally and
physically. There were times when we would just laugh
hysterically, remembering moments like Adrian urging
our catch of the night to be gentle because it was my
"first time." And sometimes we would sit and cry
because the drinking had sensitized us to the music and
we were so moved. We'd offer each other support, tell
each other that we were good enough and that someone
out there would be very lucky to have us. An entire hour
would fleet by as we sifted through our emotions before
tearing from the car to make our way down the boulevard
and into a club before it closed.

Long after we had left a drained sipper bottle and
the car behind, the music would continue to play in our
minds. We would still hear it. Somewhere on a deeper
level within. Resonating within the walls of our hearts.
Melancholy. Sensual. Heartbreaking. We became as
light as air. Our step barely feeling the ground beneath.
Ethereal. Wafting through the night like Apsaras, from
fables told to me long ago.

And when we were finally inside a club, only an hour left before that fateful two o'clock, the symphony in us resonated still; resonated in spite of the dance music compelling everyone to gyrate shirtless on the dance floor, to find someone to go home with.

While the crowd grew more frantic with the last call for alcohol, or last call for ass-a-hole as the inebriated ones called it, we remained calm in the knowledge of a little flask nestled in my back pocket. Our eyes smoothly surveyed the room rather than darting around in a panic. We felt good. We felt right. No more standing on the edge of the dance floor feeling like we didn't belong just because we hadn't spent hours in a gym and the shirts still cloaked our slender bodies. No more guilt for abandoning those that had been consigned to AIDS. No more searching for Richard and trying to sabotage whomever he was planning on fucking that night. No more holocaust of the heart.

If the eyes were mirrors to the soul, then both Adrian and I felt that anyone who looked at us was being treated to a truly rare splendor.

CHAPTER 11

LITHMUS TEST

Salman calls me. He's terribly upset because he thinks he's been disinherited.

"Bitch sister!" he keeps saying. "She's making my life pure hell, *kutri sali!* Total control queen, just like my mother. Well, to hell with them all! I just don't give a shit anymore. Let her control all the finances – and I hope she screws them *all* one day! *Hunh!* Wait till my mother gets a load of my answering machine. She'll get a heart attack when she hears the greeting, I swear it!"

On it, he has the campiest song from one of Hindi cinema's classics, *Pakeezah*. Meena Kumari starred in it as a courtesan, lip-synching to Lata Mangeshkar's "Inhi Logo Ne," declaring how she had been exploited by every man from the postman to the policeman.

This should have been the litmus test for any Indian parent to discover if a son's homosexuality. The infamous *Pakeezah* song.

CHAPTER 12

THE ART OF WAR

I remember my grandfather teaching me how to make ice popsicles in the scorching equatorial afternoons of Mombasa. Under a towering ylang-ylang tree, which provided some shade and perfumed the air intoxicatingly, Bapa would crush the ice in an old rag, insert a stick from the *fagia* before balling it up and then dip it into a cup of rose sherbet syrup. Sometimes he sat back on the cement bench and supervised my attempts at this miracle; but when my small, maladroit hands fumbled to affix the stick, his shaky (sober) hands would take custody of our project. After a little fiddling, a perfectly globular, smooth popsicle would glisten under the merciless sun.

But no sooner had I taken hold of this crimson treat would we hear the angry screams of everybody, from my grandmother to my aunty, accusing him of attempting to make me sick due to my chronic tonsillitis.

"What are you trying to do now, you *chodu?* Are you trying to kill him?" They would holler and yank me in from the verandah.

Ice popsicles were prohibited, just like ice-cold sodas and sun dried shreds of mango called *achari*, playing in the sun for too long or swimming in the ocean because I could drown just like that little boy in our community fifteen years ago. And my grandfather was definitely up to no good, even when sober.

"Why don't you just get lost instead of destroying everyone's life, *hunh?*" my grandmother would say, slapping her forehead in disdain.

He would curse back sometimes, and sometimes he would leave home and go on a drinking binge until he came back swaggering at the end of the day, his pants wet with urine. A neighbor would spot him, passed out by the bus shed in some part of town, and bring him home out of a sense of communal obligation.

My grandparents quarreled constantly, cursed each other mercilessly. Looking at their stoic black-and-white studio wedding picture, it was hard to imagine that they had ever spoken to one another in any way civil. Or that they had once been in love and had ever been intimate enough to conceive three children. Stranger still seemed the fact that they had been divorced nearly forty years and they had continued to live under the same roof. Somehow they had forgotten to move out. Whenever one questioned this arrangement, my grandmother would throw her hands in the air with pure resignation and say, "I came home one day and he refused to leave. Slept outside in the verandah. I had no choice but to let him back in. He's been here ever since."

When Bapa was dying, I flew back to Mombasa. Standing by his emaciated body, I held his frail hand and tried hard to smile, horrified at how much weight he had lost, and how he had shriveled into a look-alike for an unwrapped mummy.

I tried to forget about the times when even as a young child I had joined the family tradition of hurling insults his way and the times in my teens when I'd been tempted to hit him. That was just the vernacular we had always employed in that house. Instead, I thought about how handsome he looked in the wedding picture that hung over his bed, the picture he had refused to dislodge. I thought about his musical talents, his ability to play the harmonium, and his singing. How he had always been invited to perform at the music parties that were often hosted on the terraces of Tudor flats; many even begged for a cassette recording of his performance.

His hand barely a feather in my palm, my grandfather told me that he had been waiting to see me. His only grandchild. He knew he was dying and was afraid of it and didn't want to. I tried to console him with the notion that sooner or later everyone's time came and hated myself for doing it. I thought I had steeled sufficiently until, like a perplexed child, he had looked at me quizzically and asked, "How did I get this sick, Ali? What happened to me?"

Tears welled up in my eyes, and I fought them back so that he wouldn't see me cry. He couldn't comprehend how any of this had happened, and the irony both astonished and pained me. All that drinking. He honestly couldn't see a connection. He was entirely taken aback by his destroyed liver and his ailing health and now sounded like an infant who had played with matches only to be absolutely shocked by the burn. "I don't know how this became of me," he confessed, shaking his head slowly.

I patted the back of his hand and simply nodded in agreement to his sentiment. "I know, Bapa," I said. "I know..."

What do you say to him at such a moment? What can you say? That you did this to yourself? That this is the result of all that damned boozing?

I was back in Los Angeles when he died two weeks later. On the night of his passing, I dreamt of a newborn baby. It kicked and threw its fists in the air, remonstrating with all the anguish of birth.

After his burial I heard from my friend Zul, who had taken my place in performing the last rites, that nobody had been more distraught than my grandmother.

Her question: "What will I do without you now?"

Who would sit next to her in one of the two large sofas that sat like old dowagers in front of his bedroom window and argue the afternoons away? Who would she hold responsible for destroying her life, and who would curse back at her? Who would keep her company for all the hours her children were away at work?

She had wanted him to get lost, and now, much to her chagrin, he had gone and done just that.

Nobody could have doubted that they had loved each other profoundly. Not if one took the time to search beyond the combative guise of their interaction. Through the years that they had endured each other, they had reinvented their relationship. Although their language had been replaced from one of civility to that of offense, they had nevertheless chosen to communicate. They had begun a war and each had found comfort in hiding behind their armor. The art of war had become for them, the art of loving.

Yes, I choose to believe that they had loved each other profoundly. Forty-three years of any kind of liaison should be proof of that.

CHAPTER 13

INVOCATIONS

When I called my mother in Mombasa, our conversation started off typically enough with her clucking ruefully and telling me how much she missed me; how, strangely enough, she had been thinking about me just moments before the phone rang – making my call seem like a telepathic response to her invocation.

"You'll be here soon enough," I said, suddenly without the ire her impending visit had provoked in me just days ago. "But right now, I need you to do me a favor."

"What happened? Are you okay? Are you sick? Did something happen?" she said, without pausing for even a breath of air. I could feel her trying, wanting desperately to squeeze herself into the mouthpiece and through the cord so she could emerge on the other end, here with me.

"Yeah, I'm fine. I'm okay," I said. "It's just Richard, Mummy."

"Richard?"

By now she had heard his name several times and if anything, it had been taken as a rejection of her: *I can't talk to you right now, Richard's on the other line; I have to go now, Mummy. I'm meeting Richard; Richard will be here any minute, I have to get dressed.* And now, if after avoiding her for who knows how long, Richard had also motivated my reaching out to her, there was no doubt in her mind as to the stature he occupied in my life.

"He's sick, Mummy," I said, trying to throttle the tremor in my voice. "I don't know what will happen to him."

"What's the matter with him?" she asked.

I cut straight to my purpose. "I want you to put a *Satado* in the mosque," I said, referring to that most potent of prayer rituals in the community. No Ismaili was to request this weeklong observation for trivialities. An impending catastrophe or great crisis that involved either the entire community or one of its own was the only justifiable basis to undertake this vow.

"*Satado?*" she said, incredulous. "But, you know, he's not even an Ismaili, Ali!"

"What difference does *that* make? He's a human being, isn't he?" I said. "I mean, you would do it for me if I was in any kind of trouble, wouldn't you?"

"Yes, but, you know, that is differ—"

"Just think of him as your son, then. You must do this for me, Mummy, please. You have to!"

I must have sounded as completely possessed by my fear as I was. I felt her acquiescing even through her concerned reprimand.

"Ali, what the hell is the matter with you? You know, I'm not getting any younger here, and you know, one of these days these antics of yours are going to drive me into the ground, I swear it! You *must* stop feeling this way about that boy! What kind of spell has he put your under, *henh?*"

"I'll let him go, Mum, I promise. I just want him to come out of this alive and then I'll distance myself from him. But I need your help. I don't want him to die," I cried, verbalizing my deepest fear for the first time. "I won't be able to bear it. I won't be able to bear it if anything happens to him..."

"Ali, don't be silly now. Nothing's going to happen to him, okay? Why must you think of the worst things?"

"Maybe because he's in the damn I.C.U.!"

"Oh," she said. "He will be alright, just you wait and see."

"I need you to do this, Mum."

"Okay, but what is he suffering from, Ali? Did he get into an accident? Is he—"

"I don't know. Nobody knows...they're running tests...I don't know..."

"So listen, you know, *you* can also go to the mosque and put this *Satado*, you know?"

"I can't go there!" I said.

"Why?"

"It's just not the same here."

"What's not the same?"

"It's different," I said. "They're completely different here. I can't even relate to them..."

"What is different? Who is different? What are you saying, *hunh?*"

I didn't know where to start. Unless she lived here, it was difficult to explain the differences between Ismailis from East Africa and South Asia – not because there were so many of them but because these differences could be subtle. It wasn't just their mannerisms in prayers – *ginans* had the same lyrics but a different tune when coming from a Pakistani, preventing me from joining in. It was also the ingredients used in traditional viands that struck a different and irritating note on the palate. When I eagerly bought a plate of *biryani* from the food auction that took place after the prayers, I ended up dumping most of it into the garbage – the excess of cinnamon in lieu of cumin deprived me of nostalgic fulfillment.

Most striking was their interpretation of the faith itself and their secular view of living in an adopted homeland. Many of them, especially the migrants, segregated themselves from the world at large, the community setting the perimeters of both their spiritual and social realms. Stalwart in the crucibles of the faith, it was clear to see that they considered themselves as the guardians of tradition or *tarika*; where the East African Ismailis, who dynamically tried to integrate into modernism, came off looking more like the infidels that represented everything that had gone wrong with the community. Earlier dislocation – their motherlands of India and Pakistan had been left behind generations ago – had already sharpened their survival instinct and compelled them to forge an identity based not only on distant Hindu roots and the Muslim faith, but also on their nationality as Africans.

While my mother launched into an untimely and clichéd reasoning of the truly faithful, reminding me that one went to mosque to be with God and not other people, I suppressed something else; that all these reasons served me well when the truth of it might have been that I was simply afraid they wouldn't understand the real me. The boy-lover. The homosexual. That because the interpretation of the faith was so traditional, so orthodox, there wouldn't be any of the little cracks for a homosexual to slip through. It was in East Africa after all, with their sons – these boys that had grown into men and had since reared families – that I had first learned the pleasures of a man's cock and my place in the actuarial tables of sexuality.

"Are you going to help me or not?" I asked.

"Ali, listen to me! *Nothing* is going to happen to him. I'll go to mosque, and I'll put a *Satado* for him, okay? I promise you. But you know, you must also promise me in return that you will look after yourself. And that all this will change, you know?"

"It will."

"It *has* to!" she said, tsking away regretfully. "Ali, what do you see in this boy? Why are you acting so crazy?"

"Can we not get into this right now?" *I love him, Mummy, I love him!*

"Okay, okay. Don't you worry anymore. Everything will be alright, you'll see. Everything will be just perfect."

I quieted down and controlled myself from crying further. What was it about mothers? They could comfort you in a way nobody else could. Perhaps because they knew how, long before the child's memory.

Everything would indeed be alright now that she had agreed to do this. I didn't know if I had faith in God, but I certainly had faith in my mother. According to her – and as explained by the faith – initiating a *Satado* invoked the prayers of every man, woman and child in Mombasa and God had to listen. Concede. Give in. And so, for the following week, while Richard lay jaundiced in the I.C.U., the entire Ismaili community in Mombasa, unbeknownst to them, prayed for his life.

And my freedom.

CHAPTER 14

GREEN

I hate green.

Green was the color of the shawl they draped my father in during the first half of the burial ceremony at the mosque.

He was just lying there, so still, his eyes closed. His nostrils stuffed with cotton wool. I thought that there was something terribly wrong with that.

How would he breathe?

When my mother instructed me to kneel down and touch his feet, as is customary, I felt terrified that he would awaken and then he would be very, very angry with me. The *Mukhi*, a priest of the local community, sat on the other side of my father and awaited our prayer of absolution, upon which he dipped his right hand into the bowl of holy water and sprinkled it onto my father's stony face.

My father didn't wake up, and I felt relieved. I had never seen him look so at peace with either himself or the others around him.

When it was time to carry him away, a woman's melodramatic voice cut through the air and led the rest of the congregation into a relentless dirge. Pallbearers carried his body out of the mosque, the men now taking over, and my mother started to wail as if she had suddenly realized that he was forever gone. Her agony at that being the last she would see him, seemed to rack her body and spirit in quite the same way that he had when he'd been alive.

According to Islamic law, women are not permitted to participate in the final part of the liturgy for the dead – the burial. And thankfully so. Had we been the Hindus we had been converted from generations ago,

I'm quite sure that my mother wouldn't have hesitated to become *Sati* and fling herself onto his pyre.

I had started to cry too. Not because they were taking him away, but because, as is typical of a bewildered five-year-old, his mother and everyone else was crying. Although I don't recall asking my mother about him, I'm sure I must have. Thankfully, there were no stories of Daddy having gone on some long journey, never to return but always looking down benevolently upon us from some distant star. I don't know if this was because my mother was too young herself to summon such pretenses. It had been made clear to me, as clear as it can be to a five-year-old, that Daddy had been murdered by that "other woman." Perhaps I thought he was gone again and would return eventually, unpredictably as was his style, only with a bloodstained shirt this time. No need to worry. He would be back.

Some time after, I held that green cashmere shawl. It carried the musty smell of the frangipanis they had strung around his neck and the incense burnt by his side. I even held the stiletto that had robbed the life from him.

Blood strewn all over the room of his mistress. The mistress who they had claimed had put something in his food and cast a spell on him. What witchery that Kala-Singhi must have done to trap him? What *gangha*? A few drops of menstrual discharge in the cooking and the man would be pussy-whipped for life. Six fatal stabs. And she claimed he had done it to himself in a jealous rage at discovering her with another man. Not once. Not twice. But six times. Six times he had been enraged enough the plunge the dagger into his own breast. They bought it, naturally. Literally. She was set free. Money talks. Chai can silence all the mouths. Tip any scale to one party's advantage. Court battles cost too much, so poor Parin, now a single mother, had been quietly relieved of justice.

Nothing could bring him back.

I nestled that stiletto in my little hands. The knife was about the size of my palm. I don't know how we had gotten possession of it. There was no blood on it. No traces of rich crimson aged into a burnt sienna on its blade. Only the cold glint of the steel wiped clean of the life it had ebbed from him.

And the green of its barrel.

I hate green.

CHAPTER 15

HEAVEN

Heaven has terrible acoustics. All you hear is the thump, thump, thump of the music. You can't discern the lyrics. You can barely even make out the melody. Only the thump, thump, thump. And you wonder – no, you know, everyone in the room is drugged sufficiently not to mind.

Frankie Knuckles is spinning his house groove. Shirtless bodies everywhere. Gyrating. Stomping. Hands flailing in the air. Attitude to the hilt. Beautiful people. There is no space on the dance floor and they don't need any. No one is trying to show off any moves. This isn't the seventies. All anyone is interested in exhibiting is his anatomy.

You feel excommunicated, not built enough to shed clothing and be admitted into their sanctuary. Not intimidated enough either to stay home, cruise on-line and give up on this aspect of the lifestyle. So here you are. In the place to be. Hovering around the edge of the dance floor. Gripping your cocktail like it is a lover. Drinking. To tear down inhibitions. To feel more attractive. To feel included.

You're looking. Searching. Hoping tonight you won't have to go home alone. Or find solace in the darkness of some sex club. That some body will partake in your flesh. You've prepared yourself with so much anticipation and now stand in front of your Gods.

You are ready to be offered.

Across the room, I find Adrian talking to a tall, well-built black man. Kitty, our chubby Chinese friend with a penchant for stringy tank tops and astonishingly tight pants, is sipping some fruity concoction through a straw, focused on finding other Asian men to connect with. I glide over to the group, having tired of the mental masturbation in the room. Adrian's new acquaintance introduces himself as Noah. I start off with the Biblical jokes and ask him if he has an ark stored away somewhere.

"You never know," he says, attempting wit. "I just might."

"Well, where is it, Noah? We're ready to board."

He laughs out loud and steps back in mock shock. "*You* are *b-a-a-d!*"

"You have no idea," I say, grinning.

Adrian throws his arm around me proudly.

"You've got your two of a kind right here, Noah," I say. "All your work clearly cut out."

He shakes his head in disbelief. He thinks I'm a riot and he's damn right. I sure are. One big fucking riot. I feel powerful now, in word, if not in brawn. Muscle of the mind. Wit abounds. Even Hercules here, with two hours of daily gym workouts under his belt, is no match for a razor-sharp tongue. And it gets even easier after a couple of cocktails.

But I lose interest in him. His lack of a retort disappoints me. Bores me. He looks embarrassed. I think him weak. Unable to stand up to me. To tell me that the ark was docked right outside but that he had doubts I could sustain the stormy journey.

You see, my idea of a perfect pick-up line has never been, "Hey, are you having fun tonight?" or "So, what's your name?" or "You're cute," but "Come here, baby. I'll make your life pure hell."

The last time someone had been nice enough to ask me if I was having fun, I took one look at him and, diffused by his cordiality, said, "I was. Until now." Nobody was looking for nice guys in the bars, and any one that hasn't figured that out is either going to get his heart broken or remain in a constant state of perplexity. Everyone wants someone tormented, someone complicated and a bit dangerous. Wants sparks to fly across the room, long brooding glances full of lust, to make them feel like quarry being slowly snared. Not some accountant type who wants to know about your dreams and tells you all about the future he plans on sharing with the man he hopes to find tonight.

Excusing myself, I start to head for the bathroom. "And if the floods come," I impart before turning completely away. "Don't leave without me."

In the bathroom I bump into Roy, whom I haven't seen in months. His hair is still bleached blonde and he's doing his classic Eartha Kitt purr at some porno star zipping himself up at the urinal. I can never get used to the garish contrast of the gold in his hair with his dark Latin face.

He sees me, throws open his arms open and shrieks, "My sister! Oh, my sister in crime! I've missed you!"

The porno star rolls his eyes at us and slips past.

Air kisses and hugs. We tell each other how fabulous we both look. We're young. We're negative – or at least uninformed otherwise. And the direct deposit has replenished our bank account hours before. What more can you ask for?

"And how's the love life?" he says, winking and slapping my butt.

I shrug. "Alright."

"Hmm," he says, shaking his head. "I know that look. Men! They're all pigs," he says, throwing disapproving glances at the men around us and conveniently disregarding our own gender. "Gay or straight, it doesn't matter, they all still think with their dicks!"

"You know it."

"We should've been born lesbians, no? Gir-r-r-l, we'd be harvesting eggs by now."

Laughing, I offer him some of my Stoli, and he confesses between sips that he is going to get some China.

"China?" I ask.

"Blow," he says, nudging me.

Jesus! Whoever did coke anymore? So eighties!

"Well, wait for me," I say, breezing past the ridiculously long line of men too shy to use the urinal. Meanwhile Roy blots his face in the mirror with the special absorbent paper he carries in his wallet.

Stationed before the urinal, I force myself to release. My eyes fix upon the flier for an Asian dance club taped against the wall. I try to concentrate on it to ward off the stares of the men standing behind. It's like they're all waiting to witness my failure at this most human of tasks, one they have such a problem performing. I think there must always be a certain humiliation served to the tormented butch men waiting for the stall when a femme glides past them with confidence and pisses away with superior glee...*I'll show you who's "on top!"*

I try to ignore the man standing next to me who, not subtle enough to use his peripheral vision, is staring directly at my cock. I'm frozen. Glaring at him, I hiss, "Do you mind!" and as if electrocuted, his head jerks up and he looks away.

"Huh! Not much to look at anyway," he mutters.

Club Asia...waterfalls...psss...psss...They are all trash...Goddamn trash with their big bulky bodies...Show them who the real man is...Go ahead and piss...Piss...Piss...For Asians and their lovers...Piss...Piss...Aaaah!

Zipped up, I follow Roy to the bar and watch him sashay his way through the clamor perched around it. That's club expertise right there. Knowing how to steer through the crowds at the bar and get that cocktail. Men everywhere with water bottles tucked into their jeans are running back and forth from the bathroom, refilling them

– on Ecstasy and in need of more water than an evening's allowance can support. These days the E-boys are the only ones who look blissfully happy. I can see Adrian talking to Noah in the same spot but Kitty has vanished, and I hope they don't come looking for me.

Roy leans forward at the bar and is quickly noticed by the bartender, a muscular, shirtless Tom Cruise look-alike. We have all lusted after him at one point or another. So typical, this lusting after bartenders in a gay club, as if they have been handpicked precisely to set off a hormonal bomb in our bodies and make us drink more out of frustration. An average looking bartender working alongside him graces me with his attention. *Oh well, saved me an extra dollar on the tip.*

"Vodka," I say quickly, before anyone notices I haven't waited as long as the others.

"And what do want with your Vodka?"

"Rocks."

I pay for my drink, tempted to leave the quarters on the bar, then leave the dollar instead. The quarters will come in handy for laundry.

Roy returns to me with a fruity, grenadine-infected cocktail in his hand and takes the time to visually undress the men around him as he slinks over. "I have it!" he declares.

"You have it? How? Who gave it to you?"

He leans over and whispers, "The bartender, silly!"

"Him?" I ask, glancing at the one I'd been coveting.

He nods.

"I didn't even see him give it to you!"

"Neither did anyone else." He winks, flashing a folded napkin at me.

"Well," I say, "talk about one-stop shopping."

I shake my head, amazed that these transactions have been taking place right under my nose all this time.

Even more shocking is *who* supplied Roy with the coke:
the same bartender who refused to serve any more
alcohol to a totally wasted queen the last time I was here.
I had been so impressed with his resilience. So
responsible. Resisting the dollar bills that were being
shelled out in an effort to secure just one more drink.

Roy tells me that I can get anything from this
bartender. Coke. X. Pot. Name it. Simply the best
quality. "Just place your order a week in advance, honey,
and you can buy him too if you like. No, wait, that only
takes a few hours notice." Now my jaw really drops.
"Oh, come on!" he says. "Surely you've seen his latest ad
in *Frontiers?*"

How well I knew those pages at the back of the
magazine, crammed with ads for "models" and
"masseurs." They were my solace when, after an entire
evening of relentlessly looking for love, I returned home
feeling not like the polished man that had slaved over his
appearance before stepping out but a roach, scurrying
home as daylight approached. In that state of exhaustion,
when it became difficult even to masturbate, I pored over
the pages of the magazine, suspecting that the reason I
was such a flop as a gay man was because everyone else
had turned into hookers and porno stars. A hundred and
fifty dollars. In or out. Top. Bottom (very, very rarely).
Nine inches. Twelve inches. Rock hard. Second
available. Will travel. Get your intake of meat for the
week. And always twenty-nine years old or under.

As Roy leads me away from the bar, I take a last
look at the bartender and wonder, how the hell am I
supposed to distinguish him from anyone else in the
magazine? It's not like they showed anything above the
rippling chests and silhouettes of erect dicks throbbing
through Calvin Klein underwear – faces cut out of the
pictures to protect the innocent.

Back in the bathroom, we file into the line and
wait impatiently for a stall. Some of them note our

sudden return with curiosity. Others just know. Roy launches into a manifesto about the single life. It's not his overrated take on the pleasures of being accountable to no one that irritates me as much as his need to preach these views to everyone around us. I wonder what Adrian is up to, contribute a few insincere remarks and pray for the line to move faster.

Finally inside the stall, Roy unwraps the paper napkin and reveals the little plastic zipper bag. He scoops the powder on a key and sniffs it. First the right nostril, then a refill for the left. He turns to me.

I pause. *Do I really want to do this? Booze I can just regurgitate but this I'm going to be stuck with!*

But the monotony of the music and the phlegmatic attitude of men bound to their narcissism are rousing a feeling of ennui in me. I feel a little tired. My feet are starting to drag. There is still a whole night ahead of me, and I know I must get by because I'm not ready to go home. Or to the Vortex. There is still the chance that I might be able to pick someone up without having to pay admission for it. I feel the need for a little something to push me over the edge. To ignite a spark for an otherwise mundane scene.

And to top it all off, Mummy will be arriving tomorrow.

I lean toward Roy's key to unlock the magic.

Might as well unleash tonight.

CHAPTER 16

BOYFRIEND

Her British Airways flight has arrived on time. Thank God. Now customs. That would take at least another hour. I pace around the airport, my Motorola clutched in one hand and CK sunglasses in another. Objects that certify me as part of the L.A. culture.

A young man walked by, holding a single long-stemmed rose in his hand and rendering me mesmerized. He had rich, dark skin and stirring, mystical eyes. He could have been Indian or Latino – sometimes it's hard to tell. His plaid shirt and baggy blue jeans embody the grunge look that I've never been able to get into, but those looks and that rose...irresistible. Who was it all for?

He was obviously waiting for someone to arrive too, and they were probably in love. My own parents had been just that young when they had met and fallen in love. Could he be anything like my father? This is what he must have looked like when he had pursued my mother and turned her life upside down. Was his relationship as passionate as theirs had been? Judging from just that rose, I convinced myself that it must have been.

My eyes followed his steps until I feared losing sight of him. Then, without giving it much thought, I found myself trailing him to a lounge bar. Settled on a barstool, the rose placed carefully on the counter top, he ordered a tap beer. I watched him from a bench outside the bar. Watched him. Fascinated. His every gesture a testament to his masculinity. Restraint. Minimal. Commanding and without animation, from his strident walk to the way in which he peeled the bills from a wad to pay for the beer.

Reminding me of the want ads that insisted upon "straight acting" contenders. The ones that I am humiliated by yet almost exclusively find myself looking for.

What would it be like to approach this one? Just walk up to him and smile suggestively. The way a woman might have when suggesting a come-on. Ask him who he was and maybe slip him my card.

How easy it must be for *them* to make such advances. To do their little mating dance. No risks involved. Well, at least not any *real* danger. At best, they plan to connect. At worst, he's flattered. Or she may tell him she's already involved and wants to be left alone. There is no violence. No fists to bludgeon the face. No insults inadvertently delivered. None taken.

Instead, I relied upon the hope of the reciprocal lingering of his glance. That most primitive and sophisticated of senses. Pray that if he *did* turn around, catch my gaze and hesitate before averting his eyes, his pause would not imply animosity or offense. Or botheration. That my nervous attempt at a smile would not be countered by a sneer deforming his lips.

Instead, looked at his back. Ah, that back. So much to be said about a man's back. To see him from an angle that was his most unassuming. My eyes danced upon that vast land of plains and curves. To be able to rest my head in the concave straight of his back and close my eyes and hold him from around his waist and not feel the need to be held. Possession.

Roll fantasy.

We are not strangers. He needs the beer to calm his nervousness of meeting Mummy for the first time. We have been seeing each other for quite a while now. He has brought the rose in the hope of making a good first impression. Once he has won her over with the same charm that seduced me, he would call her "Mummy" as I do. His warm, respectful candor and striking good looks disarm any initial hesitation on her part, quickly allaying any suspicions a mother comes armed with when protectively evaluating her child's mate. He insists on picking up both her bags, so I have my arms free to put around her; walks a few steps behind us, allowing us a moment of privacy to chatter away in Kutchi and not feel the need to converse in English for his benefit; escorts us to his Jeep or Blazer or one of those masculine cars where he insists she sit in the front seat (the only time he would expect me not to insist on that privilege). She looks to me distressfully for help, and he puts the bags on the ground to help her climb up and in.

For a little while, he ignores me without meaning to, concentrates on how her flight was and tells her how eagerly he has waited to meet her.   Inside, he is still nervous. I watch him from behind and smile to myself.

Instead, I sigh, resigned to watching his back from this bench.

He stretched his arms, tired of waiting – the flight obviously delayed – the he turned around and his eyes caught mine. I quickly looked away, not wanting there to be any kind of contact, the spell broken.

When I looked back up at him, he had turned back toward the bar once again to sip his beer.

I grunted to myself sardonically, my fingers tracing the rim of the glasses in my hands. I knew I had to rouse myself and look for her, just in case she had cleared through customs.   This time, I halfheartedly hoped, they did not pull her aside for questioning on contraband items.

What the hell am I doing here?   Get a fucking grip! When I'd caught others leering at seemingly disinterested men I was nothing but disgusted and embarrassed for them.   I knew nothing about this man before and I wouldn't ever. He would remain an image in my mind. Like encounters that happened in passing. A glance or a smile exchanged in a crowded room or a bustling street. The kind of moment that stayed with you long after it had passed. A reminder through the daily struggle for the things that you really want but have lost sight of.

I tell myself that this man was perhaps nothing like my image of him; my fantasies based purely on his physical appearance were pure artifice. Who cared? Then, in settled an awareness of another deeply rooted fact: abandoning such shallow gauges and taking the time to descry qualities far more enduring was usually beyond me. Plumage had always overshadowed virtue and I'd always be a slave to the despotism of physical appearances.

CHAPTER 17

THE ARRIVAL

At five-feet-two inches, she came out of the terminal, her Dr. Scholl's slapping up against her back heels. I saw her long before she saw me. She had put on some weight, and her hair was cut so short, it looked embarrassing. Dressed like an aging mother in a beige cardigan over a nondescript cotton frock, she immediately piqued my irritation for looking so unkempt. On one arm is slung a tacky orange handbag with an orgy of dolphins and the word "Paris" flaunted over them. With the other hand she wheeled a large bag, burdened with handwritten nametags and a suspiciously large padlock securing what looked like the belly of an obese man suffocating under an altogether struggling belt. In it I knew she carried, despite her initial protests, all the things that those who have left their homeland craved and manipulated any travelers into hauling across the Atlantic for them. Months before her departure, upon catching wind of her plans to go abroad, friends and acquaintances would have come out of the woodwork to obligate her into making their not-so-little deliveries for their endeared ones. Kenya tea and batiks and *mabuyus* and *attars* from the House of Gulab.

The suitcase followed her waywardly, like a disobedient pet, and her eyes looked around frantically for me. From where I stood I could almost hear her tsking away and cursing at those she had conceded to. Bhosrina Sala! Khudda *knows why I agreed to this* matha-kuti!

Her face brightened up when she finally saw me, and abandoning the burden of her luggage, she threw her arms around me. "Oh, Ali," she said. "I was so afraid you wouldn't show up! Thank God, you're here!"

"Why would you think that?" I asked, my annoyance rearing.

"No, I'm just saying that, you know?"

She's started it already. Her games to gain sympathy. I moved to pick up the bag – to alleviate both her and the worn wheels – but she insisted, "*Ey, nah, nah!* Don't pick that up, Ali, it's *too* heavy!"

"Don't be silly, Mum. It's fine."

"Why don't you listen to me, Ali, why? Here, let *me* take care of it!"

The wheels groaned in protest.

"For Chrissake, Mum. Would you stop it?"

"*Haya*, fine! It's up to you. You know, can't we get someone to carry it for us?"

Erring on the side of caution, I decided to just pick up the bag rather than wheel it around and keep my mouth shut for the walk to the car.

She told me about her osteoporosis and how she'd been terribly sick for the past few months. How she had been driving one night when she dove into a ditch and was truly fortunate to have emerged physically unscathed.

When she didn't see a reaction befitting her expectations, she said, "But I lost one tooth!" and opened her mouth wide and pointed into it. I restrained from sympathizing and her litany subsided.

The entire time in the car, she prayed fanatically as if she had some premonition of how my driving is going to get us into a horrible accident. Barely even thirty minutes and I was already losing my patience with her.

"*Why* are you praying?" I demanded.

Then she gave me one of her signature looks. The one where she'd start to quiver and look like she was going to start crying because I was being so mean to her.

I sighed with exasperation. "It's not as if there's anything wrong."

"It's a habit, okay? There doesn't *have* to be anything wrong!"

My eyes on the road as we struggled down Lincoln Boulevard, I breathed in an attempt to regain tranquility.

"Do you *have* to drive *so* fast? There isn't any rush."

"We're well under the speed limit, Mum. If I drive any slower they'll pull us over and shoot us."

Then, her sigh. Without even looking at her, I could see her. Dejectedly looking down. Feeling that it was better to say nothing to someone as intolerant and disrespectful as me. Best to just bear it in silence the rest of the way. I didn't have to turn my head to recognize these looks. I call them her "martyr" and "after everything I have done for you, Ali?" looks. The same ones I'd used on Richard.

Why, dear God, did she always have to act like she was in some fucking movie?

I told myself, *Try. Please try with her*, but ended up stepping on the accelerator as she sped through her thirty-three bead rosary.

A reprieve: Mummy's suitcase full of staples of Kenya. Crimson sugarcoated morsels of the baobab's fruit called *mabuyus*. A sinfully rich pound of *halwa* studded with slivered almonds and pistachios from the coastal town of Malindi. Butter cookies called *nankhatais* from none other than Husseini Bakery, the trademark H.B. initials are engraved on each one – the first thing I do is run my finger over them and inhale the aroma of butter and vanilla.

The stuff of nostalgia. Foods and smells that leave indelible impressions on the canvas of a transient life. Discovering them again was like being immersed into a pool of the past. Like fingers gently drawing aside the veil between the present and the past. Remembering vaguely some of the last times you had enjoyed such dishes in a land so far away, I had only been able to dream about it for years.

There I was again in school uniform – khaki shorts and white cotton shirt – hiding behind schoolyards and on the verandah at home, devouring *mabuyus* and spitting out their dark seeds. Cowering from Grandma and Aunty's portentous hollering while Mummy took a nap in resignation, too young herself to indulge in such reproach and assume full guardianship. Or maybe just comfortable in the knowledge that I was being policed sufficiently by them. *Ey, chodu sala,* you better not be eating any *mabuyus! Au toke hero laafo mar-ni!* Who will look after you if your tonsils start again, *heh?* The fact that I already had my tonsils surgically removed years before made little difference to them. In their minds, the tonsils were still there – lurking in my throat somewhere instead of sitting in the little jar that they had dangled in front of me after the operation – phantom organisms just waiting to make me sick and keep them up all night in prayers and jars of Vicks and towels drenched in cologne water.

As I suckle the first velvety morsel, its sugared tanginess diffused in my mouth. Never in all these years had I forgotten how they tasted. Just resisted at first, and then gradually forgot to think about it as new flavored beguiled my taste buds. Just like all the other foods that Mummy could not bring – although I had heard that the introduction of vacuum packaging in Kenya had facilitated the smuggling of even those nowadays! – the meat pies from Cosy Tea Room on Moi Avenue, relished with that particular brand of *Peptang* chili sauce and limes; *khima* chapattis from the Aswan Cafe that the pack of us would customarily gorge upon after a night of dancing with our so "girlfriends" (who had been expediently dropped off at home so that we could all spout about the German tourist men that had been cruising us).

These were the diamonds in the minefields of memory.

Mummy mentioned that they closed Cosy Tea Room years ago, and like many others, the owners had emigrated to *Toron-to, Cay-nay-da.*

The recipe, I thought. *Whatever happened to the recipe?*

As she proceeded to empty the open package of *mabuyus* into a jar until now filled with jellybeans, Mummy caught me up with some of the friends and acquaintances in Mombasa. Emphatically, she pointed out that most had gotten married. And had children. Altaf had a German wife. Akil was the proud father of two and had bloated up with weight as every Indian married man did after marriage.

And Nawaz, whose father had passed away a couple of years ago quite suddenly, as she puts it – completely overlooking the fact that he had suffered from kidney problems and been in and out of hospitals – had moved to the Nyali beach colony, quite possibly the Malibu of Kenya.

As casually as I could, I ask her if he had gotten married.

"Yeah, yeah, he too got married, to some *Arabi, neh?"* she said. "Or maybe that was that younger brother of his. I don't know, I get so confused these days. I know that one of them is married and the other is staying with some married woman, can you imagine *that? Yah, Khuddah!* You know that family, they are *such* low class even with all their money!"

CHAPTER 18

THE APPRENTICE

I began my apprenticeship to Nawaz when I was thirteen and he was fifteen. He was one of the older boys who I played with in our community flats. I-Spy. *Geli-Danda*. Hide-and-seek. Where, hiding together, obscured by the shadows cast by some pillar at the Jamat Khanna, or in some vacant servant's quarters on the terrace atop a block of flats, someone's plea for a little "touch-touch" would incite us into experimental pleasures guiltily disbarred from memory until the next time we felt the *char.*

Over the years, I had witnessed his body evolve from that of a hairless athletic youth to one of an impressively muscled adult. I remember twiddling my fingers in the tuft of hair that had sprouted in the deep cavity of Nawaz's chest. That center, inches away from his beating heart, where I liked to lay my face when permitted rare moments of tenderness. In time, this sprouting had enticingly trailed its way over the hard bumps of his abdomen and tantalized my fingers down to the instrument of my adolescent enslavement.

I can still smell him. That distinct mingle of Imperial Lather soap, medicated sports cream and his sweat. I remember long, lazy afternoons in the stuporous heat of Mombasa, when we had both skipped school. And I remember dusks, the time of *maghrab*, when instead of praying at the mosque as our families thought we were, we would hasten back to an available venue for a desperate consumption of one another. My hands still feel the film of perspiration that collected upon them when they coasted over the curves of his broad back as I lay pinned to the cold, hard floor. He, begging for a count of twenty so that he could finish on top of me.

Me, responding with mock resistance to incite his desperation and force my yielding.

Nawaz taught me how to "suck cock" as he so eloquently put it. Rammed it repeatedly into my mouth even when I choked and spat out over his knee. "Learn! Learn!" he would implore, deftly wiping away with the corner of his open school shirt. "I promise you, you'll love it, you know? *Are, bwana,* then you'll be begging for it all the time!"

As I resisted whatever sick and disgusting act he was imploring me to perform, he would cajole me, telling me of his soccer match the next day, how he would be able to score all the goals if I just "sucked it a little bit."

I knew all about his athletic prowess. The soccer matches and the swimming tournaments and the volleyball and the weight lifting. And all those stupid little cunts bobbing up and down, flailing their arms in the air to catch his attention from stadium benches and the periphery of the pool. Drooling when he hoisted himself out of the pool and strutted past, beads of water glistening on his oiled body.

And I knew his girlfriend, Shairose. At noontime, Mombasa closed its doors to all trade and activity so that everyone could go home and take siestas after lunch. I sat next to her on the midday bus ride back from the Aga Khan Primary School sometimes. Between reading pages of her Mills & Boon novel, she would enthuse about how besotted he was with her. "Yeah, you know, he'll be coming to see me this evening, tee hee hee" she would inform me, giggling hysterically. *"Ay, ma!* I can't wait! Tee hee hee!"

And all I could think under my restraint was, *Yeah, neither can I, a few hours later, when he'll be plowing me into the ground, begging me for yet another count of twenty.*

I had a feeling it was Nawaz that had gotten married and not his younger brother Fareed.

The last time I went to Kenya, six years ago, I had heard about Nawaz's engagement to some outcast. Not very commendable. Unless, of course, this outcast was a *dhorki*. Then by all means you had alleviated your status, mingling whites into your bloodline. A Caucasian struggling to speak Kutchi or Gujarati meant everyone would be enchanted to hear those same words with an accent. *"Han, han,* my daughter-in-law is so *hushyar!* So clever! She can speak the language better than even I can!"

Maybe she would wear a sari occasionally and learn how to cook curries and clumsily fry *bhajias* for tea. And maybe convert too, and how you would be blessed for making her a *khoji!* A *paki* Ismaili! Your offspring would inherit that *doodh-malai*-like complexion without having to stay out of the sun, bleaching their skin with Fair & Lovely or shielding themselves under excessive clothing, even in the sweltering heat. They might even inherit blue or green eyes and what a bonus that would be! That would certainly set them apart from everyone else, no? *"Oho-ho!* Did you see those *bhuri-bhuri* eyes of hers? Tsk. Tsk. Tsk. Just beautiful, *ney?* I wish I had colored eyes. Instead mine are dark like shit!"

But Nawaz apparently had chosen not to care, thus confirming the opinions of many like my mother, who believed his family to be of subordinate class.

The news of his prenuptials had both filled me with intense jealousy and aroused me. The implication of his sexual ambiguity. His possible unavailability. I had to have him again. One last time.

I was also curious. Having lived in America for a few years, I had acclimated to a people who in supporting sexual diversity had ironically adopted the labels and classifications best cast aside if one is to be recognized as an equal, irrespective of whom they desire sexually. Back home there appeared to be no such rigid classifications, no such pronouncement, and everyone appeared just randomly scattered on that bell curve of sexuality that eluded labels. Unless of course one was flamboyant in demeanor. Straight? Gay? Lesbian? It seemed as if everyone was none of these and all of these.

Where on this bell curve did Nawaz perch now? Had time and pressure from the family reduced his appetite for other men into a long-expired phase? I wondered.

And so, like many times in the years before I had left Kenya, I climbed up the flight of stairs that led to his door but only after keeping a close vigil on his flat from the street below. I could hear the evening *d'ua* being recited from the mosque behind me, its obligatory beckon worsening the guilt of an intention already weighty with prohibition.

I paced around nervously on the street, trying to appear like I was on my way to somewhere as late attendees of the mosque hurried past, some of them carefully balancing plates of food covered in plastic film and triangular pints of milk for *nandhi*, the food auction after the prayers. Traversing the parking lot, I surveilled his flat on the third floor. Anticipating. Hesitating. Wondering. Waiting for a sign. Maybe a glimpse of him. A light switch to go on. Go off. Something.

As I stood there summoning courage, I realized how Nawaz had completely turned the tables on us during the latter part of our relationship. He had trained me in such a way, that the pleasure of someone succumbing to me after a challenge would always prove more gratifying than that of readily available sex.

When I finally rapped on his door, a panic seized me. I could hear my heart pounding within my chest, as if in the throes of a drug. That familiar rush pulsating through my body. A desire so urgent, it was acutely painful. Standing there, facing that door beyond which awaited my sexual deliverance, every second that transpired felt like an eternity. I wished I could have found a way to just extricate the flesh of my groin so as to rid myself of that knotted feeling that had me addicted to him.

But then, I had often wondered where my satisfaction truly lay. In that torment right before Nawaz, languid in the knowledge of my need, delayed opening the door after peering through the peephole – or when I lay under him, my legs encircling his torso, my soul wrapped in carnality?

Nawaz opened the door barefoot, wearing only a towel around his waist. He didn't look surprised or excited or concerned. Maybe bored. A gaze of disinterest laced with dislike. Perhaps he'd heard that I was back in town and expected me to show up sooner or later. I knew from experience not to perceive his countenance for its discouraging implication.

"I was about to take a bath," he said, and then stepped aside to let me in.

When he closed the door behind me and I heard the clicking of the lock, I knew that my visit would take a while. Seated on a gaudy sofa covered in a print of frangipanis, I watched him saunter over to the entertainment center against the wall and turn the television set on.

That seemed to be the extent of our greeting. A man I had been fucking for some six or seven years and hadn't seen in at least four. Still, it didn't feel even the slightest bit awkward. Niceties had never been a component of our relationship. And words had almost always been used only to convey lust...*Come here so I can fuck your ass...You know who this is? This is the one that fucks your* gand *calling...*

I suppose it would have been nice if he had given me a hug. Put his arm around me and given me that friendly squeeze on my shoulder like he did with his soccer buddies. Or even smiled to indicate his pleasure at seeing me. Asked me how I was doing in America. If I had become the famous artist I had set out to be. But no, there was no such civility. Nawaz acted as if he had seen me just a few days ago, and I had come back hungrily for more.

The news came on in black and white, color programming still a technology crawling into Kenya. An African broadcaster, his eyes brazenly transfixed on a handheld script, attempted to make the President's latest groundbreaking at some school sound like a philanthropic achievement in his heavily accented English. I had heard that the Voice of Kenya now had two channels of programming.

Nawaz turned around to face me. From where I sat, I could see that he was no longer the model of a youthful man's beauty. His muscles sagged, and the underside of his chin had gotten heavier. He was well on his way to being the married man who had "really put it on." None of this made any difference to me though. He still aroused in me the kind of hunger that can easily be stimulated by the memories of shared sexual encounters.

I felt weak with desire. I want to be raped, I kept thinking. Ravished. Completely gutted. Have my lusts exhumed and unfurled around us. How must I beg him so that he won't keep me waiting any longer? How to initiate what we both knew was going to happen? Perhaps if I reached out and stroked him through the towel. Started to slide my finger inside myself, there in that place where I knew he would want to go. Said something lewd and bold. Or knelt down in front of him without saying anything and reminded him of the lessons he had taught me.

Right then, Nawaz walked over and paused right in front of me, his groin inches away from my face. I sat there frozen in the moment as he looked down at me and I felt as if the blood had drained out of my body, and I was going to pass out. He could sense my weakness and it excited him.

With one swift move of his hand, he yanked his towel away and let his hardness spring forth, slapping me on my eye. Turgid and commanding.

"Is *this* what you came for? *Hunh?*" he asked.

Some things never change.

After we were done, he wiped himself with the white towel he had been wearing and said, "You suck cock like an expert now. So, how many boys have you been screwing?"

"Hardly any."

"Ah, don't be a liar. You never sucked my cock like *this* before! Aren't you worried about AIDS?"

I looked at him incredulously. How ridiculous a question was that coming from him under the circumstances? "Of course I am. But we should *all* be worried about AIDS!"

I looked at him incredulously. How ridiculous a question was that coming from him under the circumstances? "Of course I am. But we should *all* be worried about AIDS!"

"*Hunh,* all those *shogas*...." He shook his head and trailed off as if it wasn't worth commenting on.

What about them, you closeted bigot? I thought. *What homophobic crap are you going to say now that you've already sprayed yourself over me?*

"So, you even *sound* like a *dhorio* now!"

"No, I don't!" I objected at being branded a sellout, what most people in my position in this town would have been only too delighted to be perceived as. Because that would have meant they had gone abroad and adopted a superior culture.

"*Hanh, hanh,* you think you are better than us already! Anyway," he said. "You better go now, *hunh.*

My mum is going to be home soon. I don't want her to see you here."

I buttoned myself up, his treatment of me suddenly much harder to swallow. I fought the urge to tell him that I had half a mind to educate his bride-to-be about her husband's very special sexual needs and that he should be careful about where he stuck his own dick now that he was so suddenly concerned about AIDS. That all those dirty homosexuals he had rammed himself into, all those *shogas* – as he had so derogatorily called them – had been branded so by doing nothing different from what he had just done there with me.

But then again, why bother?

Nawaz would marry and in time his indiscretions with the men in his life – if there even were others beside myself – would cease. Instead, his betrayals would manifest themselves in binges with the hundreds of *malayas*, or prostitutes, of Mombasa after a few cold Tusker beers. If questioned, he would stretch the statute of limitations and claim that even a few weeks before his marriage, at the age of twenty-nine, he was doing what many boys had done growing up. Experimenting. And that now, with a wife and numerous whores at his libido's disposal, he was, as had only rarely been suspected, one hundred per cent heterosexual.

"I'm going to take a shower," Nawaz said, stretching his arms and then to my astonishment letting out a rampant fart. "We're going to Abdallah's tonight."

Disgusted, I shook my head and grimaced. This confirmed my feeling about him and others like him. Engaged to some naive woman, still doing an old boyfriend and planning on visiting the local whorehouse afterward. I stood up, wondering why should this behavior should surprise me. Was he really any different from the other men I had known growing up?

Is *this* was what our parents preferred we do, instead of just coming out and being honest and gay?

Was this man, who had just come thunderously in my mouth, gay? Or just oversexed?

I said "bye" curtly and walked out of the flat. There were no handshakes. No hugs. Not even a smile or well wishes.

Driving home, I thought about his visit to Abdallah's. I had heard the black prostitutes lay on their backs, chewing Bazookas and reading comic books while the guys fucked them, clumsy in their enthusiasm. I had been in that vicinity myself. Waiting outside in the car while my best friend, who I had been convinced was the one and only boy I would ever love and obsess over, was escorted into the shanty by two other boys to be initiated on his sixteenth birthday. I remember feeling sick to my stomach. Wanting to retch. Not because I was revolted by prostitution but because I felt ill at the thought of him spending himself on someone else, and more painfully, on someone like *that*. Someone who would actually charge him money for it while I, devoted to him, would have chopped my arm off to lie under him. I felt incapable of preventing him from touching her, that whore smacking her pink bubble gum as he penetrated her with his clean, virginal cock. Unable to stop him from mounting her and deriving pleasure from her. Images of him writhing on her, into her, while I waited muted and wracking my mind. Longing for his sperm like a boon from whichever deity could hear me pleas. So afraid that I would tear through our friends' excited imaginings of what was going on inside that shack with an anguished cry if I had even tried to participate in their endorsements.

There was this other time I waited in my car for some guy I had experimented with – he had begged me to wait on him for about a half hour at three in the morning while he satiated himself with Khadijah, his favorite one. He had been with a girlfriend hours before, at the Blues nightclub along the North Coast of Mombasa, and now it was time to expend all the excitement she had aroused in him and refused, out of virtue, to satisfy. He claimed to care for her deeply, employing the reasoning that men do about their biological need for sex, just as he had claimed his satisfaction from his favorite whore and me, the willing friend.

Many of these guys had gone on to get married. Had children. Put on some weight, gotten settled, matured. Whatever they wanted to call it. None of it, however, changed the fact that they had all been involved with me.

I started to think that, yes, perhaps labels are truly for cans of food. Not people. We are all simply sexual beings. Sometimes it took so little to tip the scales, to redirect one's sexual preference from the norm. The right timing perhaps. Or loneliness. A little too much drinking to overcome the inhibition. Or just downright horniness – sometimes that was all it took to shut one's eyes and yield to pleasure from whoever, whatever.

I had seen the scales tip more than once in my life. Many times, I must admit, I had applied the pressure.

But now, years after being removed from such an ambivalent stance, having such clarity in where my pleasure lay, having marched down Santa Monica Boulevard in full view of the cameras and onlookers (some bewildered, others still making that unsteady transition into full light), I wondered what such behavior said about those I had left behind. Those men from my homeland who would never enter a Heaven or the Vortex. Men who would never find themselves in anything even remotely comparable to a bar in West Hollywood.

I thought about men like Nawaz who would frequent Bora Bora or Florida nightclub, perhaps accompanied by their naive girlfriends – a perfect veneer of masculinity, hoping to lock gazes with some German tourist or American sailor based on the naval camp on Mombasa island.

Men whose fantasies of other men would be eventually muffled under the pressures of the norm and distending the family tree.

Would their lives have coursed differently had they been here? In a country that may still be far away from handing out equal rights but at least attempted to legitimize preferences by providing the forum and places for expression?

Would they still have gotten married, had children and disregarded past experiences as adolescent phases in a more permissive environment?

And then I thought of myself. Perched expectantly at the edge of a bar in West Hollywood. Glossed up by rigidly scheduled facials at Ole Henriksen's, admirable regimens of concealing cosmetics and alpha-hydroxy acids and some gym time to ward off the encroaching signs of aging. Searching during endless nights at the Vortex, long hardened against the guilt and sophomoric resolutions of never going back there again. Staggering in at two or three in the morning like it was second nature now to flash attitude to the very men that had been indifferent to me only hours ago at some club, but would now rise to the occasion in dark rooms and glory booths.

And I wonder, who made the right choice?

What did it make them, these friends of mine, who hadn't made *my* choice? Had they been cowards or just realistic? Practical-minded bisexuals who had modified their tastes or just suppressed individuals?

Hell, what did it make me?

CHAPTER 19

FAT LOSS

My mother is addicted to American television. *The Bold and the Beautiful* is her favorite. I came home from work to an apartment churning out the aroma of spices all the way to the end of the block and asked her what she had been up to, besides pestering God with her praying and cooking curries, so she filled me in on this passion.

"In Kenya," she said, her hand held up firmly for emphasis, "we have to rent it on the video, *khabar ayi neh?*"

How she managed to do that with a daily series, I was afraid to ask.

"Ali, you know, today I saw this advertisement on the TV for this miracle drug that burns off *all* your fat! Can you imagine? *All* your fat! I *must* have it!"

I shook my head at her, walked into the kitchen and lifted the lid to smell the simmering chicken curry. The kitchen was spotless. In an apartment that boasted modern Z-Gallery acquisitions, the grime-ridden stove had been the only embarrassment – now it actually looked unobjectionable. My landlady had renounced her responsibilities a long time ago, claiming rather sarcastically that a Santa Monica rent-controlled apartment didn't always come with a stove. Or linoleum that matched the tiles in the bathroom. Or a screen door to alleviate the heat of summer.

"Oh, this looks delicious." I carefully blew on the curry floating on the wooden spoon. "God, Mummy, don't fall for those infomercials! They're just trying to make you *chodu!*"

"What info—info—are you saying, *hunh?*" She watched me sample her offering for the day from the kitchen doorway. "I saw it with my own two eyes!" she insisted, her fingers forking at her eyes, her brows raised in wonder. "Were *you* here? No, you weren't here to see it, okay? This woman," she said, parting her arms, "she was so obese – *Yah, Khuddah!* They even showed her photo. And after she had taken this thing for just one month, my God, she had *completely* changed! You should've seen her!"

I knew that even the infomercials hadn't promised such results in a month. This was my mother's personal endorsement.

"Can you please just charge this for me? I promise I'll give you the money. I'm not running away!"

"Look, I don't care about that, okay? You just shouldn't believe all those things on TV."

"There was even a doctor they interviewed! Are you saying that he's lying?"

"Okay, fine. Good luck losing all your fat."

She sighed as I walked away from her and into my bedroom. Was she sighing at my cynicism or my impatience with her? Maybe both. *What the hell? I'll just get the damn fat-loss pills for her.*

"I'll call them tomorrow," I lobbed from my room. "You get the phone number?" But she had already moved on to greener pastures. "Oh, and Ali, do you know about this Super Thaw plate? It can thaw everything in seconds!"

CHAPTER 20

SIBLING RIVALRY

When thinking of home, it is the North Coast of Mombasa, known as Bamburi Beach, that I crave the most. I can still see the Indian Ocean from the place where I often wiggled my feet into the warm beach sand. Sometimes, when dismayed by a smear of tar on my heels from Santa Monica's polluted Will Rogers Beach, I think of the endless miles of that beach I have forsaken; the sprinkling of fishermen mending nets and towing in dawn's fresh catch from their dhows (instead of the beer guzzling, cell-phone-and-Powerbook-clad denizens of this beach); her clear waters that gave the impression I was looking through a pane of glass; laughing to myself because I thought the beach looked like a plush carpet of cocaine that I should fall to my knees and snort.

These are the things I missed most about home. People, I somehow find a way to replace over time. But I could never efface the smells, the sights, the sounds. Familiar little secrets that the land whispered to me. Expressions on the face of a land that remain hidden from outsiders, like that infernal traffic of foreigners who are met with only gratitude for gracing the country with their precious foreign exchange. They were always welcome because they were good for the economy – third-world countries could not afford the luxury of being spiteful to foreigners.

We were grateful to them. At least on the surface we were. We made great efforts to show them this. Those *dhorias* who danced awkwardly to African pop and Hindi film songs performed by the live bands at the beach hotels; coated in suntan lotions to bake themselves dark, so they could look more like the very races they had taken such pleasure extorting and condescending to.

They had forgotten that the natives had achieved *uhuru.*
But then, so had the natives frantically darting to serve
another tropical cocktail or supply a fresh towel in their
starched white uniforms, completely overlooking patrons
that weren't white.   Ah, but the foreign exchange was
needed to boost our perpetually dwindling economy, so
we consoled ourselves.   Smiled.   Displayed our dazzling
white teeth and swallowed our pride.   *Yes,* bwana.   *Of
course,* bwana.   *Anything you need,* bwana.   All teeth and
eyeballs.

     In the mind, there was this dialogue: *These*
mzungus, *they are all* unbwas! *Barking all the time for more of
this and more of that the moment they land on foreign soil. And
what the hell do they do in their own country, eh?* Hunh! *Clean
toilets, I tell you! They save up all through the year and then they
come down here with their pounds and dollars, and they boss us
around like they are royalty!* Pumbafus! *Well, let them crouch
and admire the* Makonde *carvings of ebony and mahogany and
rosewood. And let them buy these souvenirs right along with the
beads and* kitenges *and charms and try to absorb some fragment of
a true culture. Must be quite enriching after making do with
McDonald's and a national sport to constitute a culture. Let them
take their pictures of us with their telephoto cameras, which they will
no doubt be wheedled into bartering for more of our abundant
artifacts. Throw your arms around them and let them do the same,
beautiful native. See how hard they try to inosculate so that they
can take the pictures back as proof of their authentic African
vacation? To boast to their fellow toilet-cleaner friends? Why, they
have tanned to such a crisp, you can barely even tell they are
mzungus anymore! And what about their eyes? Eyes like the
devil! And that hair! No, they cannot hide that. That's a tough
one. But wait a minute. There is something that can be done!
Braid the hair! So many of them have been known to sit for hours
to have their hair braided with beads and cowrie shells. Hunh!
Do they realize how ridiculous their enthusiasm for the cultures they
claim to have saved from paganism and ignorance makes them
seem? They seem to have an inclination for everything we have to*

offer. Even sex with the locals. Please, don't act shocked now!
Surely you've heard of the sex safaris? They come down with their
hard earned money and mileage-accrued tickets, and if they have an
appetite that stretches beyond the scenery, food, souvenirs and local
pot, they can even sample the sex with local African beauties. We
need the money, you see. More importantly, we know our place.
When you get back, between scrubbing the bowls and waiting tables,
you can show everybody the pictures. You danced with the native.
You ate with the native. And you ate of the native. And for so
little money. Such a bargain. Everybody loves a bargain.

You must take a trip to Africa, white man. There they
haven't discovered what trash you are. Like babies learning how to
walk, they appear unsteady with their independence. They will cater
to your every need. And you can bark at them like the dog you are
when they are slovenly. There, in Africa, where they still think
you're Mungu, *where they still think you're God.*

That same summer I said goodbye to my grandfather, we
rented a beach cottage in Bamburi. We planned a
barbeque. We called our weekend a "*vashiah manzil*," the
destination of prostitutes. We invited friends who we
suspected were like us. Part of the agenda for the evening
included a *mujrah*, a traditional dance of Indian
courtesans, by Sunjay. As soon as he finished performing
in rented traditional garb, accentuated with befitting
jewelry and *ghungroos*, Sunjay disappeared behind the
kitchen door and emerged again to Indian cabaret music,
wearing black lace panties and bra under a sequined pink
dress for a bonus striptease. He had been transformed
from Sunjay to Rekha and then from Rekha to film vixen
Helen in the course of thirty minutes. Everyone was
infected by his performance. Soon everyone was taking
turns dressing up and performing with an almost
competitive spirit. We all laughed so hard at moments
that we cried. Akil drank so much, danced wildly in a
clumsily wrapped white bed sheet and his clownish
makeup, fell back and started to cry in the back room.

Once I had brushed his hair and asked him what was the matter, he shook his head and through globs of makeup, replied, "I'm just so happy. And I know I'll never be this happy again. I'll never be this free again..."

Life was going to change for Akil. Responsibilities and expectations had crept up and were knocking on his door. Marriage, I knew, was being imposed on him. Some Bohora girl from Kisumu or somewhere. The glass factory, which had been in his family for generations, was now awaiting his leadership. What could I say to him? I said, "Why don't you just leave this place and come with me?"

He wiped his tears with the back of his hand, smearing kohl across his rosy cheek and smiled at me. I must have sounded completely naive because I felt that he had looked up at me like a mother might at the child that tries to console her after a grown-up squabble. "You know, I'm so happy that you got away from all this," he said. "You always knew what you wanted, *ney?*"

I lay my head down upon his, while Sunjay could be heard in the other room encouraging the others to throw money at him, promising that he would return it right after his dance number.

But at that moment, I tried to concentrate on Akil and held his hand in mine. "Akil, you can do the same. *Tun mari waat sambhar*, you have the same choices, you know?"

But Akil had chosen instead, like everyone else there that night, to just continue with the suspension of time, and to hope that the night would not see the light of day.

One of our guests that evening was Fareed, Nawaz's younger brother. Although we had never spoken much before, I remembered him mostly as the athletic kid brother Nawaz and I avoided when getting together at his place. From the little we had communicated, I knew him to be a generally soft-spoken, kind and very gentle being – the virtual antithesis of his brother.

We had once found ourselves in a group of mutual friends who had converged after the evening prayers outside the mosque library. After the group had dispersed, I escorted Fareed to Safiri's *banda*, a kiosk for nocturnes where we sat around on crudely assembled wooden benches and chewed on *marungi* plant and Big G bubble gum. I was delaying going home where gloom had descended upon my family because of my grandfather's dilapidation and opted instead to shoot the breeze with my lover's younger brother.

There, at Safiri's *banda*, he had alluded to his knowledge of my sexuality and said rather sweetly, *"Bwana*, I don't care what people say. Just because people are a little different doesn't make any difference to me, you know?"

So I had gone ahead and invited him to our beach retreat. He came laden with bottles of local papaya wine and the *marungi* he had acquired a taste for from his late nights at the *banda*. By the time he arrived, Akil had recovered from his depression and was barbequing the *mishkake*. Sunjay, in his mischief, was refusing to return any of the money that had been dispensed on him, claiming "men always wanted it for free."

Fareed and I snuck away to the beach where we drained out a bottle of wine. Although we had pretended that we were only going for a walk, we both knew that sex was imminent. It was like one of those things pending for years.

There in the dunes we found a shallow basin in the sand where we stripped and lay down. The sand under my back itched and the lack of suspension for his grinding body made it doubly uncomfortable. Fareed asked me if we could "do it." When I declined, he told me about the blowjobs he had been getting on a weekly basis from this thirteen-year-old boy in our community and how it was no problem because he was going to fuck him one of these days anyway. I was aghast.

"You wouldn't! He's only a child!" I objected.

"*Hunh!* Not in the way he sucks me. You should see him begging for it," he said, grunting. "He *loves* it! He *wants* it!"

I made no attempt to conceal the repulsion on my face. It had been no different for me, I tried to rationalize in my mind. I had been exactly thirteen when his brother had initiated me, when Nawaz had first taken my hand and guided it down between his legs.

Just then, as if he had read my mind, Fareed suddenly stopped moving, and looking me dead in the eye, said, "You've been fucking my brother, haven't you?"

I was confounded. Trapped beneath him as he grabbed my face in his hand and forced me to look into his menacing face, I mumbled something incoherent, unsure of what he expected me to say and what my admission might evoke in him. *Oh, God, help me. What if he starts to get really violent or something?*

"Haven't you?" he demanded, his fingers digging into my cheeks.

"Fareed, please don't," I said, my hands pushing up against his chest. "Don't get this way..."

Then, pinning me down with his weight, he clamped my mouth shut with one hand and tried to force himself inside me with the other. I wriggled around on the sand like a fish abandoned by receding tide. But after the first minute or so, I stopped fighting him, not because I acknowledged his strength, but because I enjoyed his anger. At the sign of capitulation, he removed his hand from my mouth and replaced it with his lips, mashing mine in a mass of flesh and teeth.

He had known all along. Big brother. Swimming champion. Soccer star. Bedding numerous women. And at least one man. Perhaps Fareed had even silently watched us fucking away during those long afternoons and kept it to himself all this time. Watched his big brother and me in the bed of the servants. In the bed of their parents. In his bed. Paralyzed. Repulsed. Aroused. Now it was his turn.

When he was ready to come, Fareed pulled himself off me and just as unexpectedly, ran off into the ocean by himself. I followed him in, wading through the icy water, wanting to fuse back into him. Knee-deep in the ocean, he stopped and started to masturbate himself vigorously. I watched his face contort – a mixture, I thought, of the anger in his heart and the approach of his climax. And when he came, spurting forth over his hands like an excited child, he touched his head to my shoulder and called out God's name. And with the kind of tenderness I believed him to possess in moments other than this, I wiped his semen off our bodies with the salty ocean water.

CHAPTER 21

HE'S BACK

I'm five again. I sit on a chair, my feet dangling in the air, wearing a blue sailor suit. We are at a coffeehouse on Kilindini Road. Behind a counter that displaying an array of Indian sweetmeats, the Indian shop owner waves at me and uses baby talk to attract my attention. I ignore him completely as I relish my way through a cube of *monthar*. My father is seated across from me. I bask only in the light of his gaze. He is wearing a long sleeved white cotton shirt and dark pants, as always. A stubble has greeted his handsome face and his dark hair is combed back. He smokes a cigarette and barely eats. His piece of *monthar* sits neglected after the first bite on a plate in front of him. I see him smiling at me and watching me eat between his thoughts. My mother is not with us because she is at work. I miss her yet feel content in being alone with him.

It's a perfect moment. I keep thinking, *He's back! He's back! But he'll be gone again...Better not to think about that now. He's back at least for a while...*

And I'm happy.

CHAPTER 22

MY FIRST TIME

Nelson McGhee was one of those men whose friends consisted only of ex-boyfriends. Surrounded by much shorter, effeminate boys, mostly Asian (and never black like himself, as he was to confess to me later), he towered over them like an obelisk in the center of a thriving harem. His sometimes doting and at other times self-amused little queens formed a kind of fence around him, through which only his constantly roving eyes promised any possibility of penetration.

I first saw him when groggily weaving through Oasis nightclub (popular for its Asian influence), not long before the music was to die and the lights – which made the patrons flee from the dance floor like vampires exposed to annihilating sunlight – were to come up. That night money had been a little tight, and the free admission had lured Adrian, Kitty and myself into the club we had dubbed "Pearl Harbor." *What the hell, let's go get a hot Asian!* Adrian and I would often joke, pulling up the corners of our eyes, and yakking away in mock-Cantonese as we entered the club. Naturally this infuriated Kitty, but because his already poor English became even more incoherent when he got angry, he just turned beet-red, shook his head at both of us and managed, "It's no funny, okay? Why this cracks you up so much? Is just stupid."

From the moment I laid eyes on Nelson, I was completely arrested by lust. He aroused in me the kind of sexual compulsion that hits you smack in the gut. Made me want to press up against his body without the formality of sobering introductions and inane words. Made me want to relinquish the cocktail that I had been concealing from club security and rake myself against his beautiful, muscled body. Voltaire said, "To conquer one is not enough. One must know how to seduce." And seeing Nelson leaning back placidly against the rail with a beer bottle clutched in hand, towering over his carnival of Asian queens chattering away in a conspiratorial dialect that even he wasn't privy to, his wandering eyes subtly recruiting and betraying the feigned interest in their cackling, I felt this urge to seduce. To seduce without forethought, without a blueprint, with the disarming confidence and directness that only one too many cocktails can purvey.

And seduced he was.

The most terrifying aspect of picking up someone in a bar was the possibility of being rejected in front of others who have already thought of making the same advance but pragmatically vetoed it. Of being sized up by the companions of the pursued, of the catty discussion about you the moment you turned around and slinked away, your head heavy from the weight of your embarrassment. The original purpose of a bar, camaraderie and sociability, was overshadowed by the rule that you should never pay attention to the man you really want. But in a rum-and-Coke haze, such apprehensions vaporized and all I wanted to do was walk right up and tell him how attractive I found him and that I'd like nothing more than to suck his cock. I managed to disown my glass, saunter over and through his coterie of sexual conquests and, gently licking his ear lobe, breathe a "hi."

We spoke on the phone a few times before getting together. Los Angeles, being the natural and human disaster capital of the world, had delayed our rendezvous until the fires of Laguna Hills could be vanquished. Each time we hung up, I found myself masturbating to thoughts of him, feeling slightly awkward with my mother counting her rosary in the other room. Obtaining Nelson became a libidinous obsession. Two weeks later, having tersely explained to my mother that I was spending the night out with someone and ignoring her eyes boring holes into me, I drove down to Orange County.

While waiting for him in the deserted parking lot of a mini-mall that night, I swigged rum from my flask, half-afraid that he wouldn't show. Every minute lasted an hour as I sat there, trying to regulate my breathing and cancel the lurid images of our bodies colliding against each other. *Why the fuck did I agree to do this? I should've just insisted on picking him up from his place,* I kept telling myself. *Now what if he flakes on me? Fuck! What then? I'm going to throw myself onto this palm tree!*

But Nelson had been adamant. Having recently broken up with his lover, he was still in the process of moving out and considered it insensitive for it to be any other way. For someone who never took notice of a ring on the finger of a prospect, I ignored this as any kind of sign or an indication of poor timing.

We rented a motel room, for which I paid. As soon as I unpacked the change of clothes, condoms and a travel-size bottle of lubricant from my overnight bag, Nelson remarked that I knew exactly what I had come for. When I responded that I did, that I wanted him to fuck me, he was stunned. Of all the things he expected to come out of me – despite the audacious way in which I had introduced myself to him – the boldness of my demand shocked him. Mostly, I think, because it was so blatantly sexual.

Slowly, I walked over to where he stood, and his eyes fixated on me like he was searching my body for concealed, complex muscles, some explanation of how vulnerability and confidence could seethe together within me. I started to feel him up. "You know what I want, Nelson?" I said. "I want you to get inside me. And then when you're inside me, I'd like for you to just stay there for a little while without moving. Can you do that?"

I thought his face looked a little nervous if not flustered. "That would be very difficult," he managed, and then, assuming the dominant role that my aggression had momentarily deflected him from, drew me to him and started to knead my buttocks with his large hands. "But I'll try."

I went into the bathroom where I sunk my car keys in the toilet tank. You just never know. I pissed, hitting the side of the bowl so as to not make that crass sound I suspected might further confuse his perception of my submissiveness. The distinct sound of urine jetting into the reservoir of toilet bowl water, a sound I knew he would never even think to suppress. It was just such a man thing.

I reflected upon his discomfort as the blue of the water turned green. The struggle that he was undergoing, because, like women, submissive sexual partners were expected to yield control of the sexual arena to the man. The top. The assumed aggressor. But I had learned a long time ago that the real power in sex was in the hands of the submissive, whether they chose to reveal it or not. It was the woman, the bottom, the receiver who had the real power, the most potent kind of power, because it was completely mental. With all his grinding and heaving, Nelson would get no further, feel not much more than I would ultimately allow him to. In the grand design Nelson was but a component, like the bed that we would fuck on and the pillow I would sink my face into.

I slipped off my jeans and threw them to aside. I put the lid down, flushed the toilet and thought of my keys soaking in there. *I don't trust him with my car but I'm going to let him fuck me.* I walked to the mirror over the sink and blotted the oil from my face with toilet paper. Then I drained my flask of what was left and felt the rum burning down my body. A deep breath later, I went back out to find him standing over the bed that he would ravage me on, eagerly tearing the seal off the bottle of Wet, and accordion of condoms hanging from around his wrist. It was a sight I would never forget.

For some inexplicable reason I thought of my mother right then, sitting at home on the living room sofa that temporarily served as her bed, rapt in prayer, worried sick about me. Grappling with the knowledge that her son had grown up and was having casual sex. Mothers never needed to be told, only forced to confront what they already knew.

She must have been terrified of her suspicions, of the things she thought me capable of because she knew me through herself. How different could my appetites be from her own? How dissimilar could we be, mother and son?

For a man of his build, I found it strange that Nelson should feel so cold. He turned up the heater to high and started to turn out every light. I asked him to keep the bathroom lit so we wouldn't be engulfed in darkness. "I want to be able to see you," I said and climbed onto the bed. I sat in my unbuttoned shirt with my legs folded under me and watched him remove his pants, fold them neatly and hang them over a chair. Then he walked over to me. All I could see was his bulbous cock bobbing between his legs and I thought, *My God. Do I really want that thing inside me?*

Pushing me down with one hand, he climbed on top of me and taking his cock with the other hand, aligned it between my thighs. I could feel it, slathered with the lubricant, warm and pinguid as it pushed up against my balls.

"You ready for this?" he asked.

"No," I quipped. "Why don't we do it next week?"

"What?"

"I'm just kidding," I said quickly. "Yes."

He promised that he would be gentle and although I wanted to laugh in his face at the banality of his line, I acted nervous and told him that it was my first time getting fucked – partly because I knew they always wanted to believe this and partly because I truly feared the pain. This excited him tremendously. I imagine he felt like some great explorer charting into the undiscovered territory within my rectal walls. This precursory advice had always been Adrian's job as he lay by my side, watching. We would laugh about this in the coming week, I knew this.

"I like being the first one inside you, " he said and with that his torso gave a little thrust against me. "I'm going to make this real special, your first time."

"Thank you." I pulled his face down into the nape of my neck and with one leg over the other, squeezed my thighs tighter around his cock. I looked up at the ceiling for a moment before closing my eyes to the world.

When I woke up, I found Nelson seated across from me on the chair that he had hung his pants on. He was just sitting there, watching me intently, a white towel knotted around his waist. Even in the dim light that peered from the bathroom, I could see the faint smile on his face. I asked him what time it was and without looking at a watch, he told me it was a little past one in the morning. He asked me to go back to sleep and continued to watch me for a little while longer, the way an admirer might gaze at art in a gallery. Except I didn't feel like a painting and his gaze made me feel addled – more like an insect on formalin. I felt the searing pain in my rectum, dreadfully aware that in the coming days it would get much worse. Despite his gallant promises, Nelson had not been gentle. In the throes of passion, he had pushed me back down into the mattress and spurred himself to an orgasm as I bit into the fleshy palm that had brutally covered my face and held me down.

I wanted to pull the bed sheet up, but his gaze upon me like an invisible pair of hands frisking through my body, I forced myself to lie naked for him to look at. Nelson had liked my body for exactly what it had been. Unlike his own. There was no need to conceal myself from him. While he was fucking me, he repeated, "God, I love your body...I love how you feel..."

When first treading into gay Los Angeles, one of the rudest shocks had been that opposites didn't always attract. The clones were looking for clones. Buffed men were looking for other buff men. And the most popular of them all, the tops, were looking for bottoms who, alas, looked like tops. Only the queens weren't looking for their own kind. Ultimately though, everyone, irrespective of his tribe, was looking for the same thing: the man.

In this culture of complex narcissism, where everyone was relentlessly searching for their spitting image, Nelson desired someone dissimilar to his own physical type. I told myself I had no reason to feel self-conscious, that in his eyes my digressive physique was not a flaw but an asset.

And with that thought I continued to lie on my stomach, the sheet entwined around the lower half of my body like a classic sculpture, and I felt beautiful. I smiled faintly within. Everyone deserves to be looked at just this way once in his lifetime. To be adulated unawares at first and then with secret knowledge and calculation. This was my moment. What would probably be one of the few tender moments I would elicit from him. Yes, let him appraise this body that so few like him in this city would demand. *I will give him this body, again and again, for him to crave and drink from.* And I'll guard him from the conniving little queens that will want to lure him away from me.

And with that, I started to shift languidly in my pretended sleep, stretching my body out like an elongated landscape for his relishing eyes.

My face against the wall, I grasped the top edge of the wooden headboard and looked into the kind of insipid painting I'd found myself staring at in the dentist's office or some other lobby of eternal waiting. We were both on our knees, and I could see the reflection of his body shuffling behind me among the sunshine, sailboats and seagulls in front of me. His arm slid around my belly and pulled me higher up toward him, but I gripped the headboard tighter instead of falling on my hands. I felt his pelvis warm and moist against my behind as he prepared to plunder. When his fingers, sheathed with lubricant, started to probe inside me, I flinched from the pain but said nothing. *I'll give him all the sex he wants*, I kept thinking. And then he would need to look nowhere else. Nelson would be my farewell to the sex clubs and the nights of marauding through the string of bars on Santa Monica Boulevard with Adrian, Salman and Kitty. An end to the huddled last minute attempts at picking up someone off the curb at the end of the night – "Side walk sale! Side walk sale!" someone was always alerting. A culmination to the despondent sleepovers with friends who returned home equally disheartened and too tired or too drunk (mostly both) to drive back home at three in the morning for expiration in a lonely bed.

I closed my eyes and rested my head upon my arm, waiting for the rest of him, catching my breath every time his fingers began to feel like a hook piercing into me. But then I caught the scent of lotion and I turned around, horrified to find that we'd run out of lubricant, and him retracting his fingers and preparing to enter me without a condom. I stopped him immediately and asked him what the hell he thought he was doing.

"It's no big deal," he said sheepishly. "I'm negative."

I felt unnerved. His nonchalance made me wonder if he'd pulled the condom off before when he fucked me on my stomach, and would I have been able to detect it? I decided not to wallow and expunged the thought from my mind. Upon my insistence, he agreed to use a condom and I conceded to the lotion as a compromise. Even adherence to safety, I convinced myself, had to have practical limitations. While he fucked me, having managed to pry my grasp off the headboard and molding me into prostration, as if I had rolled out my mat and were about to give thanks to Allah, I thought fleetingly of Adrian's dead uncle and of the suffering his family had had to endure; all those disco records that Adrian had reluctantly boxed away because nobody used vinyl anymore. And I thought, *Nothing's changed. Nothing's come out of all the loss, all those deaths, and all the tragedy that AIDS has caused. Even now, millions of people this very moment, men and women, gay and straight, are fucking away in motels and toilets and homes and cars and offices. Even now, after witnessing the degradation of this epidemic, I still go to the sex clubs and bars to look for new and uncharted bodies to explore, oblivious to the virulence pulsing beneath the chiseled armor. I still afford myself the luxury of allowing Nelson to use pink, perfumed body lotion to inhabit me. I still hunger for love, but instead of holding out for it, instead of taking the time to have a conversation of any lasting significance with anyone viable for such an undertaking, I cave in to the need to get fucked instead.*

When I felt pain and cried out from it, Nelson jammed his fingers into my mouth and I started to gnaw on them. Along with the colliding of his body, his passionate utterance filled my ears and validated my long-suffering ego. There was no rent check due and no mother sitting at home counting the rosary. All – at least

for the few hours in that motel room rented on my nearly
maxed-out Visa card – was well.

CHAPTER 23

KISSES

He liked to take me on my stomach. Flattening my front against the bed, Nelson focused on that one part of my writhing body into which he soldered his own. I gave in to this whenever we had sex. Sometimes I thought that by averting my face from his, Nelson managed not only to avoid some of the emotion, but also to annihilate the disapproval of society. He had reduced me to a butt hole, that entrance that transported him into an underworld where emotions and introspection did not thrive. We rarely kissed when we made love. When we did, his fleshly lips clamped against mine, as if he was trying to hold back words that might otherwise hurtle forth or bar the entry of some vile germ I might spew from my mouth and into his. I felt at those times like the whore who he let suck his dick but not kiss his mouth.

But outside of bed, Nelson was strangely different. He caressed and persisted, chiseling through the walls that Richard and I had erected so arduously. He wanted to know what I thought of dating older men. Available men as opposed to the Richards of this world. Black men. Men who wanted to spend money on me for a change. I think I preferred it when he was distant, when he was demeaning, when, instead of looking me in the eye and expressing his desire to take care of me, he was facing the back of my head in the grasp of his hand and grunting like a beast.

It kept me from panicking, from cringing at the thought of being laid bare again. What if my heart, starved by my very own hands for all these years, should retreat, resentful from my acerbic offerings? How to open up again? And what if I should start to need him too much? I asked myself. Every time I opened up, it was to the wrong damn man. Why should Nelson be any different? The more elusive I was, the more determined he became. He wanted to hold my hand in public, to call me at work and play Nancy Wilson over the phone, to buy me gifts on holidays and get acquainted with my friends. He wanted to meet my mother, whose potential reaction to his color worried me more than that to his gender.

But when we climbed into bed at the end of a night, having conversed about everything from Richard's dejected gaze to Adrian's peculiar behavior at the club that night, from his daughter – whose photo he carried around in his wallet – to my estrangement from Mummy, who had stayed six weeks already, Nelson still refused to fuck me any other way but on my stomach, with my head smashed against the pillow and his lips so far away from mine.

CHAPTER 24

FRIENDS

As a freshman in college, Darnel Washington was the first black person I befriended on the integrating campus grounds. Removed from the preconditioned, postcolonial environment of Kenya, I forged a friendship with Dar that would facilitate my entry into gay Los Angeles.

A fashion major who had moved from Newark, Dar was the kind of flamboyant, animated artist that typified most people's impression of the gay fashion designer who went swishing through life equipped with a lacerating tongue and a brimful of attitude. He peppered all his sentences generously with drawls of "Ooh, da-r-r-ling" or "Hey, gir-r-l!" regardless of who he was talking to. He could be spotted sashaying his way through the art-cluttered corridors of Woodbury University, a measuring tape perpetually around his neck, a turtleneck on, a freshly sharpened pencil lodged behind his ear and rolls of vivid fabrics carried under his conspicuously shoulder-padded arms. His hair was coifed in the front to resemble a visor over his head; rare was the day I'd see him without the dark cat-eye glasses, which defined his attitude first and blocked out the UV rays second.

Dar's prescription for his lack of an L.A. gym body, which he despised as a condition of gay-male culture but pursued in his men, was: "Layer, honey! Layer! Layer! Layer!" And he was always swaddled in layers of meticulously coordinated clothing that he had either made himself or plucked out from various thrift stores on Melrose and then remodeled to reflect his personal style.

One night, months into our friendship, Dar and I ventured out to West Hollywood on the bus. At Studio One, where it was eighteen-and-over night, I remember perching nervously on the balcony that overlooked the dance floor and watching Dar unleash the dance steps that Janet Jackson performed on the video monitor behind him. He duplicated her choreography flawlessly, had her every mercurial move down to a science. He didn't consult her for any cues, paid no attention to the screen that mesmerized others and continued to dance on his own, focused on his inner director. As I clutched my drink (sans alcohol) and gazed only upon Dar's celebration of self-awareness, I thought, *My God! I'm here at last! I'm here at last!* And kept thinking quite stupidly, quite naively, *Now I can find love. Now I can find someone to fall in love with,* because everyone here had come to find the same thing: another man to fall in love with; not one who could substitute for a woman, not an indiscretion to be erased from their minds because they'd been horny and preferred to think themselves as straight. There are times now when standing on the balcony of yet another club, looking down at the nearly indistinguishable view of the dance floor that I think the same thing: to find someone who can take us away from this frenzied, deafening, drug-and-alcohol catalyzed milieu of nightclubs and bars. And I think, *My God, only love can make it all right.* But then the music changes, the video screen rolls away into the ceiling and a friend grabs my hand, leading me to dance with him and to stop acting so dramatic.

On the way back home, drenched in sweat from dancing all night, he and I had huddled at the back of the practically vacant bus and excitedly shared our feelings. Dar uncoiled the muffler from around his neck then slathered some balm over his chapped lips, handling the little tube as if it was a lipstick, pronouncedly puckering and smacking his lips. As I watched him, marveling at how comfortable he was with himself, I wondered if it was because he was a couple of years older or because he'd been around more. I found myself appreciative of his outlook on life in a way that I had never been with another black person. Here we were, students away from home, closeted to our parents, finding ourselves and planning our futures. There was no master or servant. No native or migrant. We had been equalized. Or so I thought.

Dar divulged the tale of his family in Newark: a mother who had juggled jobs as a seamstress and as a department store saleslady to support two children after his father deserted them; a younger sister who was pregnant at seventeen; his hesitation to reveal his sexual persuasion to his family; how he thought being black must be a little like being Latin, in that there is overwhelming pressure for a man to be macho when all Dar wanted to do was create fashion like his mother and suck dick on weekends.

I told him how most people in Los Angeles were surprised that I could speak English so well and that I could dress presentably when I told them I was from Kenya, ludicrous reactions familiar to all foreigners. That I was astounded because they expected me to prattle away in jungle gibberish and prance around in a loincloth. That I was at first insulted and then, in time, bemused by their ignorance when asked if wild animals stalked the city, posing a threat to everyday life. And that one time, while taking the bus home from college, I had derisively indulged this middle-aged woman seated next to me by fictionalizing how my mother wished I would return home to protect her from this one predacious lioness that stalked our verandah every evening – that many a time I would have to charge out with a spear in hand to repel the beast. When, instead of feeling absurd, this woman on the bus had clutched at her breast in horror and cried, "Oh no! Your poor mother, who will protect her now?" I had been so discomfited that I had clamped my mouth shut and buried myself in my art-history textbook.

"But dar-r-ling, that's all they see on TV, what do you expect?" he reasoned. "I mean, nobody thinks of going to Kenya for haute couture, do they? Kenya is for a naturalist what Paris is to the fashionable, my love."

"But that's no excuse!" I said. "People shouldn't be so ignorant!"

"We live in America, dar-r-ling. And even though it may not be the case, we like to pretend as if we live on another planet most of the time. For so many people there is no reason to pay attention to the rest of the world. Everything they need, want, is right here. Unless, of course, they plan on going on safari!" he laughed.

Once we reached my apartment in Santa Monica, trading more stories during the long walk from the bus stop, Dar and I felt as if we had known each other for years. But when it came time to sleep, I laid out a mattress on the floor next to my queen-sized bed. When he requested a sip of water from the glass I was holding, I handed him a separate glass. And I caught a hint of a look that said he was insulted. He expressed none of his humiliation through words, but his eyes conveyed that he felt belittled and disappointed by my snobbery. *What am supposed to do?* I asked myself. *I can't be expected to share my bed with him! It feels dirty.....unclean.....Even in America, he's still a* golo, *for Chrissake! Having him in my bed, lying next to me, is unthinkable! Unbearable. No, no,* I thought. *We can party together and share our secrets but some things are definitely beyond me. I'm sorry, I can't do it....*

After all the years, I think about that night when Dar had hunkered on the side of my bed on a comforter, reluctant to remove his layers of clothing; I think about the two glasses of water that sat side by side on top of the stereo speaker across the bed; and I wonder if Dar had known the real reason why I had refused to lie in the same bed or share the same glass with him. Because I felt that physical intimacy with him would have maligned me.

I think about it a lot those days, now that I shared my bed with a black man and let him come inside me.

CHAPTER 25

LOVE LETTERS

In a drawer of her cupboard, buried at the feet of her many tailored dresses in pastel and wedged among unwrapped bottles of imported perfume that she'd hoarded, my mother kept the mementos of my father's cataclysmic love for her. These were the letters and cards that he'd sent her during what he professed to be his necessary visits to Nairobi city, bundled crudely with the stray cotton sash of a discarded dress. Along with them, he had sent her several tapes of Indian film music, each song carefully selected to express the deluge of his love. One card I remember clearly. It was etched in my father's own blood. After having sat me on her lap, she'd opened it up for me to see. Letters of the alphabet were inscribed with a needle dipped in blood and crawled across the page like little rusted filaments. A triumphant look came onto Mummy's face as she said, "See? This is how much he loved me. You know, he couldn't live without me!" And then the compulsory clucks of ruefulness.

As my tiny finger ran across his writing – a declaration of the convoluted love they both claimed they'd been unable to live without, yet which he proceeded so naturally to destroy – only admiration and awe registered in my mind. There in his blood, aged to a burnt sienna by time, was all the proof I needed that theirs had been the love of legends: Heer and Rhanjha, Laila and Majnu, Romeo and Juliet. Never mind that the obstacle that had cost my father his life and damned their love was not a family feud or conflicting religious ideologies but my father's lust for other women.

Before I left for America, she dug into the same drawer to extract a small, specific picture that had been taken during their courtship. She wanted me to have it.

At first glance, the picture didn't look like anything special. It was blurry and had been taken from a distance, obscuring their features. Its focus was on a cheery young lady in sixties glasses and beehive hairdo holding a bottle of Fanta soda. Next to her in the grass was a portable gramophone player, the once-spinning vinyl now trapped in a paralyzed lapse of time. Sitting a few feet away from the picnic were my parents looking as I had never seen them. They cut a handsome pair. My mother sat on a crate and my father on bent knees, holding a white cup of tea and smiling at her.

"We look beautiful, don't we?" she said, stealing the words from my mouth. "You can have that. It's from when we were in love."

"You know what, Mummy?" I remembered, "I'd like to see that card again. You know, the one he wrote you in blood?"

Nodding, she got it and let me hold it again, years after I had first held it. "You know, he gave me this one after one of those…those horrible times," she said with a shudder. She was referring to one of the many times he had brutalized her. "Your father, he really put me through hell."

I handed the card back to her and she inspected it, almost as if making sure the writing hadn't faded. "He may have written this in blood, but it wasn't until after he had shed some of mine."

For some months, my parents, struggling to make ends meet during the early part of their marriage, had lodged at a guesthouse in Nairobi. My paternal grandmother had refused to look after her newly born grandson or give them shelter unless paid handsomely for her services. So they chose to distance themselves from her and I was consigned to my mother's family, who were ecstatic to have me, in Mombasa. My father was extremely suspicious of my mother around other people, a malaise she claimed was a projection of his own infidelity, so he often locked her in their room for the evening when he went out with his buddies. Upon returning earlier than expected one night, he'd discovered she'd gone out with one of her cousins. He searched and failed to find her, and waited up for her with a belt wound in his hands. When she came home, he beat her until he tired of beating. He took her to bed, and placing the cold metal edge of his switchblade against the throbbing vein of her neck, fucked her. He said, "If you ever do this again, if you ever try to leave me, I swear it, I will hunt you down and kill you."

Tears filmed the kohl-lined orbs of my mother's large, beautiful eyes when she relived this incident, and her body stiffened as if the wounds were still fresh and the bruises merely hidden from view. With that same pained emotion conflicting with the discomfiture in her face, my mother had gone on to admit without any embarrassment that it had been some of the most memorable sex they'd had.

The strange thing was that although these memories of irascible jealousy filled her with dread and she was thankful to have relegated them to the past, they also offered her indisputable proof of his all-consuming love for her. Her feelings about these episodes were as dichotomous as her feelings for him.

At that moment I had wanted to kiss her, to feel her tongue in my mouth as I had wanted the time she instructed me on the intrigues of sex, as my father never had. To fuse back into her. To be her. To know that these feelings that she felt were firsthand.

And then she bundled the letters back up and I went to finish packing, the memory of their courtship in my hands and her clucking in my ears.

CHAPTER 26

WAITING FOR ME

Every once in a while, Nelson and I would run into Richard at a nightclub. The first time I introduced them, they cautiously evaluated each other over a brief handshake, then each made a point to ignore the other after that. Sometimes, having drank a little too much (Richard's presence inspired me to drink more than usual), I would excuse myself from Nelson and hunt Richard down instead of going to the bathroom. By consuming large quantities of alcohol, I thought I might still be able to swim back into that space where he would be waiting for me. Into the familiar swamp of pain that had agonized and espoused me just the same. But no sooner had I opened my mouth than Richard would pronounce, "You've been drinking, haven't you?" The caution and pity in his eyes would anger me and then, regaining my steely composure, I would throw a venomous look at his companion, some white worked-out blonde in a skintight shirt, and tell him that I had to run back to Nelson. He was *waiting* for me.

Even when I stood next to Nelson, his arm possessively around my waist as we leaned against an unoccupied pool table in the bar area, my eyes studied Richard fluttering around the room, trying hard to impress someone with his hip-hop moves on the edge of the dance floor or coveting someone he hoped to go home with. I felt sorry for him. I had been right to suspect that nothing would change with him even after his illness, that he would continue to sleep around relentlessly with other men. Except that this time he would not have me, his devoted confidant, to climb into bed with at the end of an unfulfilled night, to pour his sorrows out to as he climbed upon me and clasped his arms around me, to seek advice about someone that had let him down as he buried his face within my neck, his hair tumbling across my chin.

And as I stood there, next to Nelson, his arm drawing me closer to his side and his eyes perceptively shifting between me and a seemingly oblivious Richard, I felt comforted, blessed almost for his nurturing, and found that I was gradually letting him into a place where only Richard had been permitted to go.

CHAPTER 27

NO SHOW

The rain came down in sheets. I stood outside of Oasis nightclub, where I first met you, cowering from the pelting rain, thinking wryly, there couldn't be a better setting for a letdown. Behind me, dance music blared, competing with the clamor of the rain, its vibration in the glass doors against my back. Inside the club the rites of mating had begun: drink specials spilling over from glasses on the counter, deftly penciled phone numbers on paper napkins being bartered like promissory notes, predatory treks around the bar periphery to encounter suitable prey. I could've been in there with the rest of the emotionally anesthetized regulars, with only fucking on my mind (the size of his arm, the measure of his cock, the firmness of his butt), but had been convinced into treading out of those waters, to be revived from emotional sedation into taking a chance with you, and this is where it's landed me. On the outside. Waiting for you in this unceasing rain with a Miles Davis CD clutched in my frozen hands, a modest offering for your birthday, now three days late. You'd been unable to see me. You claimed to have been under the weather.

While standing there for over an hour, avoiding the eyes of everyone that went hurriedly past, huddling together for warmth and shelter under umbrellas, I prayed that I wouldn't run into anyone I knew. I hated being alone, for people to think that I had no one. Winter was the most romantic time of the year. And the most tragic. In the cold, our bodies nestled together for warmth; we clustered in little groups even without realizing it. Only when sweltering in the summer heat did we start to repel one another, to stand further apart, to demand that compass of space around us, the space without which another body might smother us.

I craved a cup of coffee, or better yet a stiff cocktail, but didn't dare move lest I might miss you. I called home from the pay phone outside the entrance to the club to see if you had left any messages. Once, my mother answered the phone and furiously I ordered her never to answer the phone again unless the caller had identified himself to her on the machine. There was nothing from you; the series of beeps indicating this to me felt like a death sentence. I sifted through the possibilities of an impeding traffic problem, your miscalculation of time, and even plain forgetfulness, although I knew that you, Nelson, had never been the forgetful kind. But I sank with the only explanation that made any sense in light of your recent behavior. That you'd planned on not showing up, on putting me through this. Quite in synch with your failure to return any of my calls or commit to any dates. I was being sent the message that after vying unremittingly for my affections, after stripping me down, you'd seen how vulnerable I could be and were now rejecting me.

Our last real conversation went through my mind as I pulled the overcoat, one that Mummy had insisted I take with me, tighter around myself. *I care so much about you, I think we should take more time to get to know each other. We went about this the wrong way, you know what I mean? Sleeping with each other before getting to really know one another?* I remember studying the young, white-trash girl seated across from us as she sucked on her fingers and released each one with an audible sound for the benefit of her much older male companion. I remember watching the electric train chug its way along the trek of the ceiling at this restaurant in Costa Mesa, my fork toying with the scrambled eggs on my plate, my ears listening to your new slant on our twelve-week relationship as we kept getting interrupted by the overzealous waitress you'd made it a point to be exceptionally nice to. "They work so hard," you always reasoned at every restaurant we'd been to, "and they deal with such assholes that I think people should be extra nice to them." How incredibly patronizing, I had thought. Why don't you demonstrate your compassion with a bigger tip? I'm sure she'd appreciate that a lot more. I attempted to appear unscathed by your assessment of our relationship, then recalled how you had girdled me and forced yourself into my mouth on the mattress on the floor of your new apartment only hours before. I could still remember how you tasted in my mouth.

I complied with your proposal to just being friends, to changing the nature of our relationship, to save face; as you had put it, I reminded you so much of your younger, feisty sister now. All I had wanted to do was mangle your face and scream, *How dare you! How dare you make this decision after maneuvering me into opening up to you!* Did this mean I would never have you in that way again? That I would never be able to bite into the hunks of your flesh or rest my naked face against your chest after being caulked by your penis?

My loss felt more debilitating because I knew that both Richard and you had one thing in common: Neither one of you could ever be without someone in your lives. Who had become my replacement? Who were you denuding now that I had lain myself bare to you and started to yearn for your intimations? I wanted to hurl everything off the table, the plates of scrambled eggs and the orange juice and the apple pancakes you were gorging on, so that they would make a clangor over your carefully rehearsed words. I wanted to reach over and tear your T-shirt off, to search for any telltale marks on your dark body – crescents from fingernails on your back that didn't belong to me, purple bite marks where I hadn't gnawed on you. But I sat there slowly forking the overly salty eggs into my mouth, watching your mouth move, but having lost any cognizance of the words after the first few minutes; the girl across from us now drawing more attention from the other patrons; the waitress intruding on the periphery of my vision, preparing to refill your glass of freshly squeezed orange juice for the third time.

That was a week ago.   Outside the club, shuddering from the bite of the wind, from the grave acceptance of your abandonment, I dreaded returning home because Mummy would be waiting on the sofa, expecting a dialogue, my pain evident to her from the sound of my breath.

Where could you be now? I wondered. I hoped you were mangled in some car accident, your limbs torn from side to side, your neck cleaved off by sharp metal. But I knew that you were probably resting at home, the heater turned on to high, maybe even watching the rain pour down from that bare window in your room, which you had blanketed to keep the sun from rousing me – had you found matching blinds for that bare window? Maybe you had someone there with you and your bodies were jousting in passion, your every thrust increasing in vigor as you thought of me here, waiting for you.   Yes, I admitted to myself, begrudging the tears that welled up in my eyes, you must have someone there with you now.

Someone who hadn't hesitated to express how he felt about you, someone who hadn't needed all that time like me. Someone who might have blinked doe-eyed as you opened the door for him instead of scowling at the gesture as an infringement on his independence. Someone who had, by taking you away from me, sentenced me back into this infernal world of clubs and bars.

CHAPTER 28

MOTHER KNOWS BEST

She was nursing a glass of Scotch, glassy-eyed on the sofa, when I let myself in. The television set was on and *Jerry Springer* was feeding her prodigious appetite for sensationalism with an episode on midget lesbian prostitutes. Her hands turned the glass as if trying to summon courage from the movement, and the rocks of ice clanked loudly. Although her mouth opened while I shed my soaked jacket in the corner behind the door, she knew better than to say anything just then. I avoided looking into her eyes because I could feel her pain as I suspected she felt mine. I walked into my room where I started to undress. Cautiously, she followed me and paused by the doorframe. She held out a towel.

"Mum, I'm changing!"

"*Hanh, hanh,* I know," she said, nodding apologetically. "I just want to give you this. Dry yourself before you get sick."

I sighed with exasperation, more loudly than was necessary, and practically snatched it from her extended hand. "Just...can you give me a moment, please?"

She disappeared into the living room without saying another word and I shut the door after her. As I rubbed myself dry, my body covered with goose bumps, I looked down at the soaked gift-wrapped CD on my bed and I thought about taking it back to the store the next day. I thought of the music that Nelson and I had heard together and the Nancy Wilson song that he had played for me on the phone while I had been at work. How I had tittered and resolved to always think of him when hearing that particular song again. My eyes started to tear, and my body convulsed to shake the feeling off me. I wished my mother wasn't waiting for me in the other room. I wanted her gone. Back to Kenya, far away from me so I wouldn't have to hide my pain from her, so I could just mourn openly.

I was being cruel to her, but I felt impotent to do anything about it. My alienation of her made me feel wretched, but something about rekindling our intimacy terrified me. It was as if she might somehow propel me back into dependency. I calmed myself with the thought of calling Nelson the next day. He'd have a logical excuse for not showing up, and there would be no need to return the CD. I would repackage it, maybe even get him the whole Miles Davis anthology instead.

When I walked out into the living room in sweats, she was back on the sofa looking up at me. Her face quivered as if she was on the verge of tears – that look that mothers have a patent on and can speak volumes – making it clear that I had succeeded in hurting her. For the last several years, continents had separated us and afforded us a dialogue of, at best, perfunctory niceties. It was the language of a relationship forced to thrive on echoing long distance phone calls where the expense of each ticking minute and crossing wires riddled with the tidbits of someone else's conversation had mercilessly kept us from significant topics. But suddenly there she was, the landmass between us swallowed as if by the earth itself, yet our hearts were worlds apart. There was no escaping her.

Reluctantly I flopped onto the sofa and curled my knees up to my chin, my eyes fixed on the television set where a commercial for Nyquil promised relief from every thinkable ailment. The headache and the heartache medicine, that's what Salman called it. Just a few capfuls and goodbye to every kind of shit! I thought about the stiff cocktail that I never got. My eyes flirted momentarily with the half bottle of Scotch on the coffee table. It angered me to think that she probably held me responsible for driving her to drink.

I could feel her eyes resting heavily on me, and I wished she would say something. Anything. Ask me to charge more of the miracle cures she'd been gullible enough to believe in; give me the lowdown on Brook Logan from *The Bold and the Beautiful*; tell me that she hated me. But she remained silent, martyred, humiliated in a way that hollered at me louder than her words ever could. I grabbed the remote and killed the TV.

"I can't handle this right now," I said finally, starring at the lacquered screen faintly reflecting us. "I can't handle this whole...silent-treatment thing, okay?" And then, when she still said nothing, "I can't pretend to be happy just to spare your feelings, Mum."

"Don't worry. You won't have to for much longer," she said. "You see, I can't handle this either. I don't have the strength, you know." She started to cry. "I'm not going to stay around and watch this. So you can call the airline tomorrow and change my dates. If you're going to destroy yourself, you're going to have to do it without an audience."

I tried as hard as I could to hold my own tears back, but I could feel them mounting within me like a mad, violent flood. "I'm sorry, Mum. I didn't mean for it to be like this."

"Who *are* you?" she asked, her face contorted with pain. "I don't even recognize you anymore. What happened to my son? What happened to my little Ali?"

I looked the other way and squeezed my eyes shut.

"You know, day and night I pray for God to keep his hand over you because I'm too far. Because I can't be here with you. 'This poor child has nobody else,' I keep telling him. 'You have to look after him.' But seeing you like this...do you know how it makes me feel? Where did I fail in my prayers?"

I covered my face in my hands, tears filtering through my lashes, screaming in my mind, *Oh, God...I don't know, Mummy. I don't know. I've lost Nelson. I'm alone again...Why do you do this to me, God? First Richard and now Nelson. Why must you bring them into my life only so I can lose them?*

Then I grunted sardonically. "Maybe he isn't listening. Maybe we should've stopped praying a long time ago."

"Don't talk such nonsense! Who do you think has been looking after you all these years? You know, God is not some bank you make withdrawals from. He gives us whatever we need. Sometimes it's strength."

I don't want his goddamn strength. I don't want his anything! I just want the guy at the airport with the red rose. I want someone to be him...

"I don't need that crutch anymore," I said.

"Don't speak that way, Ali. Look," she said, wiping her tears on the edge of her sleeve. "I'm not going to live forever, okay? So just bear with me for now. From the time you were a little baby, I have tried to move heaven and earth to make sure that you have everything. Everyone told me, 'Parin, you are spoiling this boy *too much*,' but I never listened to them, you know. 'You will both regret it one day,' they kept telling me. 'The world out there is not going to give him any special treatment,' but I just ignored them. But now...Ali, there isn't much more I can do, and it breaks my heart to see you suffering like this."

I shrugged. The most ludicrous thought went through my mind: what if I had Mummy call Nelson? Maybe he would be more responsive; after all, he'd been dying to meet her. And then I realized with some sadness how, when heartbroken, we all became like children, needing to clutch that index finger that would guide us out of the mess we'd gotten ourselves into.

"You've made your own choices in life, Ali. Maybe you can turn all this around," she said, touching my shoulder. "It's not too late, Ali. It's not too late. Look at all your other friends."

I groaned and leaned away from her. I knew where this was heading: her son's much anticipated prodigal return from the deviant ways of the West, where innocent, wholesome children had picked up all these horrible, aberrant perversions – from those immoral white people with·their drugs and drinking and spiritual bankruptcy.

I could see in her face that my mother was perched on the edge of wining her son over in this most desperate of moments buy I thwarted her budding hopes, more comfortable pirouetting on the glossed-out floor of a West Hollywood nightclub than the consecrated grounds of the mosque she hoped to see me married in.

"Let me guess," I said, steeling up. "You want me to go back home with you – to that hellhole – and – you want me to get married and have children, right? That will solve everything!"

"Yes, but don't you think—"

"God, you just don't get it, do you?" I sprang off the couch, suddenly unable to bear sitting in the same spot as her.

"What's wrong with that? Why can't you just give up all this craziness and be like your other friends, Ali? Settle down. Find a good girl who will look after you."

"I'm not like them, mother! Jesus, are you daft? Don't you get it?"

She remained calm, shook her head and smiled sadly. "You know, I go to mosque everyday, and I too want to be proud and boast about my son when everyone speaks of their children. Your friend, Karim, you know, he got married and your friend Salim, even he got married to that girl he was dating, remember? And now, you know, they are even expecting a baby! What can I talk about? How can I share my stories with them? What do I tell them when they ask me about you?"

"So that's what matters more to you? Trading stories? Contributing to their gossip?"

"No, no, Ali," she moaned and rose to her feet. "It's just that as a parent I have dreams too. You have left that world behind, but I'm still very much a part of it. Everybody remembers you, asks about you. 'How is Ali? Are you going to see him? Are you going for his *sagaai?*' And what do I do? I keep my mouth shut, make some excuse, tell them you are still trying to, you know, establish yourself." She looks up at me. "I don't know how to handle this."

I felt the urge to say bitterly, *Then why don't you pray a little harder? Maybe that omniscient God that you claim has knowledge of every trembling leaf on each branch – that same one that permits it to skitter onto the ground where it is crushed and turned to dust – the God who you claim created me and, so I have to believe, my sexuality, maybe he can tell you why he has deprived you of the chance to compete in the community chatter and fall short of being a proud parent.* Instead, I said coldly, "I'm sorry, but I can't help you there," and walked away from her to my room.

"Wait a minute," she said and charged behind me, pushing my door open. "Don't you walk away from me! I'm your mother! We have to talk about this!"

"What do you want me to say?" I faced her menacingly. *"Hunh?* What? What do you want from me? To live a lie? To be a hypocrite just so that you can hold your head up in the community?" I waved a dismissing hand at her and turned away. "I'm not going to deal with this shit!"

"You'll have to deal with this!" she said, pushing herself in front of me. "Do you have any idea what this is putting me through? Haven't I been through enough in my life to have to endure *this* now?"

"This," I hissed, "isn't about you! This is about my life, you hear me? My life!"

"And your life has nothing to do with me?" she asked. "I've raised a son, given him every ounce of my being and now what? I'm supposed to turn to stone and feel nothing? I have no right to find out why he's so determined on destroying himself? Why he's turned into this…this…"

"Monster. Say it!"

"This stranger," she cried.

"You want to know why you don't recognize your son?" I asked. "Why he doesn't call, doesn't keep in touch? It's because of all this bullshit you keep expecting from him. It's because he can't tell you who he really is when all you see is the man you want him to be!"

She shook her head and smiled as one would at a petulant little child. "Oh, Ali. I know my son even better than he knows himself. And I don't need this…" she pulled a gay porno tape from the closet, in all its orgiastic glory, to my embarrassed face. "I don't need to see *this* to tell me who you are, okay?"

My gaze fell to the floor.

"You know, all your life, I've seen you go through this with boys," she said, placing the cassette gently on the bed. "You think I've forgotten? You remember the time with your friend, Amin? When you used to come and sleep next to me and tell me how it was hurting you here, deep inside your stomach? I'm not stupid. I remember all that." Her hand touched my abdomen. "I gave life to you. I just want to keep you from destroying it. I was just hoping that by now, that pain would have stopped for you."

No, I wanted to tell her. It has only worsened, Mum. Only now I can no longer seek solace in the folds of your skirt or excuse myself as being naïve. With time, the only things that seemed to have changed in this game are the locales and the participants; the heart seems to have an ineffectual memory of the pain that should keep it from gambling again.

"If you were at least happy," she said. "Then I could go back there and face...whatever and still be okay with it because I know that you are not suffering. But all I see it that you're unhappy, you're alone, you're lost. You'll never know, Ali, what it's like to be in my shoes."

I wanted to tell her that I empathized with her pain. The pain of someone that had been left behind to contend with both private and public expectations. With having to confront her own fears at first and then having to yarn excuses for the rest of the Ismaili community. But I said nothing from the fear that if I opened my mouth, I would break down.

As her crying deprived her of breath, she hiccupped, and I felt the urge to take her into my arms and give her everything she desired of me. This woman who had been through so much, I reminded myself. This petite little woman with a size four shoe and who still had a milk tooth in her mouth, this woman who prayed fanatically for me and strayed only for a drink of Scotch. I mustn't underestimate her because she knew what it was like to love like I did, to feel the gamut of emotions that I thought others incapable of, and had survived unspeakable tragedies. I wished I could give her all that other parents took for granted in their offspring. I wished I could have shown her a framed photo of some amiable young girl leaning promisingly onto me at a dinner table instead of the one with the fag hag who blew an outrageous kiss into the camera. I wished I could have done that instead of telling her that she would never have a daughter-in-law. That there would be no grandchildren for her to dote on, to carry on the family name, that the tree stopped here.

I could not give her any of this. I knew that nothing I could do or say at that moment could prepare her for when she returned to Kenya, loaded with the knowledge of what she had only suspected, but had now been confirmed – that her son, her only child, was a homosexual. The world would always be there in places where I could not be. In community functions, dinner parties, family weddings. She would have to face them alone, armed only with the hope that perhaps her son had found a way to educe some happiness from a lifestyle punctuated by loneliness. She would have to accept the reality of the situation, that she was powerless against what she saw as this demon that had possessed her only child. The apple of her eye, wormed, rotting from some vile infection. Everything she had lived and worked for in the past forty-eight years was standing before her. Flawed.

I would not hold her. I would not console her. I had to be firm. She had to realize that manipulations could not rescind anything. My coming out to her would not distance us but, much to my own revelation, just might bridge us. *I am doing this, mother, so that we can return to that place where we can talk again.* Where, having cast hybrid expectations aside, we can go back to being real with each other. Not like a child that cuts his parents out of his life because he can no longer talk to them. Because he is afraid they will not understand or accept. *I never wanted it to be that way between us, mother. I don't ever want it to be that way between us again.*

Her body had turned away from me. She heaved and leaned against the door of my room for support. Slowly I put my hand on her shaking back but she didn't turn around, inconsolable. "Mum," I started to say softly. "Please, can't you just let me lead an honest life? Do you really want me to be like those other people? You know them," I said, squeezing her shoulders. "There are so many in Mombasa who just went ahead and got married but still continue to fuck around with little Arab boys and prostitutes behind their wives' backs. Is that what you rather I did? To be like them and trap some poor woman into thinking I'm something I'm not?"

She turned around. "No, no, I don't want that. But how long can you go on like this, *hunh?* And what about those diseases?" she asked, her eyes widening. "What about this AIDS? What if you catch that, then what?"

"Oh, Mum…"

"You know, they say this is a disease that the gay people get, you know? Because of, you know, the…" her hand fluttered nervously, "the, you know, the way they do it. What if it happens to you?"

Suddenly the roles had been reversed, and I had become the educating parent. "Mum, it's not that simple, and you have nothing to worry about. I'll explain it all to you."

"Who is going to look after you, *hunh?*"

"Who's looking after me now?" I asked.

"When you're older, I mean. When you're older and I'm no longer around?"

She seemed to have forgotten that I had been managing without her for the last eight years. Without the haven of her arms, the smells of her cooking. In her mind her prayers had sustained me like an invisible paladin, over freeways and streets, at work and at play. Even physically removed, she had managed to stay by my side through her meditation, by coaxing divine intervention into substituting for her. She was probably right. She was worried that the God she prayed to was a hungry one. Once she was gone, there would be nobody to feed his appetite for adulation, to appease him into protecting me anymore.

"Mummy," I said, lifting her face gently in my hands. "Your God will look after me, don't worry. Isn't that what you've been praying for? Isn't that what you keep telling him? That I have nobody else but him?"

She sunk her face into my chest. "I've suffered all my life – enough, I hoped, for both of us. If you don't reap the fruits of happiness, then who will?"

I enveloped her into my arms and held her there with all my strength, and she mourned for me: the comforts of family which I would never know; the nurturing a traditional Indian wife may have been able to give me; and the sons and daughters that I would never hold up in the air.

CHAPTER 29

SHUT UP AND BEAR IT!

Many times that week, I called Adrian to ruminate over Nelson, to try to make some sense of his rejection of me. I called to cry to him, dejected since Nelson wouldn't speak to me. Nelson, who wanted to take care of me and purge me of all my pain, who gave me his cock and claimed to have given me his heart, was now acting like he could live happily for the rest of his life without speaking another word to me. I was told I wasn't good enough anymore, not for a relationship and not even as an instrument of sex. My God, I wasn't even sure that I really wanted Nelson, but I could not understand the wall he had erected. I wanted Adrian to tell me something, to help me rationalize the situation as he had done so many times before with Richard. As if there are any words, any explanations, that can make rejection more palatable.

Tell me something, I implored Adrian. Why is he treating me this way? I droned on. But this time, Adrian reacted differently. I got the feeling that even he, my link to a sane world, had crumbled under the weight of my venting. I could hear it in his voice; I had begun to grate on his nerves with the litany of my latest doomed affair. I had become chronic, just like those clients who have a penchant for screwing up their bank accounts; the same ones who charged into my office, statements clutched in their hands like emancipation papers that would liberate them from some elaborately designed scheme to keep them in the red. I was like them, always an ill-fated love affair to grieve over, always deserted, always freshly confounded.

Adrian made that sound – a kind of exasperated exhale – and said simply, "Well, I really don't know what to tell you."

"But you must," I insisted. "What do *you* think? I mean, if you were in my place, what would you do? How would you think?"

Adrian sighed heavily. "Ali, I...really, I wish I could help."

"He won't even return my calls, Adrian! I don't know what I've done. Why does he hate me? I wish he would just talk to me."

"Yeah..."

I could hear it in Adrian's monosyllabic responses...*Oh...Yeah...Well...Did he? Really? Hmmm...*They spoke a language of their own. A hollowness, a distinct detachment, that left me scalded. Adrian was always so compassionate, if contrived at times. The kind of friend from whom an honest opinion might not be possible but the comfort of hearing what you needed to could always be expected. I could hear the words that he wouldn't say – *I don't want to hear about your pain. I've grown bored of your pain. Don't you see? It won't diminish your pain to share it with me. Don't tell me anymore. Always who hurt you and who did what to you. Just shut up and bear it. Just don't talk to me about your pain anymore...*

CHAPTER 30

THOSE DAYS

Mohammad Rafi's elegy of lost love from *Heer Ranjha* – *"Yeh Duniya, Yeh Mehfil, Mere Kaam Ki Nahin"* – was one of my father's favorite songs. My mother had told me this many times, as if to explain the tragic complexion of his love. Like the many songs I'd heard my parents play, its melody had been branded in my mind and its lyrics easily retrieved from an archive deep within. When singing them, I found myself elated in a way that Streisand would never be able to evoke. While Mummy packed a cassette I was innocently playing came to that song. She launched into tears from where she sat on the couch and asked, "Why do you do this to me, *henh?* I really can't bear to listen to that music, you know? It reminds me so much of your father and *those days*, my God!"

Those days. The way she said those two simple words conveyed an awe-inspiring epoch of inexpressible anguish and passion. But she did nothing to terminate Rafi's lament. When I'd reached out to remedy the situation and change the music, she said through glistening eyes, "No, no, you don't have to stop it! It's okay, you know, just let it play," and retreated to the tormented memories of her one great love, clucking ruefully. "Those days...Those days..."

Sometimes I became confused as to whether Mummy was referring to the time that she shared with my father or the years following his death. I imagined that she probably coalesced both periods together and reflected upon them, mournfully, as her youth. The part of her life she had given to him with reckless abandon; the part of life when she'd finally lost him and somehow, with child in tow, had to forge through decades of questions that would remain unanswered; the years that had ravaged her and, in turn, earned her the wisdom of her later years.

"Yeh duniyah, Yeh mehfil" took me back too, but to a time far less painful than my mother's. My own memory of what she refers to as "those days" was different. A time without any formal discipline or paternal scrutiny. Instead "those days" transported me to finally ending the waiting game for Daddy and an era of drive-in cinemas in Mombasa.

As a child, I often saw the movie that bore this tune and so many others like it at the drive-in cinema. This was the Sunday ritual. The entire Indian community of Mombasa, would prepare for the excursion as early as noon by packing tiffins of Indian viands – *kachodis, samosas,* fried chicken, kebabs and thermoses of hot chai. Come four o'clock, a procession of cars would cause Mombasa's Indian merchant district to become a virtual ghost town, all of us on a pilgrimage through the oceanic smells of Changamwe to patiently await admittance in a serpentine queue for the extravaganza of Bollywood films. Once admitted into the cinema, kids played and people strolled and met and played cards on *sadhris*. They chomped on cumin-infused potato dumplings, memorized dialogues spilling out between mouthfuls; every Indian's eyes were glued to the expanse of that vibrant cinema screen.

Up until the advertisements came on – a handful of regulars that we could now claim we'd grown up to and which had become the symbols of modernity and good living (Else Balsam shampoo from L'Oreal, glittering Seiko watches, Palmolive soap, Close-Up toothpaste) – we gathered on the canteen grounds. In spite of the amount of food we'd lugged in the car, we'd always buy crinkle-cut fries, or chips as we called them. After dousing them with salt, cayenne pepper and vinegar, so that they were converted from their crisp consistency into a kind of spicy, squishy mush, we'd devour them with ice-cold Coca-Colas. It was a ritual like buttered popcorn and hot dogs. Sitting around the canteen patio, waiting for dusk to sanction the celluloid drama, my family would sit in rapt wonder as I recited *shairis*, many of which I'd written myself.

"*Wah! Wah!* Parin, your son is just going to kill me, I tell you!" they'd say, clutching their breast. "Where, I ask you, did he learn to draw daggers like this? *Wah! Wah!*" Among the congregation of avid listeners was my lesbian aunt Leila, who, snug with a flask of Johnnie Walker, tossed her head back for a healthy swig of it every time the punch line was delivered. I liked her best then because it was the only time she didn't scold me for walking funny or talking funny, and showered me with appreciative "*wah-wahs!*"

Shairis were mostly tragic, lilting stanzas about self-immolation and forsaken love. Only tragedy elicited the enthusiastic, heartfelt "*wah-wahs*" that are the accolade of an Indian poet's artistry. An eight-year-old writing and reciting Hindi poems about love's demise and the desire to kill himself didn't strike anyone as even the slightest bit macabre in a culture where as many songs were about the succoring values of drinking as about the burning desire of loving the unattainable. As an adolescent, all I proved to any of my attentive listeners when spilling out about the fatalistic nature of love and a bleeding heart was that I was exceptionally talented and appropriately schooled in the ethos of my culture.

Those days. My mother's long, black nylon slip, pulled over my forehead to imitate long, silky, flowing hair. I leapt onto the bed positioned against the windowsill, a lustful cabaret song blaring from the 45 on the record player. Pulling the curtains away from the window, I treated my neighbors – at first dumbstruck, then amused – to the spectacle of an adolescent's vamp mimicry. With no more than a dirty, black nylon slip from the hamper and a bed sheet knotted around my neck for a fashionable gown, I'd been transformed into glamorous Helen! *Piya tu, aab to aaja...*

They all had a field day, especially when my uncle came to yank me off my personal little stage, which also happened to be his bed, screaming and asking me what the hell I thought I was doing. "What do you think you are? A *chokdi?* Everybody's looking at you! *Be-sharam!* Get off that bed at once before I cut off your *taturi!"*

Outside, the crowd was clamoring for more, and I managed at least once to free my hand from his grasp and bounce back on the bed. There, I threw a couple more gyrations to my appreciative fans before being picked up and carried off the bed and into the other room where I would be disrobed off my glamorous persona.

There were also the long, hot afternoons when everyone was at work, and my grandmother was either resigned to impenetrable siestas or committed to a feud with my grandfather. The audience may not have been as large, much to my chagrin, but the shows were uninterrupted and much, much longer.

Those days. The beginning of the discovery of my queer self. Many times I've thought, my father must have been the only one who had seen it coming and been absolutely horrified by it. Everyone else in my family acted oblivious to my burgeoning queer tendencies after the first few attempts at reprimanding me. But to my father, that all-embodying paragon of masculinity, I must have felt like some kind of affront on his oppressive male persona.

My mother has often said, "Tsk, tsk, thank God, I'm telling you! I don't know what would have happened if he'd been alive. I'm telling you, Ali, one of you would've killed the other, I just know it! Do you think he would have stood for your lifestyle? No way! I'm telling you he would have *never* been able to accept it! You guys would've *never* gotten along. It would have been terrible!"

And a look glazes over her face as if she was visualizing some grand historic event that never took place.

Once, when trying to forge his features from the defeating memory of his infrequent visits, I looked up at the night sky – because the sky was where God and all that have returned to him are mythicized to thrive – and thought, *Well, your son turned out to be queer after all, Dad. After all your attempts at disciplining me, using your hands to strike me and your strength to shake me, your son has turned out to be a faggot as big as the macho man you were. Now that you're up there, and I hope not burning in the fires of hell for being the cruel son-of-a-bitch that you sometimes were, I hope you understand. I hope that from up there you've gained some perspective and are finally able to accept me and not be ashamed.*

CHAPTER 31

MAKING CHAI

There were tears in her eyes, but this time I knew they were not for dramatic effect.   In about an hour, she would be flying back to Kenya.   I sat next to her at the boarding gate to the flight that would take her to London and then, after an exhaustive eight-hour wait in transit, back home. As I watched other planes bellies regurgitate frazzled passengers, I started to wish I could have spared her the tedium of her journey; to have been able to not only pay for her trip, but also to have afforded her the comforts of first-class seating and a quick, painless layover. She struggled through a steaming cup of tea, crumpling her face in distaste.

"Is this tea? How can you just stick a bag in some hot water and call it tea, *henh?*"

I smiled at her, noticing her sarcasm was eclipsed by the poignancy in her eyes. "What do you want them to do, Mum? Boil you *chai* at the airport?"

"Ah! These people don't know the meaning of tea, *henh!*" she renounced.

In the past week, alongside baring our feelings and making our peace, she also taught me how to prepare tea the traditional way. How to add the pinches of *masala* and bruised pods of cardamom before the tea reached its boiling point and then pour cream into the bubbling lava and watch it dissipate like a placated volcano in a pot. I would look forward to making tea her way when she was gone, and I would enjoy it with the *halwa* she brought me. I would miss her terribly now. I wished she could stay longer now that the pretending was over. Now that I could go back to employing her wisdom with the emotions that ebbed inside me, emotions that perhaps only she could help explain. We had been mother and son first, then unyoked and at war and now finally friends.

Mummy rejected the remainder of her tea to contend with her rosary of marble beads. The focus of her worship, a photo of *Hazar Imam* carefully encased in plastic, was lying in the handbag on her lap. I knew that as soon as I left, she would bring it out and immerse herself into his image. She had left me another one; a larger, framed photo that now hung on my bedroom wall, replacing the one that I had knelt in front of when begging for Richard. She insisted I offer my prayers to it when I woke up in the morning and went to bed at night. Her pact with God could only be implemented if I too contributed to the worship.

I tried to make small talk and asked her if she was ready to go back home. I thought how funny that even after all these years I still referred to Kenya as "home."

She managed to smile and told me she'd had a wonderful vacation, playing the perfunctory part of every visitor, and that she was glad to have lost some weight. She wouldn't admit the fat loss pills didn't live up to their promise. The calcium tablets she'd decided to experiment with had made a considerable difference in her osteoporosis, and she couldn't wait to show off all the clothes she's raided from the malls. But I knew her stay was long and painful, thanks to me. She visited close to three months, and I got the feeling that she would've stayed even longer to regain some harmony between us.

"You know, I'm just so happy to see you finally settled in your own apartment," she added. "But please, Ali, try not to spend too much money, okay? You know, you spend money like water! You have no *keemet* of *paisa!* No value!"

"Alright, alright, don't worry, I know."

"Yeah, yeah, you know everything! Do you know how much one dollar here is worth in Kenya shillings?"

"Mum, please, I'm not living in Kenya. I'm living here, so I can't be thinking that way, okay?"

"Haya, fine!" she sighed. "But please promise me you will look after yourself. You know, if anything happens to you, Ali, it will just kill me, I swear it!"

"Mum, nothing's gonna happen to me," I begged for her to stop.

"Look here," she said, resting her hand very gently onto mine. "You have already told me everything about your lifestyle and now that I know, I have accepted it, okay? There is nothing I can do about it, right? I know that. It breaks my heart, Ali, believe me it does, but you know, the most important thing, I tell myself, is that you are happy. You go ahead and live your life the way you want. I'm not standing in your way, but please don't abuse yourself, you know? That's all I'm asking from you."

I squeezed her hand, careful not to encourage her getting emotional. Parting was always difficult even without wedging the breadth of entire continents between us, when calling one another would be confined to off-peak times when the rates were lower, when accord had been reached but time had run out. She'd need be to strong when she boarded that plane, I told myself. It would not do for her to unravel into tears again.

"I'll look after myself, Mummy, don't you worry. I have a reputation for being self-indulgent," I said with a wink.

"Try, Ali, not to expect too much from people. It never got me anywhere."

"Me? Expect too much from people?" I narrowed my eyes. "Nah!"

"I'm not playing," she maintained, her voice somber. "Just listen to me, really. I have spoiled you, we all have, and you know it. But it just does not pay, believe me. Your friends, your...lovers, even your own family can let you down, and sometimes you just have to learn to forgive them and not be so sensitive." Despite myself, a sadness begun to shroud me, and the muscles in my face started to droop. I knew that her advice was being prompted by my situation with Nelson, and was reminded again that despite numerous calls, a couple of which had been forlorn messages and the others just hang-ups, he hadn't bothered to call me back.

"You are just like me, Ali," she said softly now, her other hand touching my face as if she were wiping the dust off a mirror. "You feel *too* much."

I grunted. "For people who feel too little."

"Why?" she asked me. "If you must be with someone, I don't care who it is, Ali, why find someone like that? First that Richard boy, and now this...this other one," she said contemptuously, refusing even to utter his name. "All of them, the same person. Why are you creating this same situation *over* and *over* again?"

I shrugged. "I don't know, Mum. Maybe I'm trying to succeed where you failed." She looked away from me, obviously bruised. Her hand slid away from mine and fluttered onto her handbag. "But don't worry. I'm learning, Mum. I'm learning," I said, quickly withdrawing the sting from my sarcasm and finding her hand again with mine.

"I've tried my best with you. I really have. I don't know what I could have done differently, Ali."

"Mum, this is not a result of anything you did. It's not something you could've prevented."

"Your father..." she sighed. "Sometimes I can't help but think that maybe it's better that he's gone. Things would only have gotten more...difficult, you know?"

Yes. Things would have turned out differently had he been alive. Perhaps it was better that he was dead. How could he, this womanizing, macho figure, have embraced his son's homosexuality? Memories of his fury – him striking her to the ground, his hand lashing across my face and inflaming my cheek as a means of nullifying her coddling of me – flashed through my mind. It must have been at those moments, when I saw him unfurl into this tyrant – bullying us both with his strength, smashing his hands into us at will, calling me a girl – that I must have decided I wanted to be more like my mother and nothing like this man I called father. Yes, perhaps it was better that he was dead.

"And," she said. "You promise to be careful about the AIDS?"

"First of all, it's not *the* AIDS, and yes, I will be very careful, don't worry."

"Ali, try to focus on your reading, on your prayers, go out and see good movies, you know? You don't have to go out all the time and be marching on the streets with *those* people!"

"What – marching?"

"I have seen *them*," she said, her hand jutting up in the air. "Marching, marching, marching, down that...that Santa Monica street, doing all those...strange things!"

Oh no, Public Access. Probably a rerun of the gay-pride march where the cameras captured only the most outrageous behavior: men clad in leather and chains flagellating each other on a float for some sadomasochistic club; butch lesbians roaring down the boulevard on their motorcycles with their tits hanging out in a revolt against feminine archetypes; drag queens aureoled in feather boas and sequined gowns paying homage to every diva from Judy Garland to Diana Ross while lip-synching "I Will Survive" as an anthem against discrimination. These were overwhelming images even for me sometimes. It must have terrified her to think that her little boy, the child she had tucked away into bed at night, left home on a Saturday night to pursue such overt modes of expression.

"Mum, not everyone is like that, okay? There are different kinds of straight people and there are different kinds of gay people. Some gay people don't want to, you know, dress differently or behave like a woman or do anything that unusual."

She hunched her shoulders, obviously feeling that she'd never know for sure about many of these things. "Have you gone for a test?" she moved on.

"Mummy," I said defensively and started to frown. "I haven't done anything that would...put me at risk."

"Still," she persisted. "You should get one, don't you think?"

I nodded placatingly. "I will, don't worry about it. I guess it can't hurt." Oh, but it could, I thought. I'm one of those people for whom ignorance, in this case, was bliss. I wouldn't tell her that getting tested was a notion that had emerged in my mind only to be promptly banished by terror. That having come from such a hypochondriac family, resulting positive – even if the disease was benign, would induce psychosomatic reactions that would surely annihilate me long before the disease itself could. I would just rather not know.

"You know, I'm going to miss you terribly, Ali."

"It's Jerry Springer you're going to miss terribly," I said. "We'll be talking regularly now. We won't lose touch this time."

She leaned over and put her arms around me, her rosary still clutched tightly in her hand. Her handbag almost slid off her lap but I caught it. "You are all I have," she cried wistfully. "My only child."

I patted her on the back, oddly reminded of the times my grandmother used to pat me as a child when I was ill. I said nothing and continued to comfort her in my arms. I felt the wetness of her tears on my neck and the shaking of her body in a final cry. She whimpered and tsked away, as if cursing fate for taking me so far away from her. In her mind, I was still the little boy she indulged every time I threw a tantrum; vulnerable and unfamiliar with the schemes of the world. Not a man having sex, with an identity independent of his mother. She could pray day and night, yes, but seemed embittered at having to rely on faith alone.

After about a minute, she disengaged from me and wiped her tears. I handed her the paper napkin from her cup of tea, and she blew her nose into it, drawing my attention to her sparkling diamond nose ring.

"Are you alright?" I asked.

"Yeah," she sniffed. "I'm okay."

I offered to get her some water or soda but she refused, telling me there was no need for me to wait with her any longer. "You have to go back to work, don't you? I'll be fine now. You'd better go."

I glanced at my watch and smiled at the thought of the time she'd been keeping. For the past three months, her watch had been on Kenya time, a reminder that life went on somewhere else. She still had another hour to wait and I knew that she would spend it praying. I rose to my feet, then leaned down to give her another hug. "You'll be back next year," I said. "We'll make sure of it."

"Yeah," she struggled to smile. "Who is going to buy me the ticket? Your father?"

"Maybe I will," I said gallantly and shrugged.

"Will you do me a favor?"

"What?" I asked, preparing for another haul of emotional allegiances.

"Please don't forget to record *Melrose Place* and send it to me? You know, we don't get it there!"

CHAPTER 32

THE CONFESSION

Mummy must be in London by now, I thought as I headed home at the end of the day. And then I thought about what awaited me inside the apartment. I knew exactly how it would feel now that she had gone back to a land that I continued to think of as home, even though I'd claimed this metropolis as mine. It would feel bare. Desolate. Lonely. Mummy – with her bubbling pots of chicken curry and cumin infused basmati rice, her meticulously swept Pine-Soled linoleum surfaces, her blush colored spectacles, the arduously worked rosary and tattered prayer book flagrantly mislaid on the coffee table next to my Herb Ritts book – was gone.

This is what she warned me about: the loneliness that we somehow learned to forget or ignore until someone penetrated our lives and reacquainted us with the joys and frustrations of cohabitation. I wondered if this feeling became more acute with age; when, instead of craving attention only when seasonal allergies have disabled both body and spirit, we started to crave it everyday.

It was before I inserted my key and turned it, before I stepped into the darkness that through familiarity felt negotiable, that I thought about how I would suddenly have all that time and space in which to grieve privately. Now the pearl colored couch, which had been her bed, appeared somehow incomplete and mournful without her. The notion of all that space, all that silence without the clatter of conversation, suddenly terrified me.

The phone rang just in time. I had forgotten to change the setting on the answering machine and it intercepted the call in just two short rings. And there it was – Nelson's husky, substantial voice filling the room.

As my hand dashed for the receiver, I vowed to sound jovial. I would force myself not to think about his week of repudiation. If I sounded like I'd gotten over his neglect of me, that I intended on not leaving any more unreturned messages for him, maybe I could win him back. I thought quite foolishly that I could manifest this outcome by sheer will alone and seized the phone to hear his voice break off from the speaker and pour into my hungry ears.

When Nelson, sparing the pleasantries that might otherwise have felt awkward, asked me if I was sitting down, my voice still struggled to walk the line of containment. "Nelson, what's wrong? Whatever it is, you can just tell me, okay?"

In the hesitation of his voice, I pondered further. What would he tell me? What would surprise me at this point? That he felt we should stop seeing each other completely? Well, in reality, that had already happened. Maybe he wanted to apologize for having made all those promises he would fail to keep. Jesus, what if he had tested positive? Oh, God, that must be it. He's positive and has been avoiding me because he suspects he may have endangered me or wants to protect me from suffering the same fate. I leaned up against the wall instead of sitting down. It felt cold against my back. "What is it, Nelson?"

"Ali, I want you to know that I haven't been meaning to avoid you," he said. "I got your messages but I…I've just needed some time to…get my thoughts together and find the best way of saying this to you."

"Saying what, Nelson? You know there's nothing you can't tell me. I mean, I'm here for you, whatever it is."

"I know, it's…it's going to hurt you, but I think it's important that you know this. I mean, you have a right to know this."

"Tell me, sweetheart," I encouraged him. "What is it?"

"Your best friend and I have been sleeping together," he said.

"Hunh?"

"Just what I said."

"My best – what are you talking about? You mean..."

"Yeah, Adrian," he said and then sighed. "I'm so sorry. I've been meaning to tell you. I'm so sorry, Ali."

I took a slow deep breath and swallowed. Then I started to slide down against the wall and sank to my knees. I must have heard him wrong, I thought. He couldn't be saying this. Maybe he was just playing some kind of sadistic game with me. *Adrian and Nelson? Adrian and Nelson?*

"Look, I...I just couldn't keep it a secret any longer. I think you have a right to know."

"Why? Why are you telling me this?"

"Because I care about you, Ali. Believe it or not, I do. And you need to know this."

I closed my eyes. *I don't want to hear this! I don't want to know this!* I kept screaming in my mind. My body felt as if it had been hit by a truck. I was trembling but somehow couldn't feel any pain. The impact of his words had demolished me beyond any sensory awareness.

"Ali," he continued, "I wanted to tell you a long time ago. I did. I just—"

"*A long time ago?* How long has it been?"

"A few weeks. You know, Ali, I told him–"

"How many times?" I asked.

"How many times?"

"How many times did it happen?" I asked.

He paused. "I don't know. About three or four, I guess."

"Are you *still* sleeping with him?"

"No, no," he said quickly, as if that might somehow appear redeeming. "It's all over now. Look, Ali, I didn't mean to hurt you. I care about you, no matter what."

"How can you even say that?" I hissed. "How dare you say that! You slept with him, Nelson. It's not like you shared a bar of soap with him. Where was your concern when you fucked him?"

"Ali, I..."

"All this time..."

"I'm sorry, Ali. You're right, you're absolutely right! What I've done, it makes me feel ashamed. But I didn't want to keep you in the dark. The only reason I didn't tell you any sooner is because I wanted it to come from your friend, you know? I wanted him to have the opportunity to come clean but..."

The manner in which he kept referring to Adrian as my friend allowed his repentance a cunning transference of blame. It was being shifted, the transgression Adrian's more than his. *Your best friend and I...Your friend...*Not once did he call Adrian by name, as if to remind me that this deception had been co-orchestrated by none other than my best friend. As if to say that in the face of his early confession, in the face of our twelve weeks together as opposed to the several years shared by my friend and me, the more accountable party, the malefactor who had designed this hellish betrayal, was Adrian.

And then Adrian's face, his little pale face with the adoring amber eyes and prominent lashes, lashes that could make even his most venomous intentions seem benign, flashed through my mind. His callousness, the mottled, deceitful dimension of his personality started to reveal itself to me. And that's when the pain began to overshadow the initial shock. A heaviness came over me and although I could feel the solid floor under my legs, I felt as if I was being gobbled up.

"Ali? Are you there, Ali?"

"Yeah," I whispered.

"Look, I told him he could blame everything on me. I told him, but he just *refused* to come to you about this. He said that what you didn't know wouldn't hurt you. I guess he was just too scared to do it, so I just had to be the one."

"*Why* are you really telling me this, Nelson? You don't want me and this whole thing with him is over anyway! Why tell me about it at all?"

"You have a right to know, Ali. I've been carrying this around—"

"Nelson, please," I said. "This is making me sick!"

"Okay. But I *do* care, okay? You've gotta' believe that."

"And that absolves you, is that what you think? That you can just drop your pants and fuck him and you're exonerated because you've suddenly developed a conscience? Is that what you think?"

"No, no, I didn't expect that. I don't expect for you to forgive me, okay? I just wanted you to know that, strange as it sounds, you're still very special to me, Ali."

I breathed out heavily. "You've got some bloody way of showing it. Don't ever call me or come near me again." And with that I hung up the phone. For some time I sat paralyzed, feeling the vigorous thumping of my heart, my face trembling, looking at the couch from where I lay crumpled on the floor.

Then I cried.

CHAPTER 33

RED

There is pandemonium in the room. I stand barefoot, crying hysterically in my flimsy vest and underpants and I look at these two larger than life people going amok. There is shouting and screaming and a lot of movement, and it's very confusing and I can't understand what's going on. I only know that it's bad. Very, very bad. I cry harder. Louder. Wanting desperately for them to stop. Wanting to drown out their screams with my own. But they ignore me completely as they ferociously charge at each other. It looks like they have both gone mad. Again. My father hits his head against the wall in a frenzy. My mother looks possessed. Her cries are now a jumble of horror and bewilderment, and her shaking hands are raised up to her face as if she is about to tear at her own flesh as she watches him. Her dress is tattered from their jousting, and her hair is a disheveled mane. Her nose is running just like mine, the tears and mucus pooling around the gaping mouth and chin. I know I see blood, but I'm no longer sure where I see it. There is a little bit of red everywhere it seems. On the wall. On their hands. On their faces. In my mind.

I am standing in the middle of the room. Can't they see me? Why aren't they protecting me from all this? Why am I standing here watching? They've forgotten that I'm right here, that must be it. An unwilling witness, absorbing their heinous treatment of one other. They have dismissed my existence as smaller, less meritorious than their bloodthirsty paroxysm. So I continue to cry, abandoned in their strife. Witnessing something still unfathomable to a three year old.

There is rapid movement again and it jolts me. My mother is suddenly lying on the floor, unconscious, her eyes closed, her hands gnarled, open and motionless. The screaming has ceased, and my father turns away from the wall and falls to her side, looking down at her ruefully, his white buttonless shirt now stained with blood and hanging open over his knees. He calls out her name repeatedly, ignoring the family and concerned neighbors pounding on the door to our flat.

Now I hear only my own cries taking over the room, rising above his remorse, struggling over my being cast aside. I feel adrift as the only two people in sight continue to drown into the floor. I'm lost and terrified. Pushed further into the sea of their atrocity.

Why isn't somebody coming to get me?

CHAPTER 34

EVEN

I looked at Adrian from across my dining room table. It had been laid out meticulously for our dinner. Considering this a special occasion in some perverse way, I'd brought out the china that Adrian had helped me secure at a Sunday swap meet on Melrose. A jaded divorcee was eliminating every semblance of her ill-fated union at throwaway prices. Not only had he helped her wrap it diligently with newspaper, but he helped me wash it all and display it in the shelf space that separated my dinning room from the kitchen.

Some time before he had meekly rapped on my door, I surveyed the apartment as if was an arena for the final phase of our invisible war. A war of which until now I had been uninformed. A war which, unbeknownst to me, had been raging momentously. I wanted Adrian to see that my emotions hadn't spiraled out of control when I had learned of it. Just because he'd gone and fucked my lover three or four times, just because he'd turned a deaf ear to my pain over the breakup – while all the time being responsible for it – I hadn't been destroyed. The apartment he had helped me move into and renovate was still in the impeccable condition that Mummy had left it in, the way those familiar with my particular habits would expect to find it.

I considered the commendable job we had done after the Northridge earthquake had compelled me to change zip codes in Santa Monica the year before. Together, we pledged, we could accomplish anything. Two guys who would rather have facials and pay to watch a pair of typically muscled movers do all the hard work had not only managed to kindly transport all of the former tenant's banal Levitz furniture out – the mammoth chocolate corduroy sofas, and the chipped

Formica dressing table – but also moved my credit-line subsidized Z-Gallery acquisitions in. The colossal Picasso and Delaroche prints replaced the unobtrusive and functional Ansel Adams. Out went the twenty-dollar halogen lamp with its myriad settings and on came the track lights that illuminated the paintings and spherical African masks behind my glass top dinning table.

Now, here we were, in the apartment we had proudly ameliorated together, Adrian unable to look me in the eye, and me strangely calm, contrary to my celebrated reputation as a high-strung drama queen. I waited for the words to come from him. Through the course of the day, I had sifted through my thoughts with spasms of both rage and pain. Eventually, when the futility of the situation, the mere inexplicability of Adrian's actions had drained me, I had even resigned to crying. *Why had he done this?* I asked myself over and over again. *How could he live with himself?* Images of them together, scenes of their bodies colliding against each other in sweat and semen dredged into focus. The sounds of their reciprocal moans, of their limbs twisting and turning to accept one another as they erased my existence, deafened my ears. I knew even after I had decided to forgive him that the pictures of their indiscretion, their humiliation of me, would reverberate perpetually in the murky depths of my mind. Moments would come when, angered by something else, disappointed in something quite inconsequential about Adrian, I would remember this incident.

As Adrian's pathetic repentance stumbled forth, I began to wonder if I had somehow, without consciously meaning to, licensed their betrayal of me. As I struggled through the day, visualizing them together, I was horrified to realize that mangled right along with the pain and my visions was a distinct feeling of arousal. It made me question the normalcy of feeling that way. If that was an indication of an exclusive form of perversion in me. If that same perversion and the liberal and unconventional sexual situations that I had indulged in with Adrian had somehow legitimized his actions; made his deception of me appear excusable to him.

No, this was definitely different, I told myself. There is a big difference between picking up some stranger and having a ménage à trios and Adrian sleeping with my lover behind my back. What Adrian had done was wrong, I decided. We must not take that which does not belong to us. Especially not from those we call our friends. Those whose kindness we depend on during date-deprived weekends and midweek lulls when no one else cared about our lives. Even if, by some small miracle, it became available to us, we must not take that which is not ours.

Adrian started to cry in remorse. He told me how Nelson had pursued him – showed up at his place of work and the local bars, called him relentlessly at home, even cornered him when we had all been out together – until he had given in. As if that made it more excusable.

"Oh, God, Ali, I don't know what came over me…I'm so ashamed of myself," he blubbered. I had never seen him look like this – my pillar of strength dissolved into a puddle of shame. "He means nothing to me, I swear it, Ali. Nothing. There is nobody I care for more than you and I…I don't know what came over me…"

Strange, I thought. The two people who claim to care about me more than anything in the world went and fucked each other.

I looked at him without a hint of emotion on my face, my thoughts far from his act of contrition. Nothing that he said could erase his misdeed and because he was sensible enough to know at least this much, he let his words fall off and resolved instead to display his grief only through tears.

I had considered eliminating him from my life. I had considered punishing him by committing some kind of revengeful act. But then Mummy's words about forgiveness had gone through my mind, their validity, their wisdom being tested.

Would she have found this forgivable?

I began to realize as I watched him sob that I loved him dearly. The feeling saddened me, as if luminesced through this catastrophe it had confirmed my emotional fatality. Earlier in the day I had begun to see Adrian not the innocent light I had always seen him in but the surreptitious, self-serving shadows of his personality. Now, I saw Adrian in his entirety, as if for the very first time, with his weaknesses and faults prominently attached to his limbs like the rest of us mortals, who, instead of wings, had our imperfections weighing us to the ground. He had been the rock of Gibraltar in my sea of fleeting obsessions. The one who kept me from coming apart at the seams when Richard had pulled out every thread. Still the only one I considered extended family, and there were no crimes unforgivable when it came to family.

But I will never be able to look at your face again and think only of compassion, I thought. *Thank God, at last, you have been humanized.*

The chance to play the bereft victim was tempting, but I dispelled this notion. I began to appreciate that now, at long last, there was no more debt for me to repay. The ledger of his favors ran long, but by committing this single act, Adrian had equalized us in a way that only an extensive roster of reciprocated kindness or an abominable breach on his part could have accomplished. He had made us even.

I had to prove to myself that this friendship, which had prevailed for eight years and now stood on the verge of an evolution, was stronger and more significant than Nelson. The true test of any relationship was the capacity for forgiveness in its failing. I had to, as I suspected Mummy would have condoned, forgive my dearest friend for betraying me.

I reached over the table, over the plates of china, and beckoned for Adrian's hand. Still shaking, he took his hand away from his tearful face and placed it hesitantly into mine. I looked at the back of his hand studiously. It was as pale as mine was dark. There was no hair on it, and the pink of his knuckles was more obvious than mine would ever be. My fingers clasped around it, and I asked him to stop crying. "Everyone, Adrian, is entitled to one major fuck up," I said. "You just got yours. We'll try never to talk about this again."

"I promise you, Ali, I'll try to deserve your friendship from now on," he sniffed. "I took it for granted, but now I'll do everything to deserve you."

I smiled faintly, feeling knighted in spite of myself. "It..*this* can never happen again, Adrian. I don't need to tell you that. A man should *never* come between us."

He nodded fervently, using his other hand to wipe his tears. "Never."

I raised myself from my chair and walked around to embrace him, to reel him back into the grace that he so desperately sought. As he buried his face in my stomach, I felt like a sick man who had lightened the situation by being stronger than the visitor who came to lend him support. With my hands on his head, I looked at the Picasso print behind him, at the woman looking into the mirror. To me, the painting was transformed into a depiction of Adrian and myself. Two figures locked in a convoluted embrace through realms and dimensions. One of them stood expressionless, touching the other whose cheek bore the mark of what could be a tear. I remembered how Adrian had helped me, lugging the frame atop of his Acura, our gripping hands securing it through the sunroof. I realized that I had no other choice but to forgive Adrian.

I had what was essentially a lonely life littered with encounters of casual sex. The men who sojourned in my bed were weeks later reduced to nameless ghosts. My friends were the only corporeal and consistent thing about it. Without them, I was completely and utterly alone. I was the lone migrant without a family in America. A statistic of the millions of multicultural orphans of this city. My friends solidified my identity. Here, you needed someone who really knew you, someone who through the years might let you down, but truly understood you.

For someone like me, loving unconditionally in L.A. was more than just a matter of virtue.

It was simple practicality.

CHAPTER 35

HOME AGAIN

We watched Farida pluck a sizzling morsel of charbroiled steak straight off the skewer, dip it into a puddle of tamarind sauce and toss it into her mouth. Salman looked at me anguished and muttered, "How many times does she have to eat the *mishkake* before making sure it's ready for the rest of us?"

I was already laughing when Riyaz said, "Maybe she's starving us on purpose and hoping we'll get desperate enough to eat her pussy instead!" The soda sputtered out of my mouth and sprayed Anwar and Anil who were seated around us on the porch. Farida, still gnawing away at a mouthful, looked at us with narrowed eyes, her heft swelling ominously in the accommodating widow-black frock she was wearing, and prodded at us with the now stripped skewer in the air. *"Ey, ey,* what are you bastards talking about. *Henh?"*

"Nothing, *mataji,"* Salman struggled to say between his laughter. "Just contemplating the exotic menu."

"Yeah, come here and I'll give you one *thapar* and everything will start looking exotic to you!"

"What about Chastity?" I asked in hushed tones, referring to Farida's Latina girlfriend who was conspicuously absent from the barbecue.

Riyaz threw his hands open and gave us that weary look. "They're having a little cat fight again!" Then he meowed meekly and scratched the air.

Salman watched the pounds of meat being burnt to cinders, as if his whole life was being immolated on a pyre, and resting his chin in one hand pronounced with a cluck, "Oh, we're definitely being starved."

Such was the general atmosphere of the Indian get-together. Juicy gossip, loud pumping remixes of nostalgic *filmi* songs, the precious camaraderie that we all sought in clubs but never found and, if we were lucky and Farida was getting laid, some edible food as well. After what had transpired between Adrian and myself, I started to spend more time with Salman and his gang of South Asian expats. My temporary drift from Adrian had not been intentional; we had both meant to use the incident to create an even stronger bond, but we began to realize that this would take some time.

For the first time in almost the decade that I had been in America, I became reacquainted with my own people. We called ourselves Indians, although the term would not have been politically applicable considering we all came from different countries, including Pakistan and even Sri Lanka. In the end, as only total displacement and a greater love for the things that bound us than those that separated us could ensure, we just thought of ourselves as Indians. The bunch that I was introduced to by Salman became, in time, everything that I missed about my friends back home. Chatting away in an orgy of different dialects – Kutchi, Gujarati, Hindi, Urdu. An acceptance of speech that doesn't require correct grammar or an explanation for the pauses in between words. The sweet exaggerated vernacular of the Indian culture with its opera of gestures and expressions. The sardonic appreciation and extraction of camp from the world of Hindi cinema. The nostalgic, melancholy strains of *filmi* music and the evergreen voice of Lata Mangeshkar.

After years of denial, of severing myself from the tribalism of Indians, I returned to them under Salman's care and started to feel a sense of peace. There was no sound sweeter than that of being chided in Gujarati. No melody more stirring than the swoops and tumbles of the strings to a *filmi* song, accompanied by tablas and haunting vocals. And so began my incorporation back into a world where Burman and Kalyanji-Anandji claimed joint custody on the stereo with Ennio Morriconne and John Barry. Where Lata Mangeshkar ousted Barbra Streisand and poorly mastered soundtracks of old films and the digitized sounds of newer ones competed for shelf space with Western music. In the bathroom, *Stardust* shared the magazine rack with *Vanity Fair* and I wondered when *Filmfare* had grown from its little *Reader's Digest* format into looking like the rest. Fewer nights were spent at Heaven and Oasis to accommodate yet another barbecue for *mishkake* and Coca-Cola on Farida's patio. Taped episodes of *Melrose Place* were dislodged from the VCR for three hours of a wacky, over-the-top, melodrama from Bollywood, with singing and dancing interpolating every turn of the formulaic plot. Imagine Ralph Fiennes lip-synching Michael Bolton when carrying his dead lover out of the cave, only to be met with the rest of the cast and every possible extra, equally bereft, in a full production number. That's Bollywood.

So seamless was my return to the members of the Indian community (some of whom had also immigrated from East Africa like me) that I wondered why it had taken me so long to come to realize that no matter how convinced any culturally reared Indian was about his faultless integration into the West, he was only deluding himself. Having been cultivated in the opulence of his own culture, in the nurturing folds of its familial and emotionally alchemized way of life, it would prove difficult to feel complete without some kind of continual connection to it. The West, with its dazzling shopping malls and technical luxuries, its societal messages of independence and its reproval of codependency, would never succeed in eradicating the *desi* in me. These traits were inbred. The passion with which I pursued both love and life, the very quality that my American friends found so remarkable in me, was in my blood and could be traced back to my Indian heritage. The lyrics to *filmi* songs that my parents had played during my childhood miraculously found their way to my lips after more than a decade of not hearing them – a testament of my unbroken ties with India. The way in which my American accent easily fell off to allow the singsong cadences when conversing with other Indians reaffirmed that the Indian was still very much alive in me. Like furniture that emits the sterile odor of disuse over the years, Salman and the bunch of Indians had removed the covering and shaken the dust off me.

I blanketed a morsel of steak in warm *naan*, sat under the virtually starless sky of Los Angeles – the same firmament under which somewhere else bodies were being traded in the commerce of nightly sex – and listened to a boom box on the windowsill. It unleashed a new breed of Indian musicians who had ambitiously remixed the standards of *filmi* music to a house beat. Salman would tease Farida that she had contracted "laveria" (an acronym of malaria and love) over Chastity or, depending on the circumstances, that he was sure Chastity was feeling suicidal and would call any moment.

I felt as if I'd gone back in time, like I was sitting outside in the verandah of our flat in Tudor. There were little children concentrating on striking marbles into a cleft in the sand, others playing hopscotch, all of them unsupervised from the dangers that make such a carefree childhood impossible here. In the grips of nostalgia, I was back there. Salman and Farida and the rest of the bunch were still with me, and they continued to chatter away between mouthfuls of *mishkake*, but we were facing those little children playing in the dust instead of the houses cloistering us.

It felt, at least for those few uncanny moments, like home again.

CHAPTER 36

BROTHERHOOD AND BLOODY MARYS

Cameras snap and roll. We march at the helm of UTSAV, the South Asian delegation at San Francisco's Pride festival, the streets transformed into a moving river, bodies of all colors and shapes rippling under banners and confetti. Others form spectatorial walls of cheerful support or silent reprobation on the curb. From windows men, women and children sprouted – witnesses to the one act of solidarity that wondrously managed to cast aside our own prejudices to combat those of the heterosexual world.

Between sips of his Bloody Mary, Salman declared, "Fuck them all! They're going to see that I don't give a shit anymore!" He was talking not about society but of his own family back in Los Angeles, who he hoped would catch a broadcast of this asseveration. He hoped they would make all the appalling assumptions that Mummy had made when confronting the images on public access. He danced the *rasra*, his body swaying and his hands clapping away fervently in an arch from the sky down to his knees and then up again. To emulate his idol, Benazir Bhutto, he had draped a shawl over his head and wore a long cotton *kurta* that expertly downplayed his rotundity. "Today Benazir Bhutto shall walk these streets to protest the injustices delivered to all of us. Let that bitch sister and my mother see me on TV! *Mein azaad hoon!*"

The air vibrated with the infectious remix of a popular *filmi* song from the PA system of the gargantuan float behind us, and we all knew the lyrics. Some of us sang them with heartfelt joy and others laughed with nervousness and excitement. Everyone took turns holding up the ends of colorful saris and dancing down the street under its tinctured sky. When Salman tired of dancing, he threw his arm around me and I felt an unparalleled kinship with him. We passed the elixir in the plastic cup back and forth between us like a gourd of blood ritualizing our unspoken brotherhood.   A brotherhood that now stretched to the hundreds of Indians who I had never met before, people who had come from all over the country to march that day. We were all tied together by an invisible cord, a family of Indians strengthened not only by color and ethos, but also by a common persuasion.

With my arm firmly around Salman, I thought that *this* couldn't be what had appalled my mother.   If only she could have been here, standing right by my side instead of watching what was fed to the masses on TV. If she could have seen other Indians like myself uniting in this demand for fairness, grown men and women who in her eyes would still appear like boys and girls, she would not have been appalled. I wonder if she could hold up a sign in the air, remonstrating in front of God and against all those who deemed it necessary to oppress her child and deprive him of dignity. I knew in my heart that even with some difficulty she would have done so, and I thanked God for her and for the understanding we'd reached. I felt my heart overflow with love for her as we marched down the streets, bypassing a sequestered group of protesters who appeared, at least for now, to be a disgruntled minority. When they caught Salman's eye, he broke away from our embrace to dance once again, shaking his shoulders vigorously in a kind of flamboyant cabaret move, inciting them even further. A woman in the crowd cried out her curses. Even more abated, Salman flicked his tongue like he was about to perform fellatio on her cringing male companion. I thought, this is something Sunjay would've done.   Vivacious, unbothered Sunjay, who had performed a memorable cabaret in Bamburi, claimed men never liked to pay for it, and died several years later in a car accident. Taking a hefty gulp of my cocktail, I threw my own hands up in the air and danced too. I danced for the new family of friends that I had found here and for those who had gone ahead and left us behind to endure the travails of the living.

Perfect moments never last, but perhaps if we absorbed them, we could rekindle their memory to lighten the moments of darkness that would inevitably come.

CHAPTER 37

MARKS ON THE BODY

When I was a child, my mother and I used to play a game of moles.

In Indian films, the double role plot has always been popular. Twins separated at birth, grow up apart, and then meet in adult life, where the evil one somehow takes over her innocent sister's life and nobody's the wiser.

"What if someone took me away from you and then this other woman claiming to be Parin came to be your mummy? And she looked exactly like me! Then what would you do?" she'd ask me.

Terrified, wide-eyed and gnawing my fingers, I would look straight at her and proclaim, "I will hate her! I will hate her!"

"Then you must remember certain things about me," she would say, putting her index finger to her lip in a gesture of secrecy. She would tuck the wisps of hair behind her ear and reveal a tiny mole on its crest, or sometimes point out the mole on the finger of her own little hand. "See? This is how you'll be able to tell that it's not me! And what would I do if someone took you away and brought me another Ali?"

By then I would practically be in tears. Anger would rage in my heart for anyone who would do something so hateful. With eyes full of adoration and childhood possessiveness, I would look up at her, the kidnapping suddenly imminent.

"How will I be able to tell?"

Flustered, I would squeeze my hands together, unable to offer her the keys to identifying me, the knowledge of my body's trademarks still an uninvestigated mystery to me. She would take it a little further by looking perplexed, agonizing me more. "He would look just like you, you know? And then how would I know that this isn't my little sunny boy? How?"

My eyes would look up at her hopefully, expectantly, imploringly. Surely you *must* know! You're my mother, you *must* know!

"*This* is how I would be able to tell," she would finally say, her face brightening, revealing a mole on my wrist, granting me permission to breath again. "And *this* is how," she would offer proof again, lifting my shirt and touching another one on my abdomen. "And I would know that this impostor is *not* my little Ali!"

Relieved, I would throw myself into her arms, convinced that no one could take us away from each other. My mother had knighted the irrelevant marks on our bodies as guardians of our identities. Insignificant little moles were transformed into mysterious little conservators of my parentage. *Always remember the marks on the body. They will lead us to each other.*

Finally, I would crane up from the cradle of her arms and inquire, "But after I know she isn't my mummy, then how will I bring you back?"

CHAPTER 38

INDIAN

Salman's Honda trumpeted down Santa Monica Boulevard, the broken exhaust competing with the loud *filmi* music inside the car, appearing like the moribund chariot of a banished god condemned to wreak havoc on earth's disobedient mortals. *Here I come*, it seemed to announce in sputters, *prepare for intervention!*

We had just completed outreaching to three completely confounded South Asians in the last hour and were headed to our final interview for the evening. By convincing me to volunteer for an outreach group that educated sexually ambivalent Indian males about AIDS – an experience Salman promised would be mind-blowing but not for the reasons I suspected – he unveiled to me a community that had thrived in this city for decades and yet appeared untouched by its inducements. Unwilling to adopt anything foreign except the land itself, they sanctimoniously went about their lives and viewed everything that sprang from the West as morally weakening.

"We have a responsibility, *nah?*" he had said, one hand whipping in the air with conviction. "To ensure all Indians know condoms are for fucking little boys and not to blow up as balloons on *Diwali* and birthdays."

The Asian Aids Intervention Group, a government-subsidized agency located in a run-down part of downtown, had created a South Asian program for this purpose. Under the management of Mr. Chen, a sometimes intimidating, balding Chinese man in his forties ("he has little wee-wee" Salman giggled as soon as he turned his back on us) and his young flamboyant assistant simply known as Red (*"hunh*, just a wet tampon!"), the South Asian program became a kind of politically correct appeasement for the powers that be; a way to demonstrate the integrative nature of this Asian intervention team. In Salman's capable hands, this namesake program came to be known as *Saath*, meaning unity. There wasn't a doubt in any one's mind that Salman certainly had all the expertise – if not the practicality of being an open homosexual – to make this project work.

As a social health care worker for UCLA, Salman had always worked with people and championed causes like breast cancer. After being alienated from his family, he began to boldly extend his gift for communal intervention with less decorous causes. "To hell with cancer of the *booblas!*" he decried, referring to breasts in the comical Kutchi term. "It's time to get down and dir-r-r-ty," he said.

Since I was one of the few openly gay Indian men he knew, he believed that I had an obligation to educate this disturbingly repressed community, to go out into the trenches of ignorance with him, to gas stations, convenience stores, spice markets, nightclubs – wherever an opportunity presented itself.

So, armed with a box full of condoms, safe sex pamphlets and questionnaires, we hit the road and approached the envoys of the South Asian diaspora at nightfall. Most of them turned out to be Bengali. It felt strange when, despite the similarities in the color of our skin and features, we were unable to communicate effectively. Bengali was the one language that neither Salman nor I spoke, and most of them only knew perfunctory English. From behind the counter of their franchises, they would narrow their eyes and survey us suspiciously when the clipboard and pencil came out, and instead of purchasing beers we asked questions about sex. The mere mention of AIDS made them tense up. Like they'd suddenly realized that we were wielding a gun or, worse, that we were homosexual and instead of leaning over the counter and pillaging the cash register, we just might grab their balls in a bizarre ritual of homosexual camaraderie. Sometimes after sneering, they turned away from us to find a fellow worker with whom to laugh derisively at our unwitting admittance to being connected to what they considered a gay disease. In such cases, a simple business card would sometimes qualify us for some solemnity. Business cards always impressed peasant folk. In their minds, a two-by-four piece of printed card somehow legitimized our enterprise more than the rectitude of our intention.

Whenever we stumbled upon someone who was more forthcoming and able to overcome the language barrier, he would never failed to express that none of these diseases had existed "back home." The land that he had renounced to seek a better life was suddenly transformed into some kind of Utopia where no disease or injustice could possibly prevail. He would confidently boast that now that he was married with children, this AIDS thing was of little concern to him or his family and dismissed us. Upon this stance Salman often turned to me to roll his eyes or give a wearisome nod, *Yeah, yeah, I've heard it all before.* We knew the condoms and pamphlet that we were resigned to leave behind would be tossed out the moment we turned out backs to walk out.

And then there were the other ones. Salman told me how many a times he had gotten men off in the bathrooms of 7-Elevens and Mobil gas stations during their ten-minute breaks. The same ones who vaunted about their homemaker wives, their two-point-five children; men with the glint of a gold band on the very hand that clawed into his hair as he buckled under them, Salman's fingers raking down their mat of curling chest hair.

"So much cheaper than going to the Vortex. Once in a while they might even let you take a free Slurpee with you!"

He generally preferred Muslim men and insisted they utter to him in guttural Arabic while carrying out the act, almost none of which he understood. Sometimes he recognized their utterances as derogatory, but instead of feeling insulted his excitement escalated. I laughed, visualizing this. Salman observed that all of them, Muslim or Hindu, married or single, resisted anything more than a blowjob. At the end of it, they always expediently zipped up and fled, leaving him there on his knees with his mouth agape and full of their misspent seed. It was as if, up until that point, they could still return to their counters feeling relieved and yet preserve their identities as heterosexuals. "Indian men are like British men," he claimed. "All of them – *gay!*"

This time as luck would have it, the man we approached was especially attractive, and I became petrified as I imagined Salman hoping that we had arrived in time for his break. Salman's eyes drooped seductively behind his spectacles, his body swishing to the counter, his heft in jarring contrast to the sleekness of his behavior. His questions and tone of voice carried the weight of expectation, and his head danced in the intoxication of desire and challenge. I had to remind him of our purpose for being there as discreetly as I could.

"*Hanh, hanh*, I know, okay?" he shushed me, tearing his name badge off his shirt. "What do you think I'm doing, *rani mata*? I'm *reaching out*, literally!"

Muffled, I found myself purchasing some magazine in the hopes that the attendant would be more tolerant of us, outreach workers who had rushed in the moment he'd been available and slapped him with questions about the one thing that Indians are most squeamish about: sex. And that Salman would not fall to his knees and beg to give him a blowjob right then and there.

The cashier said, "You hold on for one minute, okay? I putting some ice in the machine now."

Salman smiled and gave him that look that said, I'll wait all night if I have to.

How ironic, I thought while meekly busying myself with a newly purchased *Los Angeles* magazine in the corner, and fighting over my guilt in letting Salman deal with the awkwardness of discussing sex with an Indian. We came from a culture that wrote the book on sexual relations, that practically invented the art itself. A culture that immortalized not only sexual liberty, but also its diversity on the faces of temples such as Khajuraho. Various sexual positions, group sex, homosexual practices, relations with animals – they are all there and are justly famous. Legend told that the sculptures protected the temples from lightning, and we had become a culture that is ashamed of sex. A people that, through gradual regression, fear lightning will strike at the mention of it. Parents unable to speak to their own children about the risks involved. Grown men insulted at being approached on the subject unless in jest or boasting about conquests. And us, here, at a 7-Eleven on Santa Monica Boulevard, struggling to educate an Indian. How did a period of great civilization and liberty evolve into one of the most backward cultures in the domain of sexuality?

How, I asked myself, peering over the pages of the best restaurants in the city and hearing Salman excitedly tell the cashier that coincidentally his name was Aziz as well, had the culture of the Kama Sutra been reduced to one of such incipience on the subject?

When did we lose our identity as the pioneers of eroticism and become a people paralyzed by shame?

I had missed the tail end of their exchange, but before I knew it, the cashier was hollering at Salman, who grabbed me by the elbow and began to pull me out of the store as if a bomb was being detonated. "You go right now, you listening? I don't want your filthy business here, okay? Go! Go! *Gandu, haram zade, pata nahin kahan se ajate hain!*"

In the car, I didn't ask Salman exactly what he had done or said to provoke Aziz but I suspected it had been more than just the imparting of preventive information; perhaps it had been the lethal, ironic mix of safe sex education with the relentless visual hold on his crotch that had unnerved poor Aziz.

As we drove over to the Vortex, where Salman and I hoped to encounter more unsuspecting Indians and also steal some pleasure for ourselves, we turned Lata down to a whisper and discussed what it was like to be Indian. And sex. We acknowledged that Indians were much more than delectable curries, over-the-top Hindi films, the Taj Mahal and Eastern philosophy. They were the founders, the monarchs of the ancient legacy of sex. Indians were to sex what Rumi was to mysticism. And now this same culture had appointed a tyrannical censor board, which would not allow even a simple kiss in Indian films for fear of overexciting its public. When was the last time two Indians had been seen kissing on the lips? At home, on the street, anywhere? Did they ever? No. It was all about shame, shame, and more shame.

"India," Salman said, "our dear motherland, is a raped woman. Come to think of it, the continent even looks like the shape of a woman, standing there in a sari with one hand on her hips, her elbow jutting out, *no?* Anyway, what can you expect after your mother's been gang-raped?"

I was confused. "Okay, it all sounds very profound but what the hell are you babbling about?"

Salman reached out and turned the stereo off completely, clearing the air for his surprisingly well-contemplated analysis. "First she was raped by the Moguls," he began didactically. "And then by those snooty British bastards who decided we were no better than dogs. You know what those two had in common?"

I fumbled at first. "Moguls and British...well, the Moguls were...Muslim and the British...oh, Puritans!"

"Oh," he sighed. *"Meri beti kitni akalmand hai!"*

Suddenly it all became perfectly clear. Two very different cultures with one very virulent trait in common – Puritanism – had ruled India. An epoch of lavish sexuality had been expunged by the conviction that the very quality that had exalted India was now the cause of its denigration. This attempt to redraw her face by the rulers that held her captive continued down the centuries, at the hands of the heroes who sought to alter her into what they thought she should look like instead of what she had always been. Luminaries who, in making philanthropic strides for economic and racial matters, reduced her into docility, forever obliterating her progressiveness.

Even Mahatma Gandhi had sent troops to tear down the erotic images on temples. And it was the socialist government of Nehru that for the first time in history prohibited what they considered acts against nature through article 377: No more sexual relations against nature with a man, woman or animal, whether the intercourse is anal or oral.

Mutual consent was not even a consideration in this edict. And whose nature were they referring to? Pandit Nehru's nature? Gandhi's nature? We must all have sex the way *they* had deemed it natural, these self-proclaimed sovereigns of morality. Suddenly what was natural had nothing to do with our ancestors – they had become a source of shame for us with their wanton lifestyles. Centuries of history were suddenly consigned to oblivion. Disowned. Exported to the West. There was a new India, and it wore that tyrannical face of puritanism. India and her legacy had been prostituted not only by outsiders, but also by her own children. They had reduced her to a commercial about pungent spices, Gods and Goddesses with multiple limbs and heads, and Bollywood. They had hoped that we would forget what few cultures had dared to represent, and they had been right. We had forgotten.

"We're all screwed up," Salman declared. "No wonder we're all screwed up! We are the children impacted by their shame. Unable to take anything to this arena but a funny accent and a fucking dot on the head!"

We continued to drive in silence for a little while, and I thought about what he had just said. He's right, we are all screwed up and lost. All of us. The Indians back in India, the ones that make it on *20/20* for dousing brides with kerosene and setting them ablaze all for women with bigger dowries, and us here in L.A., on our way to a sex club to feast on a banquet of cocks for a five-dollar admission. A new generation of Indians that have never even been to India; Indians who have become multicultural, not even knowing where they belong anymore; Indians who brought to the table the nostalgia of a home incongruent to the color of their skin, the syrupy lyrics of *filmi* songs, and the vague knowledge that the wanton images on the bottles of erotic massage oils were indisputably Indian, but contrary to the conservatism that they had experienced as Indian.

How could the members of such a culture, ignorant to an alarming extent of their contribution to sexual progression, truly fare amidst a seemingly fearless community marching down Santa Monica Boulevard in a flurry of shirtless musculature and pink feather boas?

We have no answers and no role models, not unless we wanted to consider the eunuchs in India, clapping away in celebration and pelting out songs in hoarse voices; or the brutish husbands who give in to blowjobs in toilets as role models.

"Everything!" Salman said. "Why does *every* fucking thing about being Indian have to be so complex!"

I grunted. "You're right, you know. Everything Indian is complex. The food is complex with all its spices, the clothing is complex with all the layers and layers, the continent is a virtual curry of languages and tribes, and the emotions, ha! Watch out!"

"That's why it gives me such satisfaction to do what we're doing," he said, turning the volume up on the stereo and letting Lata sing her little heart out. "Oh, this is one of my favorite songs!" And he sang a few words, *"sheesha ho ya dil ho, akhir toot jata hai...*I know you like this one too. It's so-o-o tragic!" and then just as suddenly he switched back. "There are other Indians out there who really need a support group, you know? They really need to know that there are others like them."

"Yeah," I chided. "I wish they'd been here tonight to see how you changed Aziz's life."

"Ar-e-e, kuti!" He gave me a playful slap on my shoulder. "Don't give me a hard time! I've worked my ass off trying to knock sense into those thick-skinned Indians. After all, I'm a lonely woman too, not Mother Theresa!"

CHAPTER 39

GOSSIP

I called Salman and was momentarily stunned by the greeting on his machine. After almost a year of being accosted by various *filmi* sirens – and Salman ebulliently maintaining that he was the hub of *Saath* – his nonpartisan, conventional "Sorry, I can't come to the phone" felt like a slap on the face. The message was now a cold, businesslike rebuff, a portentous sign. I dispelled my worry as the beep came through and left a terse message that responded to the reserve in his greeting. Rather than the usual, *"Ay*, bitch, *vashiah*, where are you? *Ay*, Gulnar, this is your dear sister calling," I left a proper, "Hey, it's me. What's up with the greeting? Call me back, okay?"

And then it occurred to me as I hung up that maybe his mother had suffered that massive heart attack that the songs on his machine had been intended to deliver!

At least once a week for over a year now, we had converged at either Salman's or Farida's house under the pennant of *Saath*. Of the six who comprised the core of this group, only two were completely out of the closet: Riyaz and myself. Notably, we shared the circumstance of living far from our families in Kenya.

Ten years ago, Riyaz had come to Los Angeles on a student visa and had never gone back. Too far away to pass judgment on his sexuality or to discover that their son was trying to find spiritually through hallucinatory drugs, Riyaz's family was the suspended clan of every son who left home to pursue freedom in a country in which he would remain imprisoned. Only after digging into his flesh with a syringe of LSD while Jan Garbarek or Nusrat

Fateh Ali Khan scored out of his Magna pan speakers did Riyaz escape the castigation of his sexuality and the lonely choices it had compelled him to make. Only then could he float outside of his own body and descry on the adversities in his life with bemused detachment. To escape from the confinements of being an illegal alien. To travel abodes of consciousness that didn't require an American passport or a green card. On such days we would not hear from him. Although he was out among the worker ants of L.A., he kept himself away from us – from other Indians – giving us no cause to express concern, only reason to gossip about him when he had failed to show up to a gathering.

For Indians gossip is as staple like chapattis and basmati rice. No one was ever spared from this customary avocation (participated in innocuously and disguised as a form of concerned colloquy), which succeeded in hurting feelings all around. One could always count on being the topic of the evening if one didn't show up at a barbecue or at some insomniac coffeehouse where the group was meeting. Everyone in the group had their idiosyncrasies:

Ay, you know how Ali gets with his drinking! Oh, Khudda! *I know we'll be attending his liver transplant party in the near future! He's just wasting all his talent away. Give him disco and drinking and it's a done deal!*

That Farida is such a lesbo! I'm just so sick of going to Palms with her every time Chastity breaks up with her and listening all night about how badly that bitch's been treating her. I think that after Farida's mother died, Chastity really took over, you know? Typical codependency syndrome, neh?

Oho-ho! She just will not stop calling me, you know? Ten bloody times a day! You know, I told her, "Hunh, look, please, hunh! *Stop hounding me at work with your pussy problems."* Yah Khudda! *What came over me, can you tell me, that I was stupid enough to give her my work number? She has climbed on my head and become a real pain! I don't know what to do about her. She's such a giving person, you know? I told her she needs to stop trying so hard. She needs to stop feeling so insecure about Chastity. But will she listen, that psycho?*

Yeah, well, Chastity does get lots of attention, you know? If Farida spent less time looking like a house and running to Artesia for mithais *and videos, she might do a little exercising!*

House? She's an entire zip code!

Dear God, you know Riyaz with his drugs! There are so many holes under his sleeve, it's like a machar-dani! *A mosquito net! I told him, "Riyaz, this is really crazy,* henh! *What is all this experimenting with all these drugs?" And then you know, he'll start with his* bhashan! *Lecturing away all that crap about spiritually discovering himself through drugs and all that* ganda-wera!

Oh, God, those bhashans *of his! Sometimes I want to poke him with his needles to make him shut up!*

He's almost forty! When the hell's he coming out to his parents, when they're dead?

Salman's not forty! Salman is thirty-three or something like that!

Hanh, hanh, same thing, okay! What kind of a role model can someone make if he's in the closet after thirty? Closets are for clothes, stupid homo, not for people!

Yeah, you're one to talk! You're also in the closet yourself!

Hunh! I'm not the bloody chairman of an outreach group, okay? It's not the same thing! Those Indians who might want to come out of the closet need someone like you, Ali, not some hypocrite like Salman who wants to sit around and fill out millions of questionnaires and harp about safe sex all the time! Doesn't he realize part of safe sex is feeling good about yourself so you don't get involved in such khatar-naakh *situations? And you can't do that from under the hangers in your closet!*

All of our lives we have been exposed to this mode of communication. Everyone, from the ailing old ladies of the *bankra* committee to members of our own families, indulged in this pastime. Sometimes, inevitably, things would backfire and a wounded aunty would appear at your doorstep, teary-eyed, demanding reparation for a comment we may have made frequently to her face, but made the fatal mistake of telling behind her back to someone who had leaked it. *Panchaat* was just a way of life for Indians, to the extent that even *Hazar Imam* had addressed the damage it could do to the community. But did anyone listen? As South Asians away from Asia, and, more painfully, away from the country of our childhood, we tried to recreate the norms of our culture. And gossiping was not only the easiest of all cultural profligacy, but it was also the most fun.

So when the truth recoiled in *Saath*, why did the group splinter irreparably? Since the core group's nature was as intimate as a real family's, gossip had never been received with much offense. Our gossip fests, though sometimes malicious in tone, still represented only unbridled cogitation from members of the family. They were like Mummy and Aunty sitting over a cup of tea and *samosas* and having an unchecked, no-holds-barred dialogue about my psychosis. At times the conversation could get brassy and impertinent – and always exaggerated – but it was still only Mummy and Aunty, and the reason they had chosen to discuss me in the first place was because, in some peculiar way, they were concerned; therefore it was their duty if not an involuntary reflex to do so.

When discord sprouted within *Saath*, it was obvious that a loose-lipped aunt had orchestrated it; someone had manipulated it as part of a personal agenda, taken what had always been innocuous and disinterred its potential for damage. After participating in flagrant gossiping about one other, suddenly everyone awoke from a deep sleep with wounds and indictments. *How had it gotten so far? How could he have said this about me? Well, do you know what he said about you? He said this about you!*

I was the first one to be indicted and, discovered in time, the only one ostracized for it.

CHAPTER 40

EXCOMMUNICATED

Salman responded to my message with a message of his own on my answering machine. I found this odd, considering he knew he could reach me at work. At such times, falling back on the answering machine became a clear indication of his avoidance of actually connecting.

Apparently he wasn't the only one.

For about a week now, I hadn't joined the group for one of our gatherings – either they had been temporarily halted or someone had forgotten to invite me. I had left messages for Farida and Riyaz as well, but neither one of them had called me back.

Instead, I reconnected with Adrian, attempting to boost some life into our impaired friendship. But I missed the *Saath* brand of camaraderie: the extravagant welcoming hugs, casual touches and gentle squeezes which became an essential part of any conversation; Farida's commando tactics when she was upset and trying to punish everybody else; Salman's dramatic expressions and sarcasm, unconsciously derived from the *bankara* committee; all the gossip and cackling. I realized with some sadness, as I threw back another potent shot at some video bar with Adrian, that *Saath* had become like a cyclone sucking everyone in. Within it, each of us familially or societally misunderstood Indians became a codependent.

The social matriarch of this extended family, Farida, had crammed each week with different plans, leaving little time for anyone else outside of *Saath*. One night it was a barbecue, then a Hindi film, another day it would be a day trip to Artesia where we could gorge on *mithais* and buy hard-to-find Bollywood soundtracks. As much as I valued our genus of culture, and had used it to spend time away from Adrian, it had become apparent that I would have to completely sacrifice his friendship. I had not been prepared to do this and had broken the cardinal rule of not attending all of the gatherings. Now I found myself uninvited to any of them.

Salman started off by providing me with the implausible yet commonly used excuse of Angelenos and almost all city dwellers: he was too busy to respond sooner. He went on to say, "And by the way, you know, I had a talk with my mother and as far as she's concerned, she said it doesn't matter what that bitch sister of mine wants! She actually said, '*Beta*, do you think that we would disown our own child? What would make you think like that?" He continued to mimic her, and I found some reassurance of our intimacy in his flamboyance.

"'Oh, *mowla!* You are my first born, and nothing can change the way I feel about you, you know?'" he cried. "So, anyway, now I feel a lot better. Just knowing I still have my inheritance! But you know, I'm going to be real busy at work, *aah!* We're doing mammograms for the pussies at the DWP during the next few days, so I guess, I don't know, I guess I'll just talk to you some time later on?"

There was no mention of the weekly outreach to all the confused Indian shopkeepers who surely had been expecting the duo like clockwork by now, and I presumed that this too had been postponed.

"Oh, and by the way, I don't think I'll be able to go out this Saturday. I'm sorry," he continued. "My parents are having some *maghenis* over for dinner, and I completely forgot about it! You know how it is with guests and all, *neh?* Okay?"

A beep signaled the end of his message and I felt rudely cut off. What? Not going out on Saturday either? How can that be? We've been planning on attending the opening of this Latino club in Silver Lake for so long! And it had been his idea to begin with! His demanding

words from weeks ago went through my mind: *"Ay,*
you'd better go with me, *henh?"* he had warned me on
being handed a flier for this club. "I need to find my
dhanni for the night. It won't kill you not to shake your
gand at those white-boys for one night! Oh, WeHo is so
eighties anyway, with its attitude and gloss! 'Look at me!
Look at me! No body fat and no brains either!'"

Salman scoffed at West Hollywood nightclubs;
places where sexuality had been reduced to an illusion
were of little use to him.   Not in the arena to battle
vanities, and burdened with self-consciousness about his
weight, Salman felt uncomfortable in such places.   He
scowled at the sweating bodies bumping and grinding
against each other. He subscribed instead to the Vortex
and those sleazy little Latino dives in Silver Lake where he
could cruise his *cholos*. Places where the air crackled with
sexuality and an aura of the subterranean.   Places that
were cloaked in humid darkness instead of the pulsating
colored lights and fluorescent walls. He thrived on the
stereotype of a rowdy Mexican gangbanger.   The kind
that starred daggers across the room and acknowledged
any mutual interest with barely a nod.   Mexican men
whose dark skins were scored peculiarly with tattoos of
voluptuous women with their tits hanging out and slang
words; whose style was comprised of the emblematic
crew cut, goatee and the unvarying livery of tank tops,
plaid shirts and boxers peeking over their low hanging
baggy denims, holding all the promise of uncut cocks.
They sent Salman in a tizzy of nervous desire. According
to him there were only two kinds of Latin men he
claimed to be fatally attracted to: the "gangbanger, gun-
packing" type or the "Taco Bell, just ran across the
border" one. Both, he claimed, represented sex in its
most primordial state.   "Ooh," he'd purr whenever
catching even so much as a glimpse of such a contender.
"Mi culo esta ardiendo!" he'd say, and start to fan his ass. I

would have to look away, anywhere, just praying we wouldn't get caught and beaten.

Once, between stops on an outreach, Salman had confided to me about the time he had been accompanied by two such men to a motel room somewhere in Hollywood. After they had all undressed, they had tied him up with bed sheets. Salman had gotten terribly excited. That is until they gathered all his clothes and his wallet and, spitting on his horror-struck face, drove off in his car.

"Can you imagine?" he asked. "After screaming my lungs out for help, who should come to my rescue? The Indian motel owner! *Ya Allah!* He breaks in with this huge knife in his hands and, for a moment I wasn't sure if I was going to die from embarrassment or if he was going to slice me up or something!"

The Indian man, an immigrant from Uganda, had gone completely insane. "You psycho!" he said, wagging the knife at Salman, still tied to the bed and trembling. "I'm not wanting this problems here, understanding? Why you bringing trouble, *henh?* You better go, get out!"

Much to Salman's relief, the Mexican cleaning lady that had followed Mr. Patel into the room had pacified him, gently taken the knife from his hands and untying a mortified and naked Salman from the bed. Then she had arranged for Salman to borrow a pair of ill-fitting sweats and spared a few of her own dollars for him to catch a bus back to his apartment. The following day, Salman lied to his parents about filing a police report, dreading that the circumstances of his entrapment would be discovered. A couple of days later, Salman had gone back to the motel to return the borrowed clothes, but Maria was off that day and all Mr. Patel could do as he mumbled his apology and thanks was look at Salman with a sneer and motion for him to disappear from his sight.

Even after that incident, Salman was not discouraged from pursuing such men. It was as if the fear of disapproval from his family fueled his flagrant behavior. Because of his lifelong struggle to conform to the expectations of his family and his culture, Salman's random assertions of sexuality had taken an extreme and daring form. These assertions were more exciting and bolder than those of most unrepressed, out-of-the-closet men. Dangerous, unrefined men were Salman's weakness and no grandeur of a dinner party thrown by his parents could have sufficiently distracted him.

So what was all this nonsense about being the obedient son? Since when did that matter more to him than anything else? I found his new responsible behavior towards family hard to swallow. I was being alienated. Not only by Salman, but also by everyone else. By *Saath*. By that Indian family that I had embraced as a refugee from the betrayals suffered at the hands of outsiders.

As long as I had known him, Salman hadn't bothered to relate to his family – save for an obligatory phone call when he'd been running low on funds and, to his chagrin, had to confront his despotic sister – and now he wanted to cancel our plans because they were having guests? I didn't buy it.

Frantic with suspicions, I decided to call the one person who had taken it upon herself to create our social calendar and enforce attendance for the past few months. I called Farida, demanding to know why I had suddenly been overlooked. Why would no one return my calls or only do so when they knew I wasn't at home? What? Had every one else also been too busy because their families were having guests?

Thank God for call waiting, otherwise I would've bumped into her answering machine just as I had for the past week. Her voice passionless, she asked me to hang on and clicked back to her previous caller, or callers, as I was to discover, when I insisted on talking to her right away. When she returned, Farida was disinterested and sounded cold. I could hear her trying to tolerate me through the wire. "I can't talk for long. You've just caught me at a really bad time," she said, the Indian vernacular that would have lightened our conversation conspicuously absent.

"Evidently it's a pretty bad time for all of you!" I said. "What the hell's going on?"

She feigned ignorance for a while, but I could feel her on the verge of cracking. I persisted, at first urging her as a friend and expressing my confusion and pain over this obvious rebuff and then irascibly as a cheated member of *Saath*. In that moment, seconds before she started to spill her guts, I felt the tormenting need for their continued friendship and the looming fear that something irrevocable had occurred.

"How *could* you! How *could* you!" she cried. "If you minded so much that I was calling you, then why the hell didn't you just tell me to stop talking to you? Why did you have to go and tell everyone that I was harassing you with ten phone calls a day?"

It took a moment. "But Farida," I said. "You *were* harassing me with ten phone calls a day!"

"So? Why not just ask me to stop? Why did you have to tell Salman that I was a psychotic with nothing better to do with my life?"

"But I *did* tell you to stop calling me so much! I told you to your face a million times before I ever said anything to Salman. And I never said that you had nothing better to do with your life, okay? That was always Salman's angle!"

"And what about – what about telling Riyaz that I called him a pathetic drug addict?"

"You *did* call him a drug addict," I said. "And what's the big deal anyway? We *all* call him a drug addict! It's practically his nickname! For Chrissake, Farida, why is this suddenly such a big deal? You know it doesn't mean anything."

She sighed. "I'm just really hurt. I mean, I just got off the phone with Salman and Riyaz and I just...I just can't believe that you had such nasty things to say about me! For your information, I *do* have better things to do with my life than be a mother to all of you and call ten times a day!"

"But we all say these things about each other, don't we?" And then, "wait a minute – you were just on the phone with them?"

She hesitated. "Yeah, they were just telling me...everything."

"*They* were telling...You mean you were telling each other about all the nasty things that Ali has been saying about each of you."

"Ali, I really can't..."

"You know what, Farida, this is all just fucking bullshit! I can't believe that we're all grown ups and we're dealing with this ridiculous situation, this nonsense! How did it get to this point? We've all talked about each other and it's always been innocent. You talk a lot of shit about Salman and about Riyaz and I've *never* told them any of it. They both talk a lot of shit about you, worse than you can ever imagine, and I *never* came to you and started poisoning your mind!"

"I need some time," she said out flatly. "I just, you know, need to take some time off from everyone. Not just you. There's a lot I'm going through, and I really can't deal with all this right now."

"What you mean is you don't want to deal with *me* right now. None of you do, is that right?"

"Look, maybe you need to talk to them, you know..."

"For what? I'm talking to you! What exactly am I defending here? I haven't even done anything that you haven't done yourself!"

"Ali, I really don't know what to say, alright? I don't hate you or anything."

"Well, I'm certainly being made to feel like you all do!"

"Just give it some time."

"And what the hell am I supposed to do while you all boycott me? You're supposed to be my friends but you're all acting like some jury trying to convict me!"

"Look, you have other friends too. Why not hang out with them for a little while?"

I felt like she'd slapped me. I was being told that they didn't want me in *Saath*. That they wished I would just get the message and leave them alone. The reason for this was unimportant. Just from talking to Farida, it was obvious that even she couldn't completely justify the charges because we were all guilty of the same treason.

"You've been spending time with Adrian lately, haven't you?" she continued in my silence. "I suggest you just spend some more time with him." And then she added, "I'm sure he won't call you ten times a day and get on your nerves!"

"I can't believe I'm hearing this, Farida."

"Believe it," she said. "Just believe it."

Part of me wanted to laugh at her, at the sheer absurdity of the situation. The other part of me felt like crying but couldn't because I felt drained. Beaten up. I felt like I was ten-years-old again, devastated because nobody wanted me on their team. No one would talk to me.

After that conversation, I feared I'd never be able to get a hold of any one of them. Before I hung up the phone, Farida, brushed with some compunction, assured me again that it was only a matter of time before the whole thing dissipated. Then perhaps we could all go back to being friends again. To the way it used to be.

I sat on the edge of my bed, feeling dazed. This is impossible. How can they do this? Salman and I had practically created *Saath*, for Chrissake. Who the hell

were they to excommunicate me from it? Nobody, only
Salman could do that. Only Salman. Salman.

It became clear. Everyone in *Saath* was following
a command. An edict dispatched from the top. The rest
of them were much too complacent, far too simple
minded to use such cunning.

Oh, God, why was Salman doing this?

CHAPTER 41

THE MEANING OF DREAMS

Draped in a printed sari of ochre and black, she stands elevated with her gaze fixed sternly upon me, assuming the capacity of my mother though I know she is not. My mother never wears a sari nor her hair knotted behind her head in a traditional bun. My mother doesn't even remotely resemble this woman's austerity and is certainly not as dark in complexion. Yet this woman addresses me as beta. I feel the urge to strike her, to demand that she refrain from calling me this at once.

Behind her, several Indian women form a filigree of performers costumed in traditional Indian style. Among them I think I also see the faces of the clerks Salman and I have approached on outreaches. Some of them move animatedly to filmi *music and others just sing. This time, the music doesn't sound sweet or resonate melancholy. The roiling of tablas and the frantic strains of its exigent strings form an unbearable cacophony. The voices are more ululation than song. Any grace in music or dance is deprived by the overwrought melody and discordant choreography. Chaos.*

If this woman, standing in the forefront, is bothered by them, it is not apparent. In fact, she seems oblivious to them and appears to be part of the assemblage. When she calls me by name, I feel temporarily relieved because I know she's made a mistake. I sigh with relief and tell her that my name is not Salman, it's Ali. But it's as if she doesn't hear me. She looks at me with conviction, and I look around to see if perhaps Salman is somewhere close. But he is nowhere around and when I look back at her, she is still focused on me.

"But I'm not your son! I'm not Salman, you've made a mistake!" I cry.

Her face hardens. She raises her hands up to her breasts and without another word, starts to massage them. I am bewildered. With her eyes shut, she throws her head back and allows an orgasmic gasp to escape her parted lips as her hands knead the

mounds of her chest more rigorously. Horrified, I beg for her to stop.
She hears me. Raising her head back very slowly, she looks at me
but her hands remain on her breasts as if priming on a weapon of
torture. It's made clear to me by the unflinching stare, the almost
demonic glint in her eyes that if I ignore her or continue to deny
being her son, she will advance into a variety of obscenities purposed
at inciting fracas in me.

"You must not fight me," she says gravely, a perverse smile
extending on her face. "I'm stronger than you."

In life, as on stage, we need props in order to enact the
roles we are required to play. The people we surround
ourselves with are sometimes the most elaborate props
enhancing our drama. For Salman, I began to think as
the gulf widened between us, I'd been the essential prop
in the homosexual phase he was now renouncing. In his
life now, peace had been made with the matriarch of the
Surani family, and as such, the Salman who had strode
admirably across the formalin of gay life had scurried
away like a roach, back into the cracks of sexual
anonymity.

In my mind, the days that had turned into the
weeks when we didn't communicate felt more like an
overnight lacuna during which he'd gone and transformed
himself completely, as if by some mythical prowess. Isn't
that how we often see people? That they change
overnight when in fact they drop little clues all along?
The Salman who had struggled to reach out to other
Indians to educate them about HIV and AIDS, albeit in
his semi-closeted and sometimes impractical way, the
same one who had even convinced me to obey the
beckon of cultural obligation, had suddenly retreated
under the bulwark of breast cancer and diabetes.

Even in his most conservative phase as a
homosexual, during the first few months of our
acquaintance, Salman had felt passionate about getting
Indians to identify with AIDS. "These *chodus!*" he would

curse, his hand shooting out as if it were being extended for an inopportune handshake. *"Nah, nah,* this Aids has nothing to do with our community! When will they wake up, these backward people? Don't they realize even Indian grandmothers in their musty *chadars* are getting it!"

But all that would cease to matter to him now. Everything had to change. It didn't serve Salman to be the spokesperson for such a taboo disease. A disease that the Indian community at large had still consigned to the rest of the world. Not if he wanted to be the beneficiary of that Surani inheritance. The rebellion was over. The prodigal son had been granted permission to come back home. The only priority now was not to develop outreach strategies, but to secure precarious inheritances by championing more acceptable causes. A disease that did not imply anything sexual. Any distraction from this newfound path would have to be eliminated.

It was time again to assume the role of the obedient son, not the family faggot.

I spent the day haunted by my dream. It was plain to see that losing Salman's friendship was taking me for a loop. Out of superstition, or habit, I went straight for my old dream dictionary. Most of the time, it defeated me with its rigid list of symbols – who ever dreamt of a lily or a goat, anyway? This time, wedged between dreams of a moth and a mouse, the old book authoritatively indicated that a mother reflected guidance and care. A symbol of nurturing and shelter. No more. Scoffing, I threw the useless tome back into the closet among old forsaken tapes and books. There was no way I was going to find any book to interpret dreams of somebody else's mother enthralled in masturbation!

Many times throughout the day, I found myself struggling to not pick up the phone to call Salman at work. I felt that if I could only corner him in person, grab him by his shoulders and shake him a little and

remind him of how close we used to be, he would end
this ridiculous plot to alienate me. If I could only tell him
how painful this whole thing was for me and that I didn't
understand the need for such a drastic course of action,
he might come to his senses. Pieces of the dream filtered
in and out of my consciousness, along with the image of
this woman's face, now dissolving with the burdens of my
awakened state.

When the day was over, I jumped into my car and
drove to his house in Beverly Hills, only to find that no
one home. Peeking through the windows I looked into
the kitchen where, drinking vodka, we had cackled away
about this and that. Where he had wickedly confessed
about the hassles of living with his lesbian, film-industry
roommate who required constant validation for the
"pretentious artsy projects" that only graced foreign art-
house theaters. On the dining room table, where we'd
gorged on *samosas* and chai, I saw the tuberose he bought
weekly, craning up from the crystal vase.

I had no clue what I would have said to him had
he been there. Maybe I would have told him about how
someone who appeared to have been his mother had
come into my dreams, mistaken me for him and then
started to knead her breasts while I watched. I'd brought
with me an old soundtrack and a novel by Vasanji that
he'd lent me a while back. But he was probably out with
the rest of the group and I couldn't help wishing I was
with them.

Dejected at not finding him, I reproached myself
for behaving compulsively and drove back to Santa
Monica, my bizarre dream in focus again. Who was that
woman, anyway? In my mind, she was Salman's mother.
The one person I was apparently holding accountable for
Salman's sexual repudiation.

A mother is, after all, the universal being who is
both nurturer and tyrant. She is creator and destroyer.
The molder of a child's life. Mine had, in her own

complex way, taught me acceptance and forgiveness. What had Salman's mother, perhaps even without meaning to, imparted to him?

In an attempt to understand why he'd felt the need to abandon our friendship, I had summoned in my dreams the one woman who is inextricable in all our lives. The woman whose rejection had fueled his rebellion toward his family in courageous acts of a homosexual. Perhaps she had sanctioned his return and demanded his rehabilitation.

The cruelest endings are those without good-byes, without explanations, just the slamming shut of a door, the startling thud of a book closed in mid-chapter. Bereft, and without the closure that only a dialogue could've provided, I was set adrift in a sea of imagined reasons as to why Salman didn't want me around. I wondered what a conversation between Salman and his mother might have been like. Or if there had been one. I imagined she would have launched into the community angle first – as my own mother had – and then, after he had defended his right to live honestly, progressed to finding some kind of middle ground; marry, according to custom and into a family of our choosing, and carry out your private shenanigans with discretion and without witnesses or cohorts. *In return, Salman, you will be welcomed back into the family and never have to beg from your bitch sister ever again.*

Not a bad deal considering Salman was never the full-time homosexual who wanted to live, work and play in WeHo. His sexual pleasures had been stolen ones, and by their very nature, he indulged in them sporadically and with compensated fervor. He could continue to do that, if he chose, just not with a partner-in-crime like myself.

"I'm sick and tired of those clubs, Ali," he had admitted at least once, when he had been brave enough to speak without hiding behind his usual camp one-liners. "Especially WeHo – dear God, how many times can you run around Heaven, sucking in your breath and holding your gut in? Ahh, I don't want to compete with those stupid queens. I just want to…be *me* and not feel so much like *nobody*, you know what I mean?" Sadly, he was probably right. As it is, few people appeared happily paired up in the community, and the paucity of those interested in an overweight Indian, as he frequently called himself, made matters more grave.

As for the sex clubs, which he enjoyed, even they had become a bit of a liability lately. "You in the mood for some seafood? No, I don't mean Farida's twat," he said over the phone, the day after he had discovered he had been struck. "I'm farming enough crabs to open a crab house. Bring your bib and go crazy!"

I couldn't help but admit that there were times when I had looked upon this lifestyle as kind of a curse. But crossing over to the other side had never even occurred to me. There had never been a choice. Its inducements were as impractical for me as a bewildered Vegan hoisted over a prime rib. The soul of a gay man, even if anatomy permits it, will not allow for the love of any other. But then, a sizeable inheritance had never been dangled in front of me.

I thanked God for my mother. For her attempt to understand that after all her sacrificing, all her love, a demand from her for me to be something I could not would have been tantamount to a much-delayed abortion. Salman hadn't been so lucky.

CHAPTER 42

THE PRICE OF PASSION

My grandmother didn't live too many years after my grandfather's demise. In death, it was as if they'd signed an unwitnessed contract to pursue one other within a reasonable time for the next leg of their journey together. These were my mother's thoughts months after my grandmother passed away, when she had broken down in tears over the phone. On the subject of my grandparents, most of us had always been dumbfounded. None of us wanted to use them as an example to legitimize notions of love, but none could deny that they had stayed together longer than most married couples.

Upon returning home from Salman's that night, when I had exhausted of ruminating over his life-altering decision, I found a message from Mummy. This time I called her right away. I reassured her about my health, my job, and then she inquired after the people in my life, about Nelson. "No," I said firmly. "We're not in touch anymore and I like it that way...Yes, everything's fine with Adrian. We're even closer than before," and I decided not to drag her into yet another fiasco that would keep her up nights worrying about my emotional well-being. The last thing she needed was to add another round of *tasbih* to her already interminably long prayer session. "Yes, I see them all once in a while, you know, mostly over a barbecue or something. But I've been kind of busy lately."

"Good, good," she said. "I'm so happy to know that you're doing well."

"And you?" I asked.

She tsked. "I miss *mama kuba*," she said, referring to my grandmother, and started to cry. "And I miss you."

I allayed her by committing to sending her a ticket next year. "Come on, now. Think of all the shopping and television you'll be able to watch."

"Things here are so rotten," she said, as if in contrast – a complaint typical of parents like her, residing far from their kids in America. Between the clucks and groans they always began to paint this bleak picture with the crumbling economy and varnished it with the escalating crime. "We've all had such miserable lives," she said. "That's why I want your life to be happy, you know? If you're going to be the last one in line, then I demand that God give you the rewards of all the good we've done. Who else have we lived for? *Mama kuba* and me?"

Suddenly I could see the chain of martyrs preceding me, and I felt bolstered for being the recipient of their deeds. My grandmother had taught kindergarten for more than twenty years. She had nurtured those children in the formative years of their lives, children that went on to be the men and women with successful adult lives and families. Pity she'd been unable to impart such wisdom to any of her own.

Until the later years of her life, when my grandmother couldn't do much more than waddle to the bathroom on the walker, she went like clockwork to mosque at seven every evening, climbed the three flights of stairs reverently and carried out her duties as head volunteer. When, debilitated with the bulbous swellings of arthritis in her legs, her only lament from that dowager sofa in the dining room was that God had taken away from her the strength to come to His home and visit Him.

My mother had followed in her devotion, taking religion's panacea against the damage of love to even greater heights. And now, defying the apparent curse running through our lineage, she was hoped that my life would turn out differently.

"You," she said. "You have to be the inheritor of all the fruits of our labor."

I shook me head at the irony. How could I tell her that I could see no such light on the horizon without breaking her heart? That although I didn't doubt how much she and my father had loved me, their parenting had been a sanctioned debacle of neglect at best. And now, years later, with him six-feet under and her enraptured in religion, it had left me with huge holes in my heart. Holes that allowed so much to seep through me. Holes that, I had been convinced for so long, could only be filled by someone exactly like my father. How to tell her all this without breaking her heart?

"Ali," she said very softly. "I know we haven't exactly been the best role models for you, but no child is free of the, you know, the baggage from his family. You must learn from our example to do differently instead of feeling fated for the same ending, you know? You can't be like those other people," she said, extracting from all those hours in front of Springer, "who start blaming everything in their lives on their parents! *Hunh!* Nothing is ever their own fault! What is important is that you realize that no matter what it looked like, we loved each other very much. Your grandparents loved each other immensely and your Dad and I loved each other too."

I flinched. I could see, hear, the screaming, the rapid swinging of limbs in assault and defense, their delirium even now. My grandmother's face floated in my mind. I missed her too. She had been, after all, more of a mother than any grandparent should ever be. "You were all so cruel to each other," I said. "There was never any peace. You all never stopped to think what it was doing to anybody else."

"But darling, we never stopped to think of what we were doing even to each other," she laughed nervously.

"Still..."

"Ali, all mothers struggle to protect their babies from the harsh realities of life for as long as they can. Until one day it just can't be done anymore. We always want our children's lives to be better, happier, than our own, you know? If I could have kept you from growing up, from feeling all this pain, if I had known how, my darling, I would have."

"I know," I said, thinking that maybe it wasn't the search for adventure but the need to escape the chaos of their lives that had driven me away from Kenya.

"You must remember, Ali, that we've all led exceptional lives. The things we've been through in this family..." she tsked. And then she said, "When you feel so much, when you love so desperately, then you also fight with the same intensity. It's just the price you pay, Ali. The price of passion."

I thought momentarily about what she had said: that their atrocities in love could only be matched by their capacity to love those that had hurt them; I felt an appreciation for all she had endured. Yes, hers has been an exceptional life. What one always thinks happens only to others had happened to her. At that moment, I wanted to reach through the phone lines and touch her. To kiss her and protect her and take away all those years of pain that she had to endure. The love of a son for his mother was perhaps the most potent, prohibitive lust. It was the first bond in the life of a human being and could be, in its consuming, impetuous nature, also the most damaging. After the disassociation that every son had to undergo, the years of severing from her persona, I felt as if I had finally come back to her as a grown man to give her the strength and reassurance she had been unable to give me. "I love you, Mummy," I said. "And I'm not afraid of what life brings me. You've taught me, somehow, that in the end we're always alone."

"Not alone, darling. By ourselves."

"Yeah," I said, impressed.

"For that I'm thankful.   That you have the courage. I know that if anything were to happen to me, you would go on and be fine, it wouldn't destroy you."

"Yeah."

"I do want you to be happy with someone though. Whoever it may be. Boy, girl, whatever. It will happen one day, I know it, *tu naarje*. You must have your faith in God."

"It's not that I don't have any faith in God, Mum," I said wryly. "I just don't trust his judgment."

CHAPTER 43

RESCUED

When night falls upon Santa Monica Boulevard, a modest stretch of its cadaver takes on a shadowy kind of life. Away from the heart of West Hollywood – that couple of miles on either side of the street littered with the mercantilism of bars and clubs, the glaring chrome and glass veneers of gyms, and late-night purveyors of pulp and video erotica – awakes another world. A world that, to the keen eye or a trained observer, simmers with life as early as dusk. But it's only when darkness finally cloaks its pavement and bus benches and buildings that it actually starts to surge and ripple, that the boulevard becomes a visible procession of sexual trade. Young boys and men stake their corners night after night as I do my banker's desk each morning. They pose in a variety of dissimulations. The lurid, unbroken stare of calculated lust delivers promises of unforgettable pleasures to the drivers that pass by. Or the oblivious and bored stance of those who are aware that even sullen disinterest has its following. The cars loop around the dimly lit blocks, around rows of structures without coruscation, unintended for any nighttime purpose – sleeping schools and office buildings and not-so-trendy pizzerias. The setting that's required for the thriving of this enterprise is just a little bit of darkness and the obscurity it promises. The drivers stealthily, and when more experienced arrantly, search out those they will not acknowledge by day. Here they will find a menagerie of sexual creatures to expiate the churning in their bellies. The seeming virgin in all his tenderness, the jaded man who looks like he's had a fight with his wife and hasn't returned home to even shave his stubble, and the homme fatale who, by virtue of his handsome looks, is fated to leave for other loves and lands. Sometimes mingling, and at other times in packs of their own, one will also find the transgendered. They all come to this stretch of the boulevard, exiled from the contrived respectability of a few blocks to the west to skulk and prey under the cover of night.

Sometimes, in a car, huddled with my group of friends on that ill-timed search for an ATM machine or a nutritional catastrophe at Del Taco at two in the morning, we traverse this area of the boulevard. And there has never, since that one night, been a single time that I haven't looked out of the car and onto that stretch with at least a decibel of anticipation.

Of course he's never there.

But my eyes, as if by some involuntary action, always survey that block on which the bank sits, outside of which on that night so long ago, he had stood with his hands dug deep into his jean pockets, his eyes drawn by our passing car.

Here – I tell myself, as if recanting nirvana, to whoever else has to listen to my drunken drawl in the car – is where I met Bill.

Bill was a hustler from Santa Monica Boulevard. He's been missing from that block since that first and last time I found him there. His phone is disconnected. Many times I think he's dead – such a fate, after all, is part of the territory when all that's negotiated before jumping into the darkness of a car is the rate for passion. Sometimes I prefer to think that he is. It makes his absence easier to accept. At other times I think that maybe he's living in Malibu with a pewter-colored dog called Rascal or Rocky, and that maybe one day, in the sprawling city of L.A., we'll miraculously run into each other again as unexpectedly as we had that night.

It was a night very much like those that culminated in a sex club. Had it not been for Bill, the evening would have ended up that way too.   After carousing with other men at a club, we headed east. We'd just drained more cash from the ATM and bickered over the sounds of pulsating dance music about the bank surcharge.   Only Adrian, always the prudent one, had come equipped with enough cash. Kitty, who had just paid his third surcharge for the evening, endorsed the bank robberies that were happening all over the city in his disgruntlement. "Is serve 'em right," he said in his own brand of English. "Why they needin' a money when they so much and steals from us?"

I slapped him on his head. "I work for one of those banks, and let me tell you, it's no fun being part of a takeover!"

Kitty became more amused. "Good! You pays for us!"

We were driving to the Hollywood Spa.   There, with a sterile white towel wrapped around the waist and a key ring fastened around the wrist, we hoped to find sexual mates for the night. Although bathhouses usually made me feel uncomfortable with the expected bodily exhibition, I'd drunk enough to override the inhibition.

As the car trudged along the traffic of onward-bound nocturnes, I leaned up to hug the front seat, my wrists nuzzling in the back of Kitty's neck, and looked out restlessly at the trade of hustlers. Some of them stood chatting in little coteries, others in deliberate solitude to appear more accessible, and a couple of them leaned into windows of cars before being extended the invitation to hop in. It was a particularly busy summer night. Outside the air conditioning of the car was a warm and slothful breeze that enabled many to dress scantily and to properly display their wares. As my eyes drifted over them I thought, how easy would it be to just pluck out one of these men and buy my sex tonight instead of enlisting in that scour at the bathhouse. What's the difference? We're still doling out cash to taste human flesh. We still

end up paying if not in currency then, in time with guilt.
The morning after, popping antioxidants and painkillers
to assuage the previous night's drunkenness, the three or
four men became a mental sludge. Looking out through
my kitchen window with a cup of coffee, the sun harsh
and unforgiving only seems to accentuate my feeling
begrimed in the night. So much easier to just invite one
of these men back home or to flip through the pages of
the *Frontiers* squashed between me and Adrian in the
backseat and summon one of them.

"They oly givin' massage, no the sex, you silly!"
Kitty said when I vocalized this.

"Don't be stupid, Kitty," I said. "Massage and sex
are like fish and chips. You don't buy one without the
other!"

"Hmm," said Adrian. "I'm going to have to tell
Burke Williams that the next time I'm there!"

"Ooh," said Kitty, delighted. "I have gif
certificates from there. Now I tell them, after massage,
before you kicks my ass out, to play with it!"

As we made out trek I even thought about
Nelson, something that I rarely did anymore. Of what it
would've been like to still have him on nights like this.
The comfort of knowing, even while rollicking around
town with my so-called sistahs, that there was someone at
home to take me in his arms and feed my hunger with his
flesh. I wondered, despite the integrity that burned even
brighter since that faithlessness, if it was not perhaps
better to go back to him. If the consolation of having
someone was not ultimately worth the assaults on dignity.

It was during the custody of these thoughts that
my eyes fell upon Bill. He was standing in the middle of
the block with an orbit of space around him. At either
ends of the same block were other workers, but he had
chosen to stand apart from all of them, in the center no
less. Our eyes locked gazes and he smiled at me – a smile
I'm sure was paraded for the benefit of all driving by him

– and I was so undone by his beauty, so flummoxed by the juxtaposition of a man who looked like him standing there on that street, that all rationale flew out of me. It was an irrevocable moment. One where, while drinking in this vision of him in a nimbus of lamp light, everything around me dissolved. Suddenly, I had to look again into those eyes. To touch him. To make contact with him. A kind of feeling tantamount only to the rapture I felt at hearing brief strains of a music score.

"Let me out of the car!" I demanded. "I have to get out!"

"We no there yet!" Kitty said.

"You okay? You want to throw up or something?" Adrian said.

"No, no, I've got to talk to that guy!" I said, pointing out the car.

They shot me an appalled look.

Despite our intentions to renew memberships and rent lockers and rooms in which to lure strangers to fuck us, an interest in picking up a prostitute was heresy. When I was undeterred, they began to moan about how it was already past two-thirty in the morning and that we should've been there long before now.

"Ali, we have to get there now, before all those stupid queens from WeHo file up," said Frankie, one of the new recruits to our group.

"Yeah, and then it takin' forevers to get in!" added Kitty.

"Sweetie," said Adrian gently. "Why waste your time with this when there are all those other men waiting there?"

But I knew with an amazing degree of conviction and clarity that there was no other man for me on that night. I would be unable to bring myself to accept any other. My desire for him felt absolute and unsubstitutable. In a way that addicts have the singular craving for their drug or a prognosticator secures the essential ingredient for a forecast, I knew that for the kind of night I longed for, the quality of experience that I sought, this man was the indispensable component.

"I don't care about those other men," I said and started to shake Kitty's shoulders until the car began to swerve and everyone became nervous. "I want to get out! Let me out!"

Granting me just a few minutes, they pulled over to let me out. I dodged cars to cross the street and stood breathlessly in front of him on the pavement. Once there, I realized with an unmaskable look of nervousness, that there were no rehearsed words to deliver. It was not a moment I had encountered before, nor one I could've prepared for. In the bars, under a firmament of painted lights, the sound of thrumming beats and the cacophony of contrived conversation, where elixirs filled plastic cups and cigarette smoke whirled into the ceiling, I knew how to behave and what to say to the guy perched on the bar stool next to me, or the guy squeezing to get through to the bar. Here, under an open sky of obscure stars, where I could actually hear my panting breath even above the disgruntled engines of cars inching forth, I had no script and no words. It all felt too real. I feared that the wit and composure that I'd been known for would betray me.

Up close, this handsome Latino looked even more startling. He possessed all the attributes of physical beauty that gay men, at least in the poster-boy culture of L.A., pursue and adulate. Bill's poise and bemusement, instead of the impatience that a hustler anticipating trade might cast on an inexperienced, flippant procurer like myself, made it look like he didn't belong on that street. His unjaded demeanor – eyes looking at me without any contrived sexuality and an almost gentle smile that acknowledged my discomfort – was perhaps his unique talent.

Bill appeared as if he had accidentally stumbled onto that section of Santa Monica Boulevard instead of claiming that region for the sole purpose of his vending. He made it look like I was nothing more than a friendly nocturnal visitor saying hello instead of a potential buyer.

Of course, the notion that just because he didn't evince the shopworn aura of a boulevard hustler meant he didn't belong there was preposterous. As if the beautiful have no place in the realm of such self-diminishment.

When I opened my mouth to speak, I was almost incoherent with embarrassment. Removed from the womb of the Mustang and slowly emerging from the inducement of alcohol, I began to feel awkward standing there. I managed to introduce myself, at which point he immediately put me at ease by saying, "Like Ali Baba?"

"Yeah," I said with a laugh. "And those in the car are my forty thieves."

"Hi," he said, accepting my handshake firmly. "Name's Bill."

"I saw you from the car and I just...I just had to come over and talk to you."

"That's cool."

"You know, I've never...done this before," I said, unable to look him in the eye.

"Oh? And what is it you think you're doing?" he asked, amused.

"I don't know. What I mean is, I've never acted so impulsively, you know, jumping out of a car to talk to some stranger? I'm not sure I know *what* I'm doing."

"Hmm. But you know what I'm doing, right?"

"Well, yeah. I suppose I do."

"I'm working," he said, just in case.

I glanced around us, drinking in the whole scene, having looked onto it and never having stood within its vortex. I crossed my arms across my chest, suddenly feeling conspicuous, as a voice inside my head (one that I would continue to ignore) said, *Jesus, what the hell am I doing here?*

"So, what are you guys up to?"

"We're actually on our way to some place else."

"Where?" he asked and his voice lowered intimately.

"Oh...to some place called the Holiday Spa or something."

"You mean the Hollywood Spa?"

I nodded as innocently as I could pretend to. "Yeah, I think that's the place."

"No need to feel embarrassed."

"Embarrassed? I'm not embarrassed! Why would I be?"

He smiled, looking down at his feet. "You just look a little embarrassed."

Was he referring to my embarrassment over the Hollywood Spa or my being there with him? "Nah, I'm fine," I assured.

Right then, a car careened around the corner and pulled up a few feet away from us. The driver, an older Caucasian man, stuck his head out of the window and cried out Bill's name, cutting rudely into our world.

Bill raised his hands emphatically at him. "Just leave me alone, okay?"

"Bill, come on, don't do this to me, man!"

"Look, just leave me the fuck alone! What part don't you understand, man? I don't want to deal with this right now!"

"C'mon, Bill. I'm begging you! Just let's...let's just talk about this, okay?"

"Shit! There's nothing to talk about. Just go!" Bill said. He turned his back on the driver and looked back at me in exasperation. "I can't believe this shit!"

"Who *is* that?"

He shook his head. "He won't leave me alone..."

"But who is he?"

That's when the driver turned feral. "Who the fuck is *that* you're talking to? Hey, who the fuck are you?" he screamed out at me.

Startled, I stepped back and Bill, infuriated, charged over to the car. "Just fuck off, man! I told you not to bother me!"

"Who is that fucker? Are you thinking of going with him?"

"What if I am? It's none of your damn business, okay?"

"Who is he?"

"Just fuck off, man!"

"Bill, please," he became plaintive. "Just get in the car, okay? We'll work this out, man."

"I don't wanna' work it out!"

Since this driver was holding up traffic, cars had piled up behind him and were honking, obviously aggravated. Someone even shouted, "Move it, you goddamn drunk queen!"

"Bill, please, just get in the car."

"No! I'm not dealing with this! Fuck, Andy, I'm so sick of this!" Bill said and walked back up to me.

Unwillingly, the driver started to roll away but only after emitting a heart-wrenching cry. I felt flustered, not knowing what to make of the incident, and even felt a little sad for the driver, but I was not discouraged. If anything, this episode in all its disturbing drama, only steeled my interest in Bill.

I felt sure that the driver hadn't completely gone away just yet. Such obsessive eruptions, I knew from experience, demanded much more to be tranquilized. I would have to act fast. Across the street, my friends became apprehensive about all the commotion. They started honking at us impatiently, and Kitty sprouted out the window and threatened to leave me there, his voice struggling over the clamor of blaring music from other revving cars.

I turned to Bill with concern. "Who was that?"

"Oh, man," he said, shaking his head. "Just some guy."

"Just some guy? That looked like more than 'just some guy'!"

"I work for him."

"*Work* for him?"

"Yeah," he replied. "He runs a modeling agency. Have you heard of Andy Jacobs?"

"No."

"Well, that's the owner. That's Andy. We were together once."

"Together?"

"Yeah."

"Not too long ago, it seems."

Bill shrugged as if that was unimportant. Such cruelty in him, even if justified by the nuisance of an embittered ex-lover, bothered me. Maybe because I could relate to the driver. Memories of Richard and the jealous fits that I'd felt driven to throw were still fresh in my mind. Mingled with that faint perturbation, however, was also the perverse joy of being in the other position. Of being the muscled blonde whom Richard had always forsaken me for.

"The guy's a psycho!" he said, his lips deforming into a sneer.

I smiled to myself thinking, Not one bigger than me, he isn't. "Well, that definitely makes him more than 'just some guy'!"

"Yeah. Anyway, I told him it was over, you know? And now he just won't let me be with anyone else."

"But *this*," I said. "*This* is much more than just *being* with someone else."

"Well, this is part of what we do at the modeling agency," he said nonchalantly. "We just don't do it from the street, that's the only difference. Anyway, I wish he'd leave me alone."

"Then maybe he likes having a say in whom you go with?"

"Who the fuck cares? He doesn't own me. I'm not gonna be there much longer, anyway."

Modeling agency, I thought. What an interesting concept. Obviously an escort service, although I couldn't picture stark-raving-mad Andy Jacobs in his blue sedan as any kind of business owner, let alone some kind of pimp and lover for Bill.

"Well, look, I have to get going. My friends," I said, throwing a look back at the car, "are getting really pissed now. You're welcome to join us."

"Where are you going? Oh, yeah, you told me. The Spa."

"Why don't you come with us? I'm sure you'll have good time."

"You want to take a hooker to a bathhouse?" he said and laughed. "No, thanks. Besides, I told you, I'm working."

I grunted. "Well, you're not going to get much work done with *him* driving around in circles, you know?" I heard my name being called from the car and I motioned to them to give me another moment. "Look, you don't have to worry about anything." I'm not sure exactly what I meant by that. I wanted it to mean everything. I wanted it to mean whatever it would take for him to get in the car with me. That I would take care of him financially for that night and his safety too, although I couldn't bring myself to say it exactly that way, at least not the financial part, not just yet.

I happened to look over his shoulder and the blue sedan was already coming around again. "Your valentine's right on time."

Bill heaved a sigh. "Christ! I'm going to kick the shit out of him."

"No, don't get into a fight," I advised. "It's not worth it. Come on, just go with me."

"How much does this place cost?"

"I'm not sure. I think about eight or something." It was more like fifteen.

He hesitated.

Then I said it. "You don't have to worry about the money or anything. We have enough." By positioning us as a group I hoped to evade the implication that I was purchasing his services. I knew no one in the car would throw a red cent his way but as long as I didn't have to hand him the cash, I felt I could absolve myself from feeling like I'd entered into the trade.

Andy Jacobs pulled up by the curb again. "Get away from him! Leave him alone!"

"I gotta go. Can't take any more of this," I said. "You coming?"

"Yeah," he said, and a smile came upon his face. "Let's get out of here."

Andy Jacobs came unhinged. "Where...Where are you going? Hey, come back here! Bill, don't do this!" And then he cried out to me, "Hey, man, don't take him with you, you're gonna regret it! He's a thief! He's gonna take all your stuff! I'm telling you, man, you're gonna be sorry!"

We began crossing the street carefully through the oncoming traffic and the possibility of Andy running us over and, somewhere in the crossing, without any forethought, our hands found each other and together we made our way to the safety of the car.

Bill lit up a joint. He shared it with everyone in the car. Instant camaraderie. Adrian struggled to cull the effects of pot again. He always claimed that he'd never succeeded in getting high on pot, so a lit joint always became a challenge for him. Personally, I'd always refrained from it. Frankie reprimanded me for showing such poor taste. "I guess it's just not the drug for control queens," he grunted and I wanted to hit him for calling me that in front of Bill.

Having Bill sitting next to me was intoxication enough. Feeling more relaxed, he removed his shirt and sat there in a white tank top. As he inhaled on the joint, my eyes lingered on the luster of his bronzed shoulder, the tattoo on his arm.

When we got to the Spa and everyone had lined up for admission, Bill realized he didn't have his ID. He explained politely that his agenda for the night hadn't included anything that would've required one. There was no stopping everybody else from going in. As far as they were concerned, this little hustler had already caused them enough delay and the pot had only been equitable reparation for it. Adrian, the first one in, had already been alerted that there was at least a two-hour wait before a room might become available and the rest of them had already given me that accusing look upon hearing the news. I called them a pack of bitches in violent heat and offered to drive Bill back to the street. Kitty would have to trust me with his new Mustang. Bill excused himself and offered to wait for me in the parking lot so we could discuss this in private. That's when Kitty vehemently said, "Just-a-forget him, will you? He fin' way back, don' worry."

"It's not him I'm worried about, Kitty, it's me. I want him! If I can't have him, I certainly don't want anything that's in there!"

He shrugged and started to hand me his car keys, knowing it was futile to argue with me. "Suit yourself. So...you come back or what?"

"No, actually I was hoping you guys could catch a bus home."

He closed his palm on the keys quickly.

"Don't be stupid! Of course I'll be back. I just don't know if I'll see you right away. Give me a couple of hours, okay?"

"Be careful, please?"

"Yeah, it's not like I'm going to some bathhouse or anything," I said wryly and pocketed the keys.

"I means with the car!"

"Oh, of course," I said.

"And of course, with him."

I practically danced my way out of that infernal place. I'd always hoped an attractive man would rescue me from those despicable places but had never quite pictured that such deliverance would come from a hustler. Outside, Bill was already chatting with a couple of guys who might have been on their way in, as he leaned against the Mustang, his shirt hanging from the seam of his jeans. Men like him, I thought, walking over to him stealthily, drew a following like bees to a hive. I felt instantly irritated, but when he noticed me and quickly excused himself from them, it pleased me immensely. On their way in, the two white boys threw me a derisive glance, and I thought, stupid little bitter queens! Nothing like other fags to horn in on your action.

"I'm sorry, man," he said.

"Sorry? Whatever for?" I asked, using the remote to unlock the car.

"You know, for messing up your night. You don't have to worry about me. You can just go in there if you like."

"And what will you do?"

"Hey, man, I can find my way back, no need to worry about that."

"Yeah, I'm sure you could," I said, walking to my side of the car. "But I don't really want to go in there anyway." *No, I'd much rather be in bed with you.*

In the car, I looked at him before turning on the engine, my fingers paused on the ignition key. "Look, I can take you back there if you want. I mean, what time is it? Three? Three-thirty? It's probably not too late for you to still make something out of this night. And I'm sure your boyfriend's gone by now," I said deliberately.

"My boyfriend?" he winced, laughing. "Andy's not my boyfriend."

"Well, your boss or your ex or whatever you call him." *Your pimp?*

"Psycho," he said.

"Okay, psycho's good. He's probably back at the Bates motel by now."

Bill thought for a moment and then shook his head. "I'll tell you what," he said. "I'm completely out of weed. Can you take me to get some?"

"Weed? Where?" I asked dubiously.

"It's not far. Just right off Western. It's safe, I swear it."

I hesitated.

"Hey, believe me, I wouldn't ask you to do anything dangerous."

I gently sighed as I switched gears and started to back out of the parking space. I tried hard not to stare at him, not to touch him, although under the circumstances it could hardly have been considered inappropriate. I wondered if he could sense my craving for him. I felt that he did. A man like him, always, even in moments of modesty and feigned innocence, knew his power over those around him and when to use his looks to achieve whatever he desired.

Had I begun my interaction with him in a manner more seductive, emitting charm and confidence as I might have in a bar, it could've been different. But I had already fallen into a role. Into a different persona. One that required me to struggle with my desire for him instead of pursuing him flagrantly, to set myself apart from those he was accustomed to and, perhaps, elicit his desire for me. All this for a hooker! I prayed that he would find a way to take us beyond such restraint. Maybe lay his hand on my lap or twiddle his fingers in the nape of my neck. Images of us naked, far beyond the point of such bridling, roistered in my mind. But he just sat there with his hands on his lap, his fingers gently and incongruently tapping to the music score that I had lodged into the cassette player.

"Okay," I said as the wheels kissed pavement. "How should we do this?"

CHAPTER 44

SHORT CUTS

We were in a part of the city that I dreaded, one that would never be depicted in glossy postcards or grace the itineraries of sight-seeing tours. Every city has its pockets of shame, even this proverbial city of angels, and Bill and I perambulated through one of them in search of marijuana. As I looked around, a feeling of depression fomented within me, an uneasiness that made me want to escape from it quickly.

The streetlights cast a uriniferous glow that felt heavy on the eyes. All around me was the commerce indigenous to such an area: the liquor store, a coin-operated Laundromat and, towering sinisterly over unkempt buildings, the billboards. Not Bijan's opulent vulgarity or Cybill Shepherd validating herself through her pre-owned Mercedes, but glamorously attired ethnic people frolicking over a bottle of liquor. They looked as if they expected a genie to pop out from the tempting oblations of dark rums and malt liquor, or, as if they were celebrating their discovery of some messianic entity that had brought smiles to their faces, making them look so much different from the patrons that wandered into the liquor stores to procure these potions. *It's what the rest of the world is hoping they'll believe too. That salvation, at least temporarily, awaits only to be uncapped from a bottle on the shelf.* Only Colonel Sanders tried to bring some unimpeachable relief with his trademark, bespectacled beam as he inquired in Spanish, *"Lunchamos?"* I'd no idea that he was bilingual.

The streets were deserted when I pulled up by a bus shelter. I noticed beer cans strewn all over the ground in spite of the trash can sitting idly by the vacant bench. The poster for a John Singleton movie was lodged into the shed's advertising panel, a film alleged to have provoked gang violence in parts of the city. How ironic that we were incapable of decoding simple messages. To grasp the intended moral in popular art. The movie exposed the perniciousness of gang life, yet it had somehow managed to trigger more of it. Everything was scrambled. We saw only what we wanted.

Sliding the gear into park, I turned to look at Bill, the discomfort apparent in my eyes as he glanced around furtively. "This is going to be quick, right?" I asked.

"Yeah, absolutely, man," he assured me. "Just drive all the way down to that McDonald's there, you see it? By the time you drive back, I'll be done."

"That one right there?" I asked, as if there were fifty of them around.

"Yup, that's the one," he said, getting out of the car. "To those beautiful golden arches."

Before he walked away, he leaned down and knocked on the window pane. I searched for a handle and then, remembering it wasn't my car, pressed down on the power button that I'd so often wished my own car had been equipped with. The veil slid from between us.

"You're not going to leave me here, are you?" he asked.

"Leave you? Why would I do that?"

He shrugged. "I don't know. See you in a couple of minutes?"

"Of course," I said, looking at him strangely. "What a weird thing for you to say."

"Not really."

"Be careful."

He gave me the benefit of his most seductive smile and a reassuring nod. A ripple of excitement ran through my body, and I nervously looked away to keep him from catching it.

"Hey," he called, and when I looked back at him, motioned for me to put the window up.

The pane of tinted glass slid between us. I put the car into gear and drove off to the comfort of the golden arches.

Driving down that desolate street, I placated myself for being convinced into coming here with the possibility of having sex with him. Between the vision of Bill's passionate lovemaking (I even found myself chanting God's name – *Ya Ali...Ya Ali...Ya Ali*) – and acknowledging that I was being a little melodramatic, I told myself, *I've succeeded in becoming a rabid, God-fearing prima donna like my mother.*

My mind raced back to Kenya. I thought about how I'd always felt something akin to terror when faced with poverty. Even as a child, I'd never felt comfortable in downtrodden areas. It wasn't that I'd feared for my safety, or that I was apathetic about the less privileged, but that I might have been able to relate too much. I had come, after all, from a family where money had always been a source of contention – my parents' absence had often been blamed on their working too hard for money; my aunt and uncle lamented how their entrepreneurship had been snubbed by the lack of it; and I'd overheard Mummy claim the reason my father had forsaken us to lay with another woman was the Rolex she'd bestowed on his wrist. Poverty and its many faces of impoverishment had always depressed me to the point of nausea.

I circled around the drive-thru of the closed McDonald's and realized that I was hungry. With all the events that had transpired, we'd forgotten our ritualistic visit to the Del Taco by Fairfax. I wondered what the guys were up to at the Spa. I imagined Kitty trundling in a room with someone: Frankie, rubbing himself concentratedly with a sweat-drenched group in the steam room; and, with some satisfaction, Adrian, still meandering up and down the staircase. In my mind, I could hear the dance music that would have been playing there. Even after hours of it at the bars, there was always more dance music to be found in the next place. Why didn't they play more sensual music in a place like that? Something more erotically conducive? Who needed more dance music? To fuck to? Did they want everything that transpired between us, whether in nightclubs or sex clubs, to feel as frivolous and detached as the music that underscored our activities? Why weren't there any ballads played in gay dance clubs? Did they presume that we only wanted to cavort with one another? That we didn't want (or need) to hold one another? Why weren't there any places where men could dress up in dark suits and listen to smoky jazz and have a martini and sway against one another tenderly? Were there no more gay people like those? Like me?

But what made me think people wanted mushy music to roll around in bed to and classy joints to slow dance in when they could throw on a tank top and exhibit the rewards of their sun worship while shaking vigorously? They all came out to forget their pain and to drink and sweat their loneliness onto the dance floor, not listen to stirring compositions of romance! Imagine Heaven playing the kind of music I was listening to right now. In two minutes half the queens would be fleeing from the bar as if an AA squad had come to gather them up, the other half slashing wrists over the sinks and sobbing inconsolably in the overcrowded bathroom.

Perfect timing. No sooner had I driven back into view of the bus shed than Bill ran back across the road and motioned to me. Once in the car, he unfolded the little plastic bag and inspected the quality of his purchase like a seasoned connoisseur. He nodded to himself. "Good stuff," he remarked with pleasure. "Definitely good stuff."

"It is? How can you tell?"

He smiled at me as one would at an inquisitive child. "Well, look here," he said, fingering the mat of green in the palm of his hand. "Lots of buds, see? And that smell!" He took a whiff, closed his eyes and gave out an elated sigh. "It smells fucking great!"

He slid it under my nose. It smelt racy but I felt no desire for it.

In the silence that ensued between Bill and myself, a short period which felt surprisingly comfortable and undemanding as he busied himself with carefully rolling his joint, my mind wandered off to the last time I'd smoked pot.

It was with Zul, who now lived in San Francisco. Sadly, our friendship had become a casualty of distance. Even in Kenya he'd smoked pot regularly. Here I remembered his ritual of foraging Venice Beach for it. The last time we'd spoken – it had been at least a few years – he'd mentioned that he'd been suffering from memory lapses. This was especially startling considering that Zul had always been a virtual compendium for as long as I'd known him. He admitted how, memory lapses aside, it was the induced complacency that had screwed him up. In essence, it had done what was incumbent upon any great drug – it had suspended him from the mundane, softened the harshness of reality.

A drug, I thought, was like a lover auditioning for future visiting privileges. Having been seduced, you discovered that with some you had compatibility, chemistry. They understood you, your movement, your persona. You decided to give them the key to your door so that they could come back in and fuck you again and again.

So we all ended up with a drug of choice, some of us promiscuously, with invitations extended to more than one to enter our bodies. Any bartender in West Hollywood could vouch for my passion for at least one of them. And there I was, an extoller of physical beauty, sitting right next to another.

And now what? I wondered. Now that Bill had collected his pot and I was, without consulting him, driving back toward the Westside? Would I find myself back at the Spa? Sullen and unfulfilled, laying down in those rooms, the ceilings of which inexplicably made me think of concentration camps? Or would I prolong my suffering until I surrendered to my bed and, conjuring up images of Bill and Nelson and perhaps Richard – no, definitely not Richard anymore – spur myself to a release?

I wasn't prepared to make any monetary propositions to Bill, although time and time again, at the mention of the hustler culture of this city, I'd claimed to feel no reservations about paying for sex. Such a hypocrite I was. Or maybe just a little afraid that it would all start to feel so terribly easy, so very convenient. That I might not ever want to bother with snaking through the bars, always demanding the instant gratification of mercantile sex.

That didn't prevent me from guessing how much Bill must charge though. A hundred? Two hundred? And just what would be include? How much for everything? Or did that ever depend on upon whom he was doing business?

How much for me?

And I want, dear Bill, more than just to suck your cock and to feel your fingers probing inside my bowels and have you splatter your sperm all over my face. How much, Bill, to kiss me like you really mean it and to enter me with all your need and roam your hands over the curves of my twisting body like you were, by making love to me, recreating me from this mass of worthless putty that I've become?

Can you make up, in one night, for not only all the neglect but also the nihilistic, cheap, meaningless sex I've been drowning myself in?

Can you, Bill, do this? Can you, with all those years of molding yourself in foreign beds with others, after supplying them with what's been expected of you while your eyes surreptitiously eyed your wristwatch, make me feel all this?

I prayed that he would keep me from taking him back to wherever else he might want to go. A decision had to be made or soon we'd be where I'd found him. And I would have to return to the spa and find myself going up and down those unending stairs with their irritating little floor lights intended to create a celestial feeling, but which, in my drunkenness, would only strike me as microscopic alien heads sticking out their tongues.

"So, Bill," I said carefully. "What do you think you want to do now? Did you want me to take you back or what?"

I felt him looking at me but didn't look away from the road. I could see the cars on Santa Monica Boulevard crisscrossing as we approached it. Highland was minutes away. My hands gripped the steering wheel tightly, and I think that for those few seconds I might even have stopped breathing.

"Let's go home," he said.

I glanced at him. "Home?"

"Yeah," he said flatly. "Why don't we go home and have sex?"

I swallowed. "There is one thing, though. I...You know, I won't pay you for it. I mean, I don't think..."

"I don't want your money. Let's just go home, okay?"

I nodded. "Yeah, okay."

Thank you, dear, sweet, God. Thank you...

This drive home offered us the opportunity – one not usually welcomed in a one-night stand – to converse. Yes, we were to fuck each other, but we were also being afforded the rare opportunity to know *who* it was that we were fucking.

The alcohol had waned from my system. What had seemed like a flurry of events blurring into one another started to unfold more systematically and to bring the discomforts of clarity. It became more evident, as we neared my beach community, that we'd left all the madness of a Saturday night and its aftermath on the boulevard far behind. That what was happening between us might be more substantial than what might have been under the army of flickering lights on a dance floor or the crowded sex clubs tonight.

But somewhere in the back of my mind, despite my gratitude for having him, lurked a concern. I was going home with a hustler. Whatever could he be carrying? Could he be infected? For that matter, God only knew what I might have been carrying! Wouldn't that be the clincher – the hooker contracts HIV from his procurer?

"So, Bill, why do you do it?" I asked him. "Is that a stupid question?"

"Why do I do it? You mean, this?"

"Yeah. I mean, this can't be what you really want to do for a living, right? I mean, you know, if you had a choice."

"No, it's not a stupid question."

"If it makes you uncomfortable to talk about it, I understand."

"Nah, I'm cool with it," he said, shrugging. "There's not much to say really. I just don't like to work. Then again, this is work too," he laughed, catching himself. "I just don't like working a regular job, you know, like a day job?"

What do you know! A hustler by choice! No sad stories about the unemployment rate and trying to survive or anything like that. He simply likes being a hustler!

When he asked me what I did for a living, I instantly became an investment banker. Just like that. What was I supposed to say? New accounts rep? At least juggling with stocks and bonds sounded somewhat passionate, not to mention lucrative. I was relieved that I wasn't driving my beat-up Pontiac, the model that has a reputation for spontaneous combustion. In this city where every third car was a Mercedes or a Jaguar, driving the right car, a sumptuously expensive one, was the essential indicator of who and where one was on the economic ladder. No longer the bored accounts officer that had to cross-sell a credit card with each account opening, I became the crucial person that deemed people's fortunes. I became Jerry Kovatch, the Armani-clad hotshot in his glass office across from my desk in the main room, for whom the Dow Jones and Nasdaq were daily chants. I felt the need to impress Bill. To make him think that he stood to benefit from me despite the fact that he'd waived his fees for me.

Dubious as I continued to feel about my own physical appeal in the presence of someone that attractive, I wanted him to feel that there were other possible compensations for his act of what I, at that moment, considered charity. There was no money forthcoming on that night. But that wasn't to say that there wouldn't be any in the nights to come. It wasn't to say that I couldn't afford him. Any hustler, I reasoned to myself, could benefit from an occasional dinner at a chic restaurant or a day of shopping at the mall. That much, if need be, I could do and comfortably live with myself for doing.

My exaggerated career impressed him. Bill felt the need to tell me about some of his own achievements, fractional but attempted endeavors nevertheless. "I went to college for restaurant management," he said. "I was real good at it too. Man, I can cook you almost anything."

I smiled to myself. Now there was a vision worth coming home to: Bill slaving over the stove, bare-chested with a ladle in hand, redolent hollandaise sauce dripping from it, and a rock-hard erection rearing through his boxers, maybe even catching some of the falling droplets for me to lap off. Who wouldn't be willing to pay to have that every night?

"The only thing I couldn't do was that damn ice-sculpting shit, you know?"

"Ice sculpting?"

"Yeah, you know, sculpting herons and fishes and all those things for displays on the food table? Presentation stuff?"

"Oh, yeah," I said.

"I couldn't do that shit to save my life. So, anyway, I dropped out."

"You dropped out because you couldn't sculpt?" I asked, doubtful. "And those were the only two career choices?" *Dad, I'm either going to be a chef at the Peninsula or a hooker on Santa Monica Boulevard when I grow up!*

"I just lost interest after a while. And no, those weren't my only two choices. I told you, this is what I enjoy doing. Not everyone is cut out to be some banker. You can't understand that, can you?"

"On the contrary," I said. "I admire very much that you do this out of choice. It must take the pressure off your clients who think you're with them just for the money. In order to do any job well, the enthusiasm counts more than the desperation. So, you must be very good at it."

"Haven't had any complaints so far."

"Only repeat clients, huh?"

I felt his eyes assessing me. Calculating the things he would do to me when we got home. I had half a mind to pull over and let him fuck me right there and then.

"Anyway, I won't be doing this shit for too long."

"Careful," I said. "Your love for the profession is sounding shaky."

"I met this guy a couple of months ago. Older guy. Wealthy guy. He's got a pad in Malibu. He wants me to move in with him, and he says he'll take care of everything and I won't have to worry about a thing, you know?"

"You mean, like a sugar daddy?"

"I can even take my dog with me. Oh, man, I can just work out all day and surf and live the good life, you know?" And then he punctuated his dreams with, "That is what everyone wants in the end, isn't it? I'm just taking a short cut."

A short cut, I thought grunting inaudibly under my breath.

It amazed me that even as a prostitute, Bill possessed such naiveté, such a vision of fulfillment in his future. I would have thought that the acrid, fatalistic view on life's imperfect constitution, its mandatory drills of suffering to even qualify for some happiness, would have come from him and not me. He told me that he hoped someday to have his own business. A little restaurant where they served healthy portions of culinary delights instead of the scrimping portions that most people expect fine cuisine to be served in. The man in Malibu was going to help him attain this dream. He asked me about my aspirations.

"I'd like to write a book," I said.

"Aha!" he said. "Now I get it with all these questions!"

I smiled at him. "A book is too much work to base over someone you've known five minutes and will probably never see again." I didn't know why I said that. Maybe I was already seeking some kind of reassurance.

"Good decision. They won't buy it anyway," he said, smirking. Then he quickly added, "The story, I mean. America wants *Pretty Woman.* Not – *Here Comes the Happy Hooker.* They're not ready for the real shit, man."

"The real shit? What's the difference? You're just like Julia Roberts being whisked off to Malibu instead of the Beverly Hills Hotel."

"Hello? *She* was rescued by Richard Gere *and* she fell in love with him," he said. "I'm *not* in love and he's *not* Richard Gere by a lo-o-ng shot! Only thing I love is my dog."

"Your dog."

"Yup. Rascal."

"Rascal? That's his name?" I laughed.

"Yup! He's a rascal like me. Mean old husky. You got one?"

"Me? A dog? No," I said, thinking, the closest I'd come to pets were the poor fish I'd systematically killed one by one.

"What, you don't like dogs?"

"Not particularly," I said, keeping my eyes on the road. "But God knows, I've slept with plenty of them."

CHAPTER 45

NAKED

I made gimlets. Having sobered up considerably, I felt the need to be alleviated by the relaxing cloud of intoxication again. We had depleted the bottle of Bacardi before entering into our night, so I settled for that tangy concoction of English gin and lime cordial, which so reminded me of my partying days in Kenya with my friend Akil. I lowered myself onto the floor with drinks in hand and handed Bill his. He smiled appreciatively. We leaned our backs against the sofa. I thought instantly of my mother as the back of my head pressed into its cushion and my eyes toured the dimpled texture of the ceiling. How I missed her. Months had passed. I often came home after nights of frolicking with the guys and, in bed, pretended that she was asleep on this sofa, a silent seraphim, watching over me. I was glad that she wasn't there on that night though, reminded of the reason she would relent and move here. I knew that the task of slowly disassociating from her had involuntarily begun again, except this time, I wouldn't distance myself completely. Only enough to staunch my loneliness for her.

I closed my eyes for a moment and that's when the room began to spin slightly. I wasn't as sober as I'd thought. I reconsidered the need for the drink in my hand but then I took one look at him and decided, yes, I could definitely use it.

"Do you mind if we listened to something with words in it?" Bill asked. We'd been listening to music scores, and he wasn't in-synch with my mood. "I'm just feeling kind of sleepy, you know? I need something that will wake me up."

"What would you like, dance music?" I asked, just a touch irritated but eager to please.

"No, not necessarily dance music, it can be something mellow."

I crawled over to the stereo languidly. "How's Sade?"

"Sade's great," he said, thumbing at me. "Perfect."

Sitting next to one other, neither one of us rushed into what I breathlessly awaited. Sade began her requiem of unrequited love in her velvety vocals. I again noticed the tattoo on his arm and, without asking, touched it gently with my finger. It appeared to be a derivative of a swastika; a cross with some dots around it. I could tell that it had been done amateurishly with a sharp piece of glass or a knife or something. There was nothing artistic about it. In fact, it was almost crude in appearance. He looked over his shoulder as my finger traced its matrix. Excited at the feel of his skin, I felt within me an urge to bite. To eat off the bulk of his shoulder.

"What is it?" I asked him.

He looked up into my eyes for a moment and then, falling back to it, said flatly, "It symbolizes my hatred for black people."

Speechless. I didn't know how to respond. My finger slowly slipped off his arm and fluttered on my lap awkwardly. I continued to look at him inquisitively. He explained that he'd belonged to a gang that shared this feeling.

I wanted to say something stupid like, *But you don't look like that type*, or, *But, you can't possibly be, you're colored yourself! And, you're here with me!*

Black people, I thought as my finger rose to touch his shoulder again, had it tough from every angle. From Caucasians, Asians, to Latinos. I couldn't deny though that the racism I felt, some of which had been reduced through my assimilative efforts in America, and even oddly through my relationship with Nelson, paled in contrast to the conviction grazed in the golden flesh of his brawny arm.

"Who are these people?" I asked.

"What do you mean?"

"I mean who are they, the members of this group? Are there whites in this group too?"

"Mostly people like me," he said. "You know, biracial people, part Mexican, and part American-Indian."

I grunted, shaking my head. This sounded even more fantastic. A hooded KKK member on an alabaster horse galloped through my mind. I tried to picture a Latino like Bill under the disguise, an image both repulsive and confounding.

"I can't believe that," I said. "I mean, I never knew there was anything between, you know, your kind and...blacks. I mean, anything *this* intense."

"There's more anger when the den's tiny and there are too many mice crawling around in there, you know what I mean? These black monkeys, man, they're always crying about all the damn injustice that's been done to them and all that tiring shit. What about *us?!* *We're* the ones that have been cheated and deprived. I mean, this," he said, jabbing vehemently on the floor, "this was *our* land long before any of *them* moved in."

His comment jolted me. The "go back to where you came from" remark always infuriated me. And I felt ashamed because the same remark coming from Bill, from someone I was sexually attracted to, didn't compromise my desire for him. "But *they're* not the ones depriving you of anything! They're fighting for the same things you are!"

"Well, we're sick of listening to their sorry-ass problems. They have more than we'll ever get from this country. What are they crying about? It's time they stopped using that dragged-over-from-Africa excuse and just got on with their lives, you know? Or they can just go back to fucking Africa. My people, shit, we went through just as much and we're still waiting for some justice."

I let it rest there, and again the image of the flag went through my mind. Bill was one of those little specks as well. A blazing, scalding, red one. For him, and others like him, America would always be the stolen land, and the flag a reminder of their oppression. I was convinced that there was more lurking in Bill's life that had reared this hatred in him, something I probably wouldn't discover in a single night. Unwilling to compromise my purpose in bringing him there that night, I refrained from making any sensible mediation on behalf of the recipients of his abhorrence. There would be nothing gained. I, of all people, knew that each of us carried within us, our own brand of daggers. Ones that were sheathed in smiles, rarely revealed by admittance, and with which we'd find an opportuned stab every now and then.

Bill's prejudice, I justified, even in all it's repugnance, revealed an honesty that deserved both admiration and pity. On a night when our meeting had been conceived by a flux of chance and timing, he became an open book, and I his determined, unflinching reader. Instead of feeling put off by him, I told myself that by revealing this offensiveness in his personality, Bill had allowed a sincerity that most couldn't reach until the masks had been pulled off. He was unashamed for both his choice in being a prostitute and for being racist. He had, in a complex way, permitted my understanding of him to be as naked and unapologetic as the love we would make; paved the way by revealing what he truly felt, for me to touch any tenderness that might have, that surely, lay within.

I just wanted to fuck him. And thinking that way made everything so much easier.

When he asked me if it was alright for him to smoke his joint, I collected an old copy of the *L.A. Weekly* for him to shake the ashes onto. I noticed that he'd barely sipped his drink and with a few brisk gulps, I had already drained mine. I replenished mine, tossed the empty bottle of gin and settled beside him again. I began to feel ashamed.

Bill had inadvertently reduced me. For professing to be something I wasn't. For trying so hard to impress him when all he had been was himself. For trying to sell myself as some hotshot investment banker that probably had a BMW or Jaguar in the garage instead of the firetrap in the carport. In that aspect, I suppose, we were both whores, no?

I sipped my drink, learning with some ambivalence that in the dark porches of my soul, instead of being repulsed by someone like him, I was beginning to find a curious and illegitimate salvation.

Having smoked his joint, Bill returned to his drink. Although his face twisted at its taste, he said nothing and emptied his glass. We'd been sitting there for close to an hour now, our backs leaning against the sofa and our minds embraced by an unexpected comfort. I was to discover that Bill had only just begun to reveal himself.

Without much probing on my part, he began to tell me about his childhood. By now, he had convinced himself that he was to be the subject of my great American novel. Bill told me of an abusive father who just couldn't get it through his head that it was his wife he should have been fucking, not his five-year-old son; the sanguinary depths of domestic violence that composed the fabric, it seemed, of all those who have nose-dived into emotional dysfunction. There were the years he spent in juvenile prison, which educated him further in hate and survival. Bill revealed to me in sparse, difficult and incisive strokes of the unequivocal horrors that made him who he was today. Bill the molested son. Bill the gangbanger. Bill the hustler.

By the time he'd finished telling me what I'd only gently encouraged, I wanted to roll another joint myself and lodge it between his lips. Such confiding from Bill appeared both rare and painful: to aerate passages that seemed barricaded forever; to shed, albeit momentarily, the tough-guy image that street-smart dwellers required almost by genetic inherency.

On that night, I watched Bill struggle through his demons, knowing even as it transpired, that this was indeed an exceptional and cathartic happening. It had taken him considerable effort to articulate his feelings. Between the pained expression on his face and the hint of tremor in his voice, there had been the occasional winces and the hesitation before the words could leave him.

Why he had chosen me to lay himself bare to, I would never truly know. Of all the men Bill must have spent only one night with, I found it difficult to imagine that any of them might have served as his confidante. Perhaps it was because he wasn't on the clock. Since he wasn't performing, he could be himself. I wanted to think that perhaps he was feeling the kind of indescribable attachment that I was feeling.

Then, as a caution to what I considered our ground-breaking connection, he said, "I don't want you to get all attached to me, okay?"

I paused and then turned to him. "Excuse me?"

"I don't want you to start getting all emotional about me, you know what I mean?"

"Where did that come from?" I said.

He raised his hands. "Just…letting you know, man."

"Hey, I didn't ask to hear your confessions, okay?"

"All I'm saying is that, you know, I don't want you feeling all involved…"

"Well, you should've thought about that before you started telling me all this! And what the hell makes you think I need such a warning, anyway?" I asked, trying my best to sound calm, but not managing.

He shrugged. "It's happened before."

"Oh, so you've done this before! This is part of some routine, then!"

He closed his eyes and shook his head regretfully. "Okay, let's just forget about it, okay?"

"How can you be *so damn* condescending!"

"Hey, Ali, I said forget about it, alright? I just feel, you know, like we've crossed a certain line here, okay, and I don't want you to...you know, fall in love with me or something like that because I'm not going to be around."

I grunted. "Fall in love with you? Well, *hunh*, thanks for the warning. It'll keep me from asking you to move in tomorrow."

With that I turned away from him. Why couldn't I just laugh at him? Why couldn't I just make him feel stupid for saying something like that? Reacting this way only confirmed his suspicions. *Well, fuck you, Bill!* I felt him looking at me. But instead of frustration, I could sense the hint of a smile lingering on his face. *He's amused*, I thought to myself, my irritation vexing. *He's fucking amused that I'm so pissed at him!*

I started to finish my drink, my eyes transfixed on the dead television set. The music had stopped playing, and the silence was heavy with anticipation. *The incredible nerve!* I screamed in my mind. Yes, it was true I was already feeling involved. That the thought of this being the only night we will share together, long before we'd even touched each other, was already unbearable. Still, how dare he!

That was when, in the elongated seconds that my irritation pulsed in my throat, his arm coasted around me on the sofa and he leaned over to very slowly run his warm tongue under the nook of my ear lobe. I felt the breath escape from me in an unguarded shudder. My head arched slowly back and up against his face, my glass balancing delicately in my hands. His mouth foraged farther into the slope of my neck, into intimate valleys long forgotten and neglected, his moist tongue gliding upon every gaping pore of my thirsty skin, bringing to them a long awaited recompense. These were the tender, embittered parts of my body that went untouched at the Vortex. Here were the secret, silent erogenous zones privy only to those who knew to look deeper.

I wondered as Bill, breaking into a tension-releasing guffaw, carried me with mock gallantness into the bedroom, which of us felt more vulnerable?

Him for having unmasked himself? Or me, for being the one-time recipient of what would remain unparalleled? For knowing more than I should about a one-night stand only to dismiss it all the morning after?

We bathed in the amber glow cast by candles masted on wrought-iron candelabras. In shadows and light our bodies entwined further until I felt disembodied – my limbs were no longer mine, my lips were now his. There were not two bodies rising and dipping within sheets, but one strangely formed, multilimbed creature jousting away in space, performing an ancient dance, a primitive ritual to indemnify itself from everything that had pained it in the past. We vacillated from astounding tenderness to fervor, extracting from one other emotional nuances that even the most intimate of lovers sometimes forbear. I drifted in and out of consciousness. Every once in a while the music playing in the living room would waft into my awareness, and then again I would be carried away into a wave of sensation that would remove me from everything that didn't emanate directly from Bill. He understood, like the elixirs veining through me, the ebb and flow of my body, the properties of my dance. How to lift me over him when I began to arch backward and my head sunk into the pillows. When to gently brush the hair away from my face and look into eyes to imprint his image in them before kissing me. For the irretrievable hours we shared that night, Bill made me feel completely understood beyond the agency of words, in spite of the fact that the path to being understood had always been prescribed through ages of conversing. But then Richard and I had spoken too much. Probed much too deep. And neither one of us had ever been able to find or provide such fulfillment for one other.

Perhaps, I was to think later, it was part of Bill's expertise to make me feel this way. His presumptuous warning against falling in love with him didn't come out of nowhere. Perhaps his impassioned and well-synchronized performance was meant to make me feel like he had this rare, unspoken insight into me. Perhaps he had known, from the moment that I had stood breathlessly in front of him on that street, what I'd needed and how to provide it.

After all, the man made love for a living.

CHAPTER 46

ARTIFICIAL MOONLIGHT

I leaned sideways against the wall of my bedroom, looking out my window onto deserted streets, the homes that fostered their resting dwellers and, above them, the sky that would soon be filled with predawn light.   I thought about *parorie*, the early morning time of prayer at the mosque; the taste of hot Kenyan coffee steeped in cream, its aroma in my nose; the warmth of the cup in my hands.   I thought of that mosque in Mombasa, so far away, where I'd petitioned for months by waking at four every morning and praying until dawn so God would grant me passage to Los Angeles. I thought of Mummy, who continued that devotion for the safekeeping of that dream.

The streetlight's glow filtered through the iron grill on my window, bore through the slats of vertical blinds, bathing my naked body. They gave the illusion of being sent from a source far more heavenly than the lampposts standing guard.   In my ears, I heard the *muezzin's* call to prayer from atop a distant minaret, the docking toot of ships approaching the island's harbor, and dawn's silence embracing them: the triumvirate of coming dawn. I was back in Mombasa again and I felt a profound peace in my heart. I imagined, suspending all reality, that in these hours, everybody else in the world was either asleep or giving thanks to God.

It had been a long time since I'd had someone in my bed. Just the two of us. Without Adrian to share him. It had been a long time since I'd had anyone, in fact, who hadn't been with Adrian sooner or later, if not at the same time. That's when I remembered John. He had been one of the first men Adrian and I had brought home together. Even as friends, we'd behaved more like lovers that had been together a long time and made a pact to share a third person every now and then just to keep the relationship invigorated. Both John and Bill had tattoos. Maybe that's why, from the countless others we'd lured back, he was the one that came to mind. John with the N/A carved on his left shoulder. John, who'd been in the military and had been reminded of Paris because of the incense I'd burnt and who'd fucked me vengefully and who I'd refused to look at when he was leaving. How would things have turned out if I hadn't acted like such a bitch that morning? If I'd turned around from laying on my stomach and acknowledged him as he'd prepared to leave and maybe even smiled at him for fucking me? Would he really have recoiled at catching a good look at me in daylight? Maybe we'd have seen each other again. How would it have turned out, for that matter, with any of those other innumerable men that had spent themselves in this room, on this bed, had I behaved and, ultimately, felt differently?

I heard the rustling of sheets, a faint creaking of springs, and then Bill was standing behind me. Together we looked out, the light framing our naked bodies like a benediction from an approbating God. I felt his arms encircle me from around my waist, his skin moving against my skin, and then he pulled me back against him, the hard ridges of his body kissing against my back.

"Artificial moonlight," I said.

He rested his chin on my shoulder, his facing sharing in its soft glow with mine. "Much more reliable. Now I know your secret."

I moaned softly and touched his cheek. "Why'd you have to go and do that? Now I'm afraid I'm going to have to kill you."

"You can do with me as you wish. You've mesmerized me."

Mesmerized you? You, who warned me that I would be left devastated? I turned my face to the side and kissed his eye.

"It was something else, wasn't it? I wish we could just stay here. Just like this."

Bill said nothing. He just held on to me and together we looked toward the light.

"When I'm finally with someone," I said. "This is exactly how I want to be made to feel. *This* is how I want it to be."

Still he remained muted. His silence synonymous with the gnawing fear of never finding such companionship, that brand of lasting intimacy. It was as if there was nothing he *could* say. I preferred to think that it wasn't for lack of what he might have been feeling. That perhaps he too felt overwhelmed and was at a loss for words.

And then again I thought, *He did warn you, didn't he? He knew you'd feel this way after he was done with you.* I recalled his conceited admonishment and began to negotiate in his silence that others must have been made to feel this same way too. But surely there was something different here? How to explain this difference? It was beyond words yet distinct in feeling. A fusing of vagrant, kindred spirits. The melting of two solitudes. The deliverance from much loneliness.

Maybe he was just being realistic and it was better that he didn't endorse my fantasies. Could such rewards, after all, be expected of a single night? Could such feelings last a month down the road? And then his arms tightened around me just a bit more and I laid my head back on his shoulder to welcome his lips against my neck. *That* registered as ample reciprocation. As confirmation of a shared fantasy.

I turned around, away from the light and faced him, now drenched in it. The shadows of tree leaves and limbs traced themselves across the chalk-white walls of my room, forming a decorative filigree behind him. His hands clasped my hips, his thumbs stroking my ileac crest. Again I was confounded by his beauty, wished for

the hundredth time that I could take his picture. I
wondered, *What is this man doing here with me? How can I,
what must I do, to keep him here?* And deeper still, I heard
myself respond with some melancholy, *Nothing, Ali.
There's nothing you can do.* I held his face in my hands,
knowing with some certainty that I wouldn't touch or see
him again. His eyes fell from mine, registering my pain,
feeling perhaps, some of his own. Now it was he who
was hiding from my gaze.

I kissed his forehead.

And then his eyes.

His nose.

And then his lips.

The way Mummy had each time she'd put me into
bed at night.

With some uneasiness, I touched the mark of
hatred on his shoulder, and then slowly bent down to kiss
it. Part of me balked at myself for doing this. The other
part reminded me that it was not because I endorsed his
creed that I had revered his mark, but because I
acknowledged the experiences that might have driven him
to it. I had found the mark on his body, the one Mummy
had taught me to look for. And then, with a desperation
unbeknownst to either one of us, we made love all over
again.

CHAPTER 47

KISS AND TELL

The phone rang a third time, and the answering machine attended to an enraged Kitty. "Hey, where you goin' my car, huh? Where you? You late already! We here waitin' for already hour now! You better on your way!"

It was past seven in the morning, and the group was calling us probably from some phone booth outside the Spa. I pictured Kitty's pudgy face turned beet-red as he broke into a nervous sweat and stressed into the phone. I kissed Bill.

"We have to go," I said. "They're going to kill me!"

Reluctantly, I sat up at the edge of the bed. With my back facing him, I tried to regain some control over myself and stared absently at the pile of crumpled clothing lying at my feet. The struggle of having to tear myself away from him was burdensome and demanded superior effort. Slowly, I started to select my articles from his.

Bill pressed up against my back and nuzzled at me disobediently. "Let them wait. Come back here to me."

Although his touch extended no further than my neck, I felt a tingling sensation at the base of my spine. My groin ached and, with the kind of desperation a sleeper cancels morning tasks to capture more sleep, I considered damning the whole world in order to burn into him again. In the last couple of hours, Bill, to my amazement had come a few times. I had not. It wasn't sensible not to come, when, after such a long time of searching, I had found someone like him to bring home. Or, on those nights without a Bill, before leaving a sex club to go home. Both instances of which I was now guilty.

I handed him his tank top, resisting looking at him. "Another minute with you and I'll have alienated everyone I talk to."

For just a moment he rested his head against my back. I thought I felt his need in the pressure he applied against me, in the silence of just those few seconds, as his hair, eyes, lips mashed against my spine. Then he grunted softly at his thought, pulled away and mercifully stopped persisting. I pried myself off the bed and gathered the rest of our clothing from the floor. Taking a shower was out of the question so we both dressed up, still filmed with a lingering scent of each other. Besides, I didn't want to wash him off my body just yet. I felt that I wanted to carry the redolence of our sex like the remaining morsels of a meal, only to be scraped out for satiating later on.

Dressed, I went around the bed and picked up the soiled condoms that lay on the carpet. As I walked over to the wastebasket in his corner of the room, I saw him zipping up with a resplendent grin on his face. His macho pride excited me immensely. Because he'd relentlessly gone through those condoms, he carried the expression of someone who'd delivered what he'd promised. *I'm going to fuck you silly*, he'd said the second time he'd entered into me and, accidentally knocking his head onto mine as he moved on top of me, broken into childlike laughter. And he'd done just that. Fucked me silly. Like some heaven-sent adjuster for past deprivation.

I wiped the sliminess from the condoms on the side of my jeans, and he asked if I'd ever been tested. Now this was different. Shouldn't I have been asking him that question? I shrugged and replied that of course I had. I asked him the same. He nodded.

"Why do I feel like we're having this conversation in reverse?" I said, laughing at the irony. "First the sex and *then* the inquiries."

"What difference does it make, really? These days you can't trust what someone says, anyhow. Just because someone claims to be negative don't mean he isn't shitting you. You shouldn't take their word for it."

"So, why bother to ask?"

"Because I know you'll tell the truth."

I swallowed.

"Most people can't be trusted," he said, shrugging. "Rest of the time I just presume everyone is. That's the safest thing to do."

"Sounds so...I don't know, clinical."

"That's sex in the nineties for you, man."

"When did you last get tested? How long ago?"

"Oh, a couple of months ago. They arrested me. Whenever they do that, they have to get you tested."

"Arrested you?"

"Yeah, motherfucking cops, man," he said, scowling while clipping his beeper to his jeans. "They just love busting our balls, you know? Like they have nothing better to do in a city like this but give us shit."

"Well, I suppose they could give out more speeding tickets."

For the past couple of hours, when we'd talked in between lovemaking sessions, Bill's language had been refined. Now, the "man" and curse words crept back in as he assumed his other role. I didn't tell him how his comments basically revealed he worked the streets more frequently than he'd indicated. "God, what's that like? Getting arrested?"

"Oh, no big deal. Sometimes it's just an overnight stay. Other times it's..." his voice trailed off. "But when they do that, they get you tested because of *why* they arrested you. They know what shit you've been up to. Hey, can I use your phone?"

Bill walked out into the living room and I remained, absorbing his experience. I began to doubt his entire story about the modeling agency and Andy Jacobs.

There was no doubt in my mind that the lunatic had been somewhat of a pimp for him and that they had even slept together. But I began to think of the whole modeling agency element as a fabricated attempt to legitimize his prostitution. If he'd slipped in his story, he didn't seem bothered or aware of it.

Oh, well, I thought. He did say he was negative, and I'm still here in my apartment with all of my things intact. And, I did have a fucking great time. So, why not lighten up and stop dredging myself through unnecessary paranoia? Mustn't give myself so much drama, drama, all the time!

My eyes spotted another condom, possibly the last one we'd used, by the foot of the bed. I walked over to it, wondering who he was calling. Was it the psycho from last night? Returning a page from a customer? I knew he wasn't calling to tell mother he'd be home soon. I tried to eavesdrop as I fell to my knees, wanting to pick up the condom with some degree of respect and curiosity, like an artifact, but his voice seemed deliberately low and I could only hear mumbling. Carefully, I pinched the condom up between my fingers and realized that it still contained some of his sperm. As I held it up to take a good look at that quintessential part of him that had been denied a merger into me, it collected in the reservoir at its tip. And then, as my fingers pressed upon its pregnant belly, droplets of it, heavy and glutinous, trickled into the palm of my hand.

I looked at them, confused.

I began to inspect the condom closely, pressing the tip of glassy sheath's tip that spurted little beads of his sperm onto my fingers, and felt a wrenching in the pit of my stomach. Horror shrouded my face and I gasped, focusing on the source of the tributaries now pooling into my palm.

There was, at the tip of its emaciated latex barrel, an invisible and traitorous tear.   And the drops were trickling away mutinously, right in front of my eyes.

After picking up a disgruntled pack of friends from the Spa, more than an hour late, Bill asked to be dropped off at a rather shady motel between Sunset and Hollywood Boulevards. I wondered who he might be meeting there but didn't ask. Kitty quickly took control of his car, throwing nettled glances at me. "We thin' you have car acciden! We all worry!"

Crammed in the backseat of the car, I held Bill, arms around his waist, head resting on his back; I thought about how I might not see him again and about the condom. I felt so pathetic. How could I need him, or anybody else for that matter, so much after only one night of something only suspectfully mutual? I wondered what such rapid overindulgence for someone I'd only just met made me. Why hadn't past hurts made me more resilient? More independent? How could it still be so easy for me to latch onto someone after everything I'd been through? Still so vacuously needy, had I learnt nothing of the purely fictional, romanticized nature of my obsession?

I couldn't deny though, that just holding on to the girth of his torso, laying my head on the musculature of his back, like a strong tree trunk, made me feel so damned good. But it could have been anyone. That it came down to the human body's need to be touched, to touch, to be reminded; because it was a living organism, every pore of it breathing and alive.

As the guys pattered on about the various men they'd sighted at the spa, those whom they had been unable to attain, Bill and I remained silent. He smoked a cigarette, comfortable in my embrace, neither of us contributing to the bathhouse confessions. We pulled over by the motel, and before he jumped out of the car he kissed me, and, pulling a little card out of his pocket, handed me his phone number. "Give me a call," he said. "This is the number at the agency."

When did he write this down? Did he always keep one ready, just in case? I kissed him again, appreciative, and then freed him to the swamps of the city. We drove away, feverish with sleep deprivation, and I fought the urge to run back to him or turn to see him diminishing with distance. That's when *they* vented at me again for keeping them waiting so long. They fussed about it for a few minutes, especially Kitty, who had been terrified that his new car had been in the hands of one who he considered a reckless, uninsured driver. "I can't believe you do this! Din' you not hear the phones ringing? Is not right. I call you how many time? Three time! Is completely not right! Thisa' so *very, very* inconsiderate!" Adrian, who would normally have defended me, sat silent, and I knew he was annoyed.

But I didn't care. As a child I'd learnt to win my battles by throwing myself on the ground and wailing until granted my demands. As an adult I'd become an expert at belittling any crisis that had worked out to my advantage. I scoffed at them for overreacting, knowing all along that I'd have been inconsolably furious in their situation.

As we drove down Fairfax, I sank into the back seat next to Frankie, who obsessed over some nine-inched stud who had inveigled him in the steam room. This man had apparently confided to having been straight – whatever that constituted in light of him being there – and to have a wife and two kids at home. Naturally this excited Frankie. Tremendously. It automatically increased his worth as some kind of a prized trophy. For being the man who, after fucking Frankie with the zeal of a prisoner during conjugal visits, returned to his cell to put the same cock back into his wife. Frankie had scribbled his phone number on the establishment's little business card, the other side of which allowed one person to rate the person on a star system, and this man had apologized for being unable to give his number out but promised that he would call Frankie for more of the unforgettable sex they'd had.

"Oooh!" Frankie cried. "He looked completely like Clooney! What a fucking stud!"

We all knew Frankie was prone to exaggeration, that he indulged himself lavishly in aggrandizing his encounters. The rude shock of discovering what a person truly looked like in the light of the lobby had never happened to Frankie. Apparently everyone had been on Frankie's hot little trail, including Clooney. So we all listened with mock excitement. (Later someone would attest to how drunk little Frankie, when walking in front of others, had taken to purposely dropping his towel to reveal himself and pretended that it had slipped off him; that he'd also groped everyone in sight, incapable of exercising such discriminating taste). Candid encounters filled the car. A dialogue about penile size, stamina and the assortment of men. Everyone, it seemed, bragged about conquests. And I thought, fags that we were, we still thought with testosterone-choked brains of straight men. Perhaps that's why sex for us, as it was for so many heterosexual men, was promiscuous and competitive. Restricted from freely expressing ourselves in public, having to seek out zones where we could get away with acting queer, inevitably resulted in a kind of blind desperation to do as much as possible when permitted.

The whole time, my fingers rubbed the coarse piece of someone's business card, on which Bill had scribbled his number. I looked out the window along Santa Monica Boulevard, at recumbent forms of sleeping bums, elderly Polish couples on the way to a market, depleted and washed-out nocturnes slavered from a rave, and either the remnants or early morning workers of the hustler trade. I thought about when it would be okay to call Bill. I could barely wait to get home so I could masturbate to his memory. I thought again of the leaking condom in the wake of our lovemaking. Fuck! Something always had to fuck up, didn't it?

Frankie nudged me, pulling me out of my reverie. He suggested I make it up to them for keeping them waiting by buying breakfast. I rolled my eyes. "Yeah, keep dreaming. I'm surprised you have any appetite left after all the dick you ate in there."

"Oh!" Frankie shrieked, clutching his breast. "Listen to Miss Virgin Mary, here! I'm not the one who took off with some hustler, you know!"

"Honey, only one of us didn't pay to get any tonight, and it certainly wasn't you."

"So, did you tell him it was your first time?" Adrian teased.

"Yeah," I said, sensing a tinge of bitterness. Sorry to rob you off your one meaningful contribution to the world of good fucking. "But then I gave him instructions on every position in the Kama Sutra and my story fell apart."

"Well, I hope you were careful, at least," Frankie said, his trademark paranoia kicking in. "I still can't believe you'd take such an incredible risk and take someone like him home with you! I mean, you don't even know this person! What if he'd, you know, done something, Ali? You did use a condom, right? Please tell me you didn't let him do it without a condom!"

"Several, as a matter of fact. Until we ran out and he wrapped his dick in Saran Wrap instead."

"Was he big?"

"Do you see me walking?"

"Was he cut?"

"Just as nature created it."

Frankie let out an ecstatic hoot, something he'd picked up from a black woman who worked with him.

"I'm glad you were careful, Ali, because as studly as he was, we did pick him up from the boulevard."

Everyone started to exchange reassurances on having had safe sex. Consolations of safety after a night of sexual decadence; sex, nineties-style. I tried not to say anything more about my night.

"You're acting strange," Adrian remarked from the front seat. "Is everything alright? Did you have a good time or what?"

"You din' pay him, do you?" Kitty asked, glancing at me from the rear view mirror. "I hope you don' paid the boy!"

"Of course not! He didn't want any money."

"He din' aks you?"

"No."

"Well, that was one generous worker," Frankie said. "Will you be seeing him again? I wish you'd stop acting like your life is over, though. Jesus, you just got laid, what are you mourning for? Would you snap out of it?"

"I'm fine, okay? I'm just a little tired."

"No, you're acting romantically delusional again. That's what you are," Frankie pronounced. "A romance junkie! Everything turns into a soap opera with you. Why can't you just accept it for what it was?"

"You had a good time and you'll probably see him again, although personally, I don't think that's such a great idea, but you know, if you want to, you can," said Adrian.

Kitty began laughing and excitedly bobbed up and down in his seat. "Yeah, yeah, thas' it! Drama queen! Drama queen!"

They were right, I was a romance junkie. A drama queen. I'd always been that way. Every event colored and spiced with tragedy and romanticism. Vetoing orgasm, creating impalpable connections with men, pursuing that which appeared unobtainable. I orchestrated, even welcomed, only situations and people that contributed to this opera.

Perking up in an effort to avoid telling them about the condom, I inquired about the CPA Kitty had encountered in the video room.   But in my mind, as everyone honed in to gorge on more details about the specifications and application of an accountant's cock, I could think only about the sperm that had dribbled onto my hand. In my mind's eye, I could see that condom within me, flawed, with a fishlike mouth, emitting, as it might have, Bill's sperm into me. I envisioned droplets of blood hitting a pool of water and dispersing in whorls, unsure of its significance.   Maybe contamination. Or maybe just the familiar swelling of a hemorrhoid. Sinister images performed a freakish gavotte in my head. The time Nelson had fucked me with perfumed body lotion. Men who I'd yanked out from inside me when realizing they'd forgone protection. Times when I'd been forced to use every ounce of strength to push them off me. Kicking my legs around. Close to screaming out. None of them had been even the least bit unattractive.   Or appeared to have had any self-esteem issues that could have propelled them into such irresponsibility. Men who had not only epitomized physical beauty with their arduously worked-out bodies, but who also gave the impression that no destruction could come upon their galvanizing looks even through their own intention. Now, having slept with Bill, who I felt confident had lied about his sexual history and probably disseminated into me, I thought about all the times that I had put myself at risk. I felt sick to my stomach.

I unlocked the door to my apartment, relieved to be alone, and reminded myself that I was over-reacting again as was characteristic of me. I was just being a dramatic Indian.   Every unsafe encounter didn't necessarily translate into HIV-positive status. Surely it was more difficult to contract AIDS. All the information I'd crammed during *Saath* relayed through my mind.

Undressing, my eyes on the rumpled bed marked with patches of dampness, I consoled myself that no one I knew had been 100 percent safe, regardless of their fervent allegiance to proper procedure. Not even Salman, who made it a point to vocalize his allegiance to safe sex and repeatedly swore by mint-flavored condoms. There had been times when, like a reprimanded slave, Salman had subjugated himself to the soiled floor, unaware of my presence as I awaited my own deliverance in the same dark and musty room at the Vortex. Not once had I seen him pause to plant the mint condom before plunging into the task of obediently lapping the man up. And at the end of the night, on our way out through the lobby of the Vortex, packed with vending machines and the ritualistic cooler of mouthwash, I even saw him absentmindedly leave the condoms behind on a rack of magazines, like tokens to be gleaned by fellow agents in espionage.

It would be alright. I'd pray. I would shut it all out of my mind and concentrate only on the romance I'd helped create in the night. I wouldn't recognize this as a sign to either alter lifestyles or coerce me into getting tested. One of these days, I smirked, climbing into bed, they will just come up with that damn vaccine. And everyone who'd been too terrified would bandwagon to the clinic and turn over their arms for a quick jab. An antidote to the sickness suspected to be incubating within them, which no one dared confirm. Then all this shit would be just like the flu or malaria or something. An inconvenient trip to the clinic.

I pulled the sheet around my legs and reached out for myself with a hand slathered in lubricant. My eyes closed, my mouth parted, I thought about Bill and inhaled the smell in the bed. I began to rub myself more vigorously. His arms came around me, his cock up inside me, his lips gashing against mine. I heard his voice in my ears. *I'm going to fuck you silly,* he said. *I'm going to fuck you silly...*

Among the three groups of people after the advent of AIDS – those who abstained, those who had never stopped fucking (and maybe only mildly altered their behavior), and those who floated between encounters – we belonged to the latter. Assuaging such sexual indulgences with untimely, obligatory discussions felt as incumbent as confessions to a priest. Some time the next day, having returned to the mundane, perhaps when driving from work on the freeway, shrapnel of guilt would poke me, as it did everyone. Some of us would make quixotic promises of avoiding sex clubs, reverting to stashes of pornography for satisfaction. Not me. I'd be the one to allay them over the phone, to reassure them that provided they had practiced safe sex, they had nothing to worry about. Feeling guilty about enjoying sex was unnatural, a result of being conditioned that way in the nineties. I'd tell them that under these circumstances, what we were feeling was normal. A denouement for not consistently indulging in sex.

What I wouldn't tell them was that a condom could tear. About my condom. I'd keep this to myself. For the first time, after years of having sex with strangers in stench-ridden cubicles and the romantically prepared atmosphere of my room, the nudging fear of my HIV status kicked like an ill-conceived pregnancy. It wouldn't help to share this with them. They'd all insist I get tested.

CHAPTER 48

JUST LEAVE

Richard stops by unexpectedly. He'd been rollerblading in Venice Beach, and was laden, as usual, with tales of lustful glances exchanged on the boardwalk. How, as always seemed to be the case, believably and irritatingly so, they all wanted him. He told me excitedly of unbelievable chemistry between him and other vagrant bladers from half a mile away, chemistry that was foiled due to bad timing.

Gay men cruise everywhere. It's like breathing. With every breath of polluted oxygen is that lustful espying of a potential fuck. On the freeways, in the supermarkets, in a drive-thru, in the gyms and on the beach. Even sport is an opportunity to cruise. Jogging is not just jogging. Rollerblading is not just that. It's the chance to hunt.

I let him ramble on as I ironed my clothes for a party in Long Beach. Trying not to appear scornful, I threw him a contrived smile or a suspiciously shallow reinforcement at the required pauses in his conversation. He bored me. Where his fantasies of other men once filled me with rage, they now inspired something akin to pity. My mind was far away from his tortured ecstasy. As long as I maintained a safe distance from him, I no longer craved his lust. I was also unable to live vicariously through the attention that he commanded anymore. In some twisted way, being attached to that which others wanted to possess helped me to fill my own void once. Now that was not enough. I was reminded, as he absentmindedly riffled through his black day planner (the one that I had despised with the passion a wife reserved for the other woman), that despite the multitudes that have been inked into it, little nuggets of sexual details to help him remember bracketed beside each name, Richard remained, essentially, alone. Unavailable men, ultimately, were always available.

I wondered when he intended to leave. I wished he would just leave. Or take a shower, which is what I suspected he'd come for before embarking on the second leg of his journey into West Hollywood. I tried, while his description of some boy's muscled torso wafted over my head, to be more tolerant. To remember that he was not the only one caught in a cycle of addiction. I may have managed to outgrow him but that only meant that I'd emerged from Richard's spin. My own patterns were far from completely broken. I was still lying there like an *almost* completely laundered article of clothing, awaiting another cycle in the washer. So I couldn't be so arrogant. I had to be humble.

But, by God, looking at him over my shoulder as he vied for my attention over the jeans I'm steaming – at that same man who once drove me up and down the spires of emotion and now had me fighting impatience – it felt so darn fucking good to be over him.

CHAPTER 49

POST NO BILLS

Certain special moments give you mileage. Having experienced them, one could go forever without another one, gassed up on sheer memory. My night with Bill was such an event. Once I had found a way to suspend all the fears about the leaking condom, I was able to feel bliss, even without knowing when I would see him again. For a couple of days, I didn't even think about calling him, although I thought about him all the time. Whenever the urge to speak with him possessed me, I educed sustenance from the memory.

A few days later, Bill called. "Hey Ali, I hope you remember me," he started to say on the machine before I grabbed the phone. "It's Bill...I love Sade." As if I need that tidbit to remind me. He went on to say that he'd missed me – missed me! – and he couldn't wait to see me again. "You've mesmerized me," he repeated.

"Okay, enough with that. You've gotta find a new word for the day."

"Alright," he said.
"Hypnotized...captivated...fascinated..."

"Wow! What a vocabulary," I said. "Maybe *you* should write the book."

We made plans. He said he was going to clear his schedule so he could come over starting Friday and we could spend the entire weekend together.

"Oh, good!" I giggled. "Then you can fuck me silly again!"

And so the plan was made and in my mind we were a couple; Adrian and Salman and the rest of them could eat shit and die because I'd found my man and it didn't matter one bit that he was a hooker. The unlikelihood of such a pairing, the very inadvisability of it, made it all the more wondrous in my mind. This, I told myself, is how love happens — with the most unlikely soul, when it is unplanned, suddenly and quite irrevocably.

I didn't hear from him for the next few days, but I didn't feel even the slightest need for it. I anticipated Friday when my argosies would come, loaded with the joys I had already started celebrating. Lata's songs of doom and devastation in love were forsaken for those of jubilation: *Na Jaane Kya Hua Jo Tune Chu Liya; Jaise Radha Ne Mala Japi Shyam Ki; Aap Ki Nazro Ne Samja Pyaar Ke Kabil Mujhe*...Those few days became Bollywood fantasies in which Bill, his hands stretched out magnificently and his body arching back under piercing blue skies, sang his declarations of love to me in fluent Hindi; somewhere on that same ice-capped mountain or blooming field, I stole my eyes from him coyly, waiting to reciprocate my love but in Lata's voice, of course.

But Friday came and went. And there was no Bill. I called his number, and it was disconnected.

As the city rushed out to parties or to be with their loved ones, I huddled in bed thinking that something must have happened; he was supposed to be here with me. Our brand of moonlight still poured in from the window, but this time its pearly light only felt like it was excoriating my flesh.

The celebratory music in my soul started to die, and slowly, the poignant, loyal soundtrack returned.

Where are you, Bill?
Where have you gone?

The next night, by which time I could barely breathe, I went in search of him. Adrian, Kitty and even Frankie called and left frolicsome messages, but I didn't call any of them back, letting them assume I was with Bill.

I returned to the same spot where I had first met him, as if by some small miracle, he would be there, under the lamppost, looking cool and collected, and we could begin our courtship all over again. This time, I couldn't even pray. Something in me just couldn't. I no longer had the heart. Or maybe, because prayer was often used as a corrective and employed when something had already come to pass, I was unwilling to admit that I had somehow lost him and had to work at regaining him. As if my yearning for him, the desperate roving of my eyes, my spasmodic breathing wasn't prayer enough.

Bill was nowhere to be found.

His spot stood vacant. Even the lamppost mourned for him, a spotlight missing its star performer. Every once in a while a worker would walk across it, and mercifully, scurry to more obscure spots. As I waited, parked by the curb, some even made eye contact and hovered around the car, but I looked away quickly and faced the boarded building to my right instead, upon which, painted crudely across to discourage anyone from sticking posters and fliers, were the flagrant words Post No Bills.

After about a couple of hours, it was time to leave but I couldn't go just yet. I had to say goodbye or know I would be returning to this spot every night, searching for Bill. Something in my heart told me he would never be coming back. Then my head fell in my face and I just started to cry. No prayers, no words, no thoughts, nothing to accompany the deluge. Just tears.

I don't know how it was possible, but I couldn't remember or imagine missing anyone more than him. Bill had done something different. There had been no deception. He had given me two things: passion, which even Nelson and Richard before him, had provided; and, in the few hours we had spent together, the truth.

For this, Bill deserved, not the anger that came from a broken heart but the appreciation that came from a sad but grateful one.

CHAPTER 50

LABYRINTH OF LOST SOULS

I couldn't go back home, to that empty apartment; it
would only remind me of the love that should have
unfurled through each room that weekend. I made the
fatal error of thinking that if I tried hard enough, I would
be recompensed in someone else's arms or crouched at
someone else's feet. I would do my best, knowing all
along that it was futile, to recreate some of the magic, to
manufacture some rapture with another stranger.   I
needed, like an ailing patient that craves human touch, to
be felt, to be reminded that along with my heart, Bill had
not erased my corporeality as well.

I have been back several times since.

I'd been waiting in line for twenty minutes already. It was
three-fifteen in the morning. No one had been let in since
I arrived, and behind me, the line to get into the Vortex
was getting longer. Some people even arrived, surveyed
the queue of people – restless yet patiently waiting – and
decided to go to another sex club instead. The city was
now littered with them. There were membership wars
going on. Trade in your old membership for one at ours.
Sex clubs had begun to imitate that other gay institution,
gyms; many would argue that business, in the age of
AIDS-enforced sexual repression, ironically, had never
been better.

I was beginning to feel increasingly tired myself,
but convinced that once inside, I'd have no problem
staying up. Besides, Alex, a forty-year-old Italian whose
face was like that of a thirty-year-old, was keeping me
company. Another man Adrian and I had shared at the
Hollywood Spa. When I'd last bumped into him at Axis
in West Hollywood, wearing his signature black tank top,

which he insisted upon sliding off his shoulder like a bra strap, Alex claimed to have given up the Vortex. He had made it sound like a drug. "I'm done with that shit, honey," he said with a look of invincibility. "I have a new boyfriend now, and if he ever catches me going there, honey, he's going to pull a Lorena Bobbit on me!"

But I'd seen him here only the week after, scurrying from room to room, unaware that I'd been watching him without being the least bit surprised. When he'd seen me as he approached the queue, shaking my head and smiling wryly at him, he'd covered his face dramatically, like a vampire shielding off sunlight.

"Whatever happened to you boyfriend?" I asked him, pretending this was the first I'd seen of him lately.

"Oh, honey," he moaned. "That bitch turned out to be an even bigger slut than I've ever been!"

He asked me where Adrian was, as he always did. "She went home. The bitch is getting old, you know what I mean? She gets tired at midnight these days. You, on the other hand, look like you're shedding off the years," I lied. "What's your secret?"

Alex framed his face with open hands, pouted his lips and flashed me a look of contrived sexuality. "Only be seen in the right lighting, honey."

Boosted by my compliment, he danced in his spot to the techno music playing inside, and I wondered if any of us could ever break away from this place. Without having a boyfriend or a lover, that is. Just how long can any of us go without finding that one special person, or at least a functional one, before caving in and falling upon the threshold of where anonymous arms were always ready to touch us and alien tongues eager to bathe us?

At his age, Alex was wearing a black tank top at war with an abnormally developed chest, giving the illusion of having breasts. I'd known him for years but was suddenly surprised that I could know someone so insignificantly for so long. I didn't consider him a friend because we never called or visited one other; but I'd slept with him and even seen him get fucked by a total stranger at a "Suds and Studs" party, where everyone stripped down to their underwear before gamboling neck-high in foam. At one point that night, as I slithered amongst the naked dancing bodies, Alex had reached out and grabbed my wrist for support as he leaned over in a melting of pleasure and pain. So now I considered him an acquaintance, a permanent fixture of the scene; like the bottles, the barstools and the boys, he was always there. I too must have seemed that way to him. All of us passengers on this doomed ark that never seems to find land.

When I finally stood before of the cashier, having waited thirty minutes in line, he informed me that my membership had expired. And I thought, *So, okay, what the hell are you expecting me to do anyway? Don't you realize that most people are practically out of money by the time they get here?* I knew they accepted credit cards and had even added an ATM feature; but I told him in all honesty that I had no idea it was renewal time – it's not like they send you a reminder in the mail – and convinced him to charge me the dues on my next visit.

"Come on, you know I'm good for it. You know I'll be back," I said wearily.

Even he agreed, and with a wink buzzed me into the labyrinth of lost souls.

My jeans hang around my knees. Sandwiched between two men, one of whom I can tell is black from touching his hair, and the other a Caucasian who followed me into this darkest of rooms, I allow myself to be consumed like mauled prey that still quivers with ebbing life. Their hands feel harsh and rending. One rubs his cock between the walls of my ass as another pulls away at my balls so forcibly that it hurts. When I consider cutting out, I think, *but I want to forget. I must forget.* What it is that I'm trying to forget I cannot even remember anymore. All I know is that I want oblivion.

I don't want to walk around tonight and save myself for that special person that everybody else will try to coerce in a dark room. The one who won't put out until half have given up and others have been distracted by someone else. I don't want my hand brushed off by anyone here tonight. And I won't brush anybody's hand off me. I want to tilt my head back and rest it upon any available shoulder. A sculpturesque shoulder, a flaccid shoulder, any shoulder, I don't mind. As they say in Gujarati, *Chattur kagro goo upar bese.* A picky crow ends up perching on shit in the end.

Here in this sightless room with night advancing, my patience for holding out, my demand for perfection, has seeped away. In fact, it is my particularity, my inflexibility, to settle for anybody who didn't fit my rigid image of "the man" that has led me here, to a room marinating in the relentless heat of sweat, semen and shit. It's not until I enter a room like this that I actually realize just how foul human beings can smell. Just how intense and repulsive the aroma of conglomerated sex can be. How even while alive, the tissue of human flesh can emit such a rancid odor of death and rot. The kind of smell exacerbated by the cheap disinfectant, aimed at snuffing it out.

Tonight I want to forget this perfect man that never comes. Or the man who just cannot stay. Tonight I want to be washed in desperation that does not emanate from me but from someone else instead. Let them touch me, let them ravage me, this body that I have only opened up to those I mistakenly assessed as worthy on merit of their appearance alone. And those who may have had more to give but wanted so much more.

The guy behind me asks if I have a condom. I tell him I don't actually want to get fucked. I just want to hear myself say those words. *Fuck me. Fuck me. Please fuck me. Or maybe it's my mind, my heart I want you to fuck so that I can stop thinking for a little while.* But I don't want him to penetrate me, at least not just yet. After futile pleading, and calling me a cockteaser, he continues to slap up against my buttocks and I squeeze my legs together to provide him with as much constriction as I can. Meanwhile, the wetness of a warm tongue flickers over my cock, and soon I'm enveloped in the moist oven of a mouth. Engulfed in the long luxurious lapping of an eager tongue, I implore myself to let go and enjoy the experience of being sucked off. This isn't something I've been able to allow myself. The moment that a man has fallen upon his knees to gorge me has always been my most disappointing moment of sex. I believe in roles and this just wasn't mine.

As the guy behind me starts to grunt away, we draw attention from others. Shapes of bodies close in around us like scavengers hankering for a kill. Everybody wants to join in on a thriving scene. For food. The vultures don't wait. Instead, claws materialize from the dark to partake of the cadaver, and in time, there is barely a part of my body that isn't being tended to by tongues or fingers.

The next time I say "fuck me, fuck me," my words resounding among hisses, groans and garbled murmurs of shock and excitement, the fellow pushes my head to make me fold over and prods forcefully into me. I wiggle myself to elude him, inadvertently pulling myself out from the black boy's mouth also. Irritated, he pulls away from me and says, "Do you want me to fuck you or not? Make up your mind, will you!"

I'm only talking dirty, for Chrissake! Don't you get it? By then, the others have managed to squirm between us by taking advantage of the rift, and I'm separated from him. In what feels like a slow wave of bodies swaying back and forth in the crowded room, I find my mouth pulled toward another mouth and feel fingers digging deep into my bowels. Recoiling from the pain, I yank that hand away from me and begin to decamp. Someone says in my ear, "Hey, piss on me, man." When I don't answer him, he repeats himself more urgently.

"No, I'm not into that."

"Shit," he grunts. "What the hell are you into then?"

I'm into music I want to say ludicrously. *Not the pounding, insufferably meaningless stuff playing right now, but the melodious, swoops and tumbles of a lush score. I'm into kissing forever and forging his face with my fingers and exploring the demons that move him...I want to lay on a bed somewhere and feel his weight upon me, his body fixed into mine, his eyes looking into mine, his hands webbed into mine...*

"Not this," I say. "Not this."

And pulling my pants up, I jostle my way out of the blind room.

The music has gone from my mind. I try hard to listen to the strains of a melody but my brain feels beaten and bare. What I hear now are not the internal, private dulcets of Lata or Doyle but the grating, oppressive cacophony of dance music. With leaded legs I drag myself from room to room, tarrying from immersing myself into any one of the marshes of flesh. I am tired. I want to leave. I want to go home. But a voice within me says, *You've paid ten fucking bucks to get in here, and what do you want to do? Leave all these men here only to go home and masturbate! What the fuck is wrong with you? Any sensible person would latch on to someone here, anyone at all, and at least come first before leaving. Stop your theatrics at once! Stop trying to burden sex with meaning! Find someone, anyone, and come or you'll be sorry! Look around you – able, providing men everywhere! Please stop looking for* him, *for someone like* him, *for someone to be* him.

Bathed in the dim, salacious red light of a corridor lined with booths – some of which are occupied with men who have closed membership to those gaping over swinging doors – I head for the bathroom. Some of these onlookers reach out over the doors, longing to meld into the excluders.   I'm bemused at my mind's reprimanding locution as I walk by them. *Come first before leaving. Come first before leaving,* I keep saying over and over in my mind like a mantra. But I know I don't need someone to rub my cock or to pinch my nipples or to exchange blowjobs to come. I can accomplish that all on my own. What I have been coming here for is something that this place is almost guaranteed *not* to provide and almost always leaves me yearning for more.

Filing behind some six or seven men, I think, at first, that I used to come here after participating in the tedious games at the nightclubs. A kind of delayed recompense. To finally extract, after hours of affectations over cocktails and meaningless conversation, the touch of another human being.   To obliterate everything that waited out there. The absence of love. The rejection from Richard. The distance of family. And even the virus. In time, the freshness of sex's copious availability gave way to deeper urges ebbing within. I now come here for a sense of ecstasy. For the fulfillment of all the yearnings I cannot express. All the feelings I cannot act upon on my own. For the ousting, at least temporarily, of all the sadness and failure of being alone. I come here for the warmth of another human being. The warmth that comes from the embrace of another man as our torsos melt in a sweaty bond. The way two lovers, consumed by their desire to merge in one another, find themselves convoluted in a pleach of sticky limbs. Or for the embrace of a father who enfolds his son. For the chance that something miraculous might happen within these dark mazes and corridors. And when I catch glimpses of this in a couple that is spent and exhausted, slumbered in a twined embrace on a couch, I'm encouraged again to think that such a thing can happen here. Sometimes I sample moments of this elusive warmth with someone, only to never find him here again. It is no wonder then that instead of leaning up against a wall that has been splattered with semen, I'm constantly trying to lead someone to the soiled sofa where we can settle into languid lovemaking instead. Yes, I've come here week after week to educe romance and tenderness from men who might have come for the same but settled for a simple uncomplicated orgasm instead.

In front of me, a young Asian boy is approached by his friend and they chatter away, their eyes constantly appraising those who walk by us as we wait our turn. There are nights when this place is chock-full of Asians. On such nights Adrian has been quick to crassly announce, "Welcome to China. On your way in, please pick up a condom and a pair of chopsticks for your eating pleasure." I miss Adrian and wish he was here with me, but he can no longer stomach this place. Without him by my side there is no one to share acrid humor. No way to ward off thoughts freighted with introspection. Appreciating – with some bitterness – the lithe, bare upper bodies of these Asian boys and their rambunctious excitement, I'm learning that these excursions at the Vortex, these forays into brief ecstasy have another cumulative cost. Even as I continue to reject those who are older, others around me are beginning to look much younger. I have remained in this place like an aging nightclub patron who hasn't settled down and suddenly finds a younger generation has moved in. A fresh haircut and concealer under the eyes can work wonders but nothing can bring back the physical awkwardness, the elflike animation authenticated by youth. The gradual settling of the face, the ease and relaxed gait of being accustomed to one's features, to one's own body, alas, becomes the betraying feature of age.

This place is no longer a refuge. The absence of love won't go away. The distance of family won't go away. The virus won't go away. They are all out there like hoodlums waiting to spring on me from the dark and I am tired of making temporary escapes only to return to their fear. And Bill, dear Bill, you never come back. Perhaps I should have phased out of here too.

I am tired. I want to go home. But first I will go to the bathroom. With all the money they make in this place, why can't they provide us with more bathrooms? How could anyone justify one bathroom for all the men foraging in this place? Perhaps I should just leave and piss by the car. But then Alex comes by to tip me off about some obnoxious guy begging to be pissed on. "Ay, what does she think this is? Basic Plumbing? I told her, honey, this girl's got a vagina and she needs to squat on a toilet to tinkle!" He tells me that he's just about ready to leave but will do one last round to look for some Mexican guy who had fucked him here once before, leaving him unable to walk for a week.

"How did you explain that to your boyfriend?"

"Oh, hemorrhoid," he says casually and darts off behind a group of new arrivals.

There are still four people ahead of me in line. None of them interest me. At least not here in the light. The Asian boy has defected from the line to pursue the same group of men that Alex went after. Disappearing around the corner and in the direction of a couple of little less popular rooms on the second floor, I spot someone who arouses my interest. I get more impatient. Then a little desperate. Finding it increasingly difficult to keep still, I decide to follow this guy up the staircase. Perhaps I'll just bend over and get fucked like Alex. I'll let him fuck all the wearisome insights out from me. Find this guy and see if he's willing to do what was being offered to me only minutes ago. Forget romance. Forget tenderness. Some brutal physical aggression might just be the trick to snapping out of it.

I pick the room on my right. Upon entering it I face a TV monitor that bombards a porno at the three people in the room. There is the guy I followed up here, a twenty-something brunette, standing in a corner with his muscled arms folded across his chest and his eyes transfixed on what, at such close range, looks like the core of a rotund peach being pummeled. And there is a black guy slumped on a couch on my left, his jeans around his ankles, his body slender compared to the astonishing size of his cock, curving upward to him like an obedient pet responding needily to his fondling.

There is too much space in this room. It's paralyzing. A single step toward either one of them will feel like a pirouette across the room. For a little while all three of us remain locked in our positions. And then, with a supreme effort I surrender the comfort of leaning against the wooden wall, looking at the brunette, thinking, what the hell, what's the worst that can happen? For a second my eyes meet his and my intention registers in them. As if to respond to my question, he throws me a mean expression that withers me completely, as if to say, don't even think about it. Then, without as much as a second glance, he walks out of the room, establishing his disinterest in both my ardor and the size of the other boy's cock. He can live without either one of us.

Dejected, my head falls to the ground and I sigh gently. When I look up, the black boy has sunk deeper into the sofa so that his torso is extended further out and his cock rises from him magnificently. He stares at me as if to say, "Isn't this what you came here for? Look at it! I know it's probably the biggest cock you'll ever see. I've been told that all my life and now I'm letting you touch it. He languorously runs his hand up and down its glistening shaft, his eyes fixed upon my gaping face. I hesitate only for a moment and then walk over to him and reach out to hold it with a kind of reverence etched upon my face. His hands fall away, allowing me complete autonomy. And then, just as I am about to kneel down between his parted thighs to offer worship, to take it with both my hands and rub it against my face and suckle him in my mouth, he says, "Hey, you wanna' piss on me?"

Jolted, I straighten up and let go. He looks up at me and sighs disappointedly. With his head crooked to the side and hunched shoulders, he says, "C'mon, man! C'mon!"

A fleeting silence. Even the synthetic sexual sounds of the porno are unheard. I remain rooted to my spot, feeling the pressure in my abdomen, my eyes locked into his, my body paused over him. A welling tide wars within the walls of my stomach. "Come on, man, just do it!" he says, and closing his eyes, rests his head back and starts to rub himself eagerly. Slowly, I unbelt myself. I position myself over him, between his parted thighs, his knees locking against mine. At the moment I'm poised over him, I'm removed from myself. I pretend that this is not happening to me. It's not me here, hanging over this man's naked body, preparing to urinate over him. Not me, who came here for tenderness and paternal embraces and chance occurrences of love. When that doesn't help, I close my eyes and try to block out his face with the parted lips and the tensed body squirming in anticipation under me. *Concentrate. Concentrate. You can do this, just like the urinal. Piss on the motherfucker. Piss on him! Piss on him and you'll be pissing on all the others. Piss on him!*

I can feel him rocking as he beats off, his knees knocking against me, his quivering voice emboldening me to defile him. *I can do this...I can do this...*In a paroxysm of images, the eternal wait for the bathroom goes through my mind. Then Richard's face is dredged up from some inner dungeon. His unforgettable eyes, the bed of chest hair in which I had loved to bury my face, and which, he often insensitively bragged, his tricks liked to gnaw at while he fucked them. And Adrian's legs frame Nelson's shoulders as he enters him and their mouths find each other, the kisses I was denied being lavished on him. And Bill. Beautiful bigoted Bill who had straddled over my twisting back, shaking in his climb towards an orgasm repeating *I'm going to fuck you silly...I'm going to fuck you silly... Don't fall in love with me...*And Dad, who had held me in the parking lot, his "sunny boy," in his arms, saying, "I'll be coming back soon. Look after your mother. Look after you mother while I'm gone," a fatalistic promise from someone who would be snuffed out only hours from then. The feeling that stirs within my groin is tantamount to wanting to subject them to the same. To mounting them and fucking them up the ass, just as I've longed for them to fuck me. To give each of them the alloyed, anguished fracas of unfulfilled love and promise, just as each of them have given me. I'm filled with a strength derived from pure, unadulterated vengeance. And then, within a minute of this invocation of emotional betrayals, the hot urine gushes forth from me and splashes over this boy's dark skin as he beats himself frantically. I throw my head back, groaning in relief, my waist pushed forward and swaying from side to side until all of him is covered with me.

When I open my eyes, the boy is bathed in piss and sperm. On his face is an ecstasy that is both repugnant and enviable. His hands smear our discharge over his chest like sacramental balm. Life source and waste. I button myself up quickly. He thanks me and slowly starts to reach out for me, but I back away and practically run out of the room and down the stairs. I've got to get out of here. Dear God, what am I doing? What have I done?

I storm past others swishing mouthwash in the lobby, past those purchasing snacks from the vending machine and those checking in their belongings. I can feel the bile rising within me steadily and think I'm going to retch. I throw the door open, pushing a bystander out of my way as he emits curses, and explode into the open air, into the parking lot and all the way onto the street.

Away from that place where everything that is different between animal and human has been diminished.

CHAPTER 51

SUNDAYS

Sometimes I think that the reason I stay out so late on Saturday nights is to eradicate Sundays altogether. Whenever I awake on a late Sunday afternoon, at the tail end of what the world over has always known as a traditional family day, I find myself slightly grateful that I've been spared from the dosages of solitude I'm being force-fed. There were the Sundays in Mombasa at the drive-in, which had been the highlight of my youth. And there are the Sundays of my adult life, when all I have to look forward to, if I decide not to turn back and reenter a bar for more carousing at a beer bust, is the stark emptiness of a young man who has woken up alone and has therefore made no progress.

It's about ten-thirty in the morning as I look out of my window and find myself confronting silence. Outside, I see the pot-bellied neighbor who had once called me a "faggot" for refusing to keep my bass down, tending to our garden with the dedication and serenity of a monk. This, I tell myself, cradling a warm cup of coffee in my hands, is what I've been avoiding for so long. The chance to rest, to free myself from the two lives of work and play, to examine my soul. To seek some kind of solution, some new resolve, to a youth that feels unnaturally stretched under a myriad of lights and limbs. But nothing comes. Instead I continue to see my obese neighbor, scratching his hairy belly as he pipes water out onto the garden, each flower, each leaf, in supplication to his nurturing.

One of my neighbors had told me about how Mr. Klaus' wife had left him with custody of one of their sons after eleven years of enduring his cantankerous personality. The nurturing he was apparently unable to bestow on other human beings, I think, he has found a way to cascade into his flowers. And as much as everyone in the apartment complex dislikes him for his inability to co-exist – he's also been known to pull the plug out on laundry cycles because they're too noisy after 9 P.M. – all of us appreciate him for the beauty his gardening adds to our world.

There is just this one isolated patch, right outside of my door, which has always remained barren. Nothing seems to thrive there. I'm convinced that this is deliberate on his part because out of all the people in this building, he seems to be the only one that resents me. Once, on the rare occasion that I did greet him and we began to talk about the roses that were blooming, he seized the opportunity to point out the barren patch and grumbled, "That's because of all your friends who keep us up till two in the morning. They've been stampeding in there and throwing all kinds of trash until they've killed everything!"

As I continue to watch, unbeknownst to him, I think about his son, the one who has remained with him, the one who often waters the gardens bare-chested, much to the delight of all my friends, and who appears mired with introversion and pain. This is the tenet of all love stories, I tell myself. That they begin, and have their foundation in people and events long before one appear on the scene. I think of my mother and father, of my grandparents, all of them links in a chain of atrocities committed in the name of love. That has been my legacy, I think. And this is where it ends, with me, a man who no longer possesses the youthful heart which made the events of the last decade thrilling, and instead of having evolved, instead of having moved closer to a promising future, has only grown older. The family, or at least those whom I can acknowledge as family, are gradually disappearing. Now there is only my aunt and my uncle and Mummy. And in time, even they, one by one, will begin to drop off, leaving only me in the end. This is what Mummy warned me of, I thought. Of Sundays.

Damien, my neighbor's son appears in the picture. No, he isn't wearing a shirt this time either. Father and son stand next to one another as he points out to his son the patch of flowers that have been infested and need insecticide. I have never once seen them touch or even smile at one another. But as they stand there, side by side, looking down at the single withering rose plant, there is an undeniable sense of communion between them. The last thirty years of my life have brought me here to this moment. To the sight of an emotionally alienated father and son connecting through an infested rose bush, the morning after I urinated all over some guy as vengeance against the men who alienated me.

Where are these men now? What must they be doing? Richard, who continues to call me occasionally, and whom I am quick to turn away from when I feel myself softening, is still hurtling between various men, unable to give of himself and quick to point out how they have all left him disillusioned. Bill, who knows? For his sake, I hope he's surfing somewhere in Malibu, far from the intimidating prospect of having to ice-sculpt herons and fish, and looking out from the waters onto a sun deck where his provider is petting his dog. Nelson, whom I run into every now and then, has gotten older, and it's become easier to smile at him and touch his cheek and wish him well with whoever is perched on his arm, throwing nettled glances at me. He asks me about Adrian every time I see him, and I tell him, without any discomfort, that he's doing okay and that yes, we are still very much friends. Salman, I know from running into his lesbian roommate Meenaz, has moved back in with his family, thus completing his phylogeny into the ideal heir and extender of the Surani lineage.

When I'm about to turn away from the window, Damien turns toward me as his father walks away. For a moment it seems I'm caught in his gaze, but then I remember that light travels to the eye and that he isn't able to see me. It just feels like he can. I remain, marveling at his strong, youthful body, the chiseled, determined face which, I suspect, belies his vulnerability, and pretend that defying the laws of physics, we are in fact looking steadfastly into each other's eyes. Then, just as casually, he turns away as if quietly sensing me; and when he has sauntered away, I'm left looking out at an erratic gardener's vision again.

The stirring of desire within me brings an imperceptible smile to my face. That my imagination has not been slaughtered by life fills me with gratitude. I was footsteps away from being committed to bitterness. Bitterness, which attaches itself like an unshakable tumor. Bitterness, which kills desire and dries up all the fuel for living. I am grateful for the space between these two states. That's not how I want to end up. Alone, perhaps, but not bitter. Never bitter. I want to continue to feel desire because I want to continue to live.

I drink the rest of my coffee, walk over to my briefcase and reach into it for a mailer that was sent to me from the *Saath* center. Despite my complete disassociation from them, I have remained, as people disinterested or dead often do on their mailing list, and continue to receive occasional invitations to meetings and workshops. Shortly after my resignation, a new, vibrant young woman who had just emigrated from India took over the post of the South Asian coordinator. I unfold the flier from the envelope, noticing again, that my last name, Khosla, is still spelled wrong. Ali S. Khoshla. They will be gathering at the junction of Santa Monica and Sunset Boulevards in Silver Lake in about an hour to perform free HIV testing. I fold the flier back up, stuff it in the back pocket of my jeans and walk out of my apartment, cell phone in tow.

Outside, I find Mr. Klaus looking down at the barren patch, shaking his head, hands planted on his waist.

"We found out what was killing your flowers," he says without looking up at me. "That damn lady upstairs has been dumping cleaning detergent in here."

Taken by surprise, because for once I'm not evil incarnate in his eyes, I stammer, "Oh, well, that's completely...not right."

"No, it certainly isn't," he says. "I'm going to have a talk with her about this." He points to the freshly planted shoots in the moist soil. "Soon we'll have this part looking as good as the rest."

"Thank you," I say and lock my door. "The garden looks really great."

"Damien," he says, nodding his head. "Damien's being working really hard on all this."

"You must be very proud of him then."

"Yes. I must say I'm very impressed with him."

Just when I think a little breakthrough in communication has occurred and I begin to walk away, Mr. Klaus launches into a complaint about the music last night – as if he is unable to let any conversation end on a pleasant note. But this time, instead of rolling my eyes at him or lashing back, I simply continue walking. I'm thinking of my name spelt erroneously on the invitation, and I smile to think that there are advantages to an unkempt mailing list.

Sometimes they come back.

GLOSSARY

Many of the words in this glossary belong to more than one dialect or language, as is typical when cultures assimilate. Some words, although attributed to a specific language, are only used regionally and remain largely unrecognized in the official directory of the language. In some cases, regional peoples develop entirely new words or phrases; these have been left unattributed to a specific background.

Aap ki nazro ne samja pyaar ke kabil mujhe (HINDI): your eyes have considered me worthy of love; song from Bollywood film *Anpadh;* sung by Lata Mangeshkar.

Achari (SWAHILI): any type of relish.

Aga Khan: philanthropist and religious leader of the Shi'i Imami Ismaili Muslims; presently the forty-ninth direct descendent of the Prophet Muhammad.

Apsara: a supernatural female being in Hindu mythology who can take you to your doom is she desires.

Attars (URDU): perfumes.

Au toke hero laafo mar-ni (KUTCHI): I will give you such a slap/beating

Banda (SWAHILI): kiosk or shack.

Bankra (KUTCHI): benches.

Bapa (KUTCHI): grandpa.

Bechari (HINDI): poor thing.

Be-sharam (HINDI): shameless.

Beta (HINDI): son

Bhagat (KUTCHI): devotee

Bhajias: potato fritters

Bhashan (HINDI): lecture

Bhuri-Bhuri (KUTCHI): used to describe someone with light-colored eyes; like saying someone is fair.

Bohora: Muslim Shi'i sect.

Booblas (KUTCHI): slang, boobs.

Bwana (SWAHILI): brother.

Chadis (HINDI): knickers.

Chai: Spiced Indian tea.

Chapati: Indian flat what bread similar to a tortilla.

Char (KUTCHI): itch.

Chodu (KUTCHI): fucker.

Chokdi (GUJARATI): girl.

Chattur kagro goo upar bese (GUJARATI ADAGE): a picky crow ends up perching on shit in the end.

Dam maro dam mit jaye gaam (HINDI): take a puff and your sorrow will be erased; song from Bollywood film, *Hare Rama Hare Krishna*, sung by Asha Bhosle.

Dhanni (KUTCHI): husband.

Dhorias (KUTCHI): whites.

Dhorio (KUTCHI): white male.

Dhorki (KUTCHI): white female.

Diwali: Hindu celebration; the festival of lights for Ram's return to Ayodhya after years in exile.

Doodh-malai: desert made with milk and cream.

D'ua (URDU): prayer.

Fagia (SWAHILI): broomstick.

Gandu (HINDI): faggot.

Gangha (SWAHILI): witchcraft.

Gand (KUTCHI): ass.

Geli-danda: a game involving a piece of wood, sharpened at both ends, and propelled by the use of a wooden bat; its rules resemble that of cricket.

Golo (KUTCHI): black.

Goras (HINDI): whites.

Gujarati: language of Gujarat, India.

Ghungroos: ankle bells.

Ginans: religious hymns.

Halwa: sweetmeat invented in 1750 by the ruler of Multan after whom it was named.

Han, han: yes, yes

Haram zade (HINDI): bastard.

Haya: okay.

Hazar Imam: the present Imam or spiritual leader of the Ismailis.

Hushyar (KUTCHI): clever.

Ismailis: Shi'i Muslim sect that believes the Prophet Muhammad was succeeded by a uninterrupted chain of Imams.

Jaise Radha ne mala japi Shyam ki: just as Radha wove Shyam's garland; based on Hindu mythology's love legend of Radha and Krishna; song from the Bollywood film, *Tere Mere Sapne*, sung by Lata Mangeshkar.

Jamat Khanna (KUTCHI): mosque or prayer house for the Ismailis.

Kaunda suits: a two-piece men's suit named after Kenneth Kaunda, Zambia's former president.

Khabar ayi neh (KUTCHI): you know, right?

Keemat (HINDI): value.

Khatar-naakh (HINDI): dangerous.

Khima chapatis: Mombasa cuisine; pan-fried bread stuffed with eggs and spiced ground beef.

Khoji (KUTCHI): female Ismaili.

Khudda (KUTCHI/URDU): God.

Kitenges: traditional and colorful African clothing made of cotton.

Kutchi: language from Kutch region in Gujarat state of India.

Kutri sali (KUTCHI): damn bitch.

Lunchamos (SPANISH): let's lunch.

Mabuyus: morsels of baobab fruit that are cooked in sugar and dyed red.

Machar-dani (KUTCHI): mosquito net.

Maghenis (KUTCHI): guests.

Maghrab/maghrib (URDU): dusk.

Makonde: an African people who lived in the Savannah highlands of East Africa.

Malayas (SWAHILI): prostitutes.

Mama kuba (SWAHILI): matriarch or grandmother.

Manzil (HINDI): destination.

Marungi: an African plant eaten raw; a stimulant.

Mataji (HINDI): mother.

Matha-kuti (KUTCHI): fuss; headache.

Mein azaad hoon (HINDI): I am free.

Meri beti kitni akalmand hai (HINDI): my daughter is so intelligent.

Mi culo esta ardiendo (SPANISH): my ass is burning.

Mishkake (SWAHILI): barbecued meat.

Mithais: Indian desert.
Monthar: Indian sweetmeat.

Mowla (URDU): Lord.

Mujrah: traditional Indian dance popularized by the courtesans.

Muindis (SWAHILI): Indians.

Mukhi (KUTCHI): the chief (male) religious priest in the Ismaili community.

Mungu (SWAHILI): God.

Mzungus (SWAHILI): whites.

Na Jaane Kya Hua Jo Tune Chu Liya (HINDI): I don't what happened now that you've touched me; song from Bollywood film *Dard*, sung by Lata Mangeshkar.

Nandhi: food auction after evening prayers, the proceeds of which go to the Ismaili community.

Nankhatais: butter cookies.

Paisa: money.

Pakeezah (URDU): title of a Bollywood film; also means pure.

Paki (KUTCHI): complete or firm.

Panchaat (KUTCHI): gossip.

Parorie: prayer from 3:30 AM to 5:30 AM for Ismailis.

Pata nahin kahan se ajate hain (HINDI): I don't know where they come from.

Piya tu aab to aaja (HINDI): lover, please come to me now; song from Bollywood film, *Caravan,* sung by Asha Bhosle.

Pumbafus (SWAHILI): stupid.

Rani Mata (HINDI): queen mother.

Rasra: traditional Gujarati folk dance.

Sadhris (KUTCHI): mats.

Sagaai: engagement.

Satado: dedicating a week's worth of prayers to a specific calamity or cause in the Ismaili community.

Sati (HINDI): ancient Hindu practice where a widow immolates herself on her husband's funeral pyre.

Shairis (HINDI): poems.

Sheesha ho ya dil ho, akhir toot jata hai (HINDI): whether it's a heart or a glass, eventually it breaks; song from Bollywood film *Ashaa.* sung by Lata Mangeshkar.

Shogas (KUTCHI): faggots.

Silsila (HINDI): title of a Bollywood film; also means chain of events.

Taqat (KUTCHI): seat or throne of God.

Tasbih (URDU): rosary.

Taturi (KUTCHI): penis.

Thapar (HINDI): slap.

Tun mari waat sambhar (GUJARATI): listen to what I'm saying.

Uhuru (SWAHILI): independence.

Umbwas (SWAHILI): dogs.

Utsav (SANSKRIT): festival.

Vashiah (HINDI): prostitute.

Wah-wah (HINDI): praise, bravo.

Yaar (HINDI): friend.

Yeh duniya, yeh mehfil, mere kaam ki nahin
(HINDI): this world, this gathering is of no use to me;
song from Bollywood film, *Heer Ranjha,* sung by
Mohammed Rafi.

Yeh kya jage hain, doston (HINDI): what is this place,
friends? Song from Bollywood film, *Umrao Jaan,* sung by
Asha Bhosle.

A

HE MARKED THE END of even a fleeting affair with a ritual of personal destruction. Some punish plastic, others gorge on food to fill the infinite void left by love, the hope of it, but he needed to raze something, to actually remove something from him, his realm.

Just as an amputated arm continues to inflict phantom pain, so too the fading of something as precious as a feeling for another must be marked by a corporeal act of obliteration, no matter how small.

Sometimes this took the shape of something as inconsequential as the breaking of a cocktail glass, seemingly accidental as he poured into it a shot of warm, unpalatable vodka at the end of a bitter night and before climbing into bed without praise or gratitude for a God that had deprived him yet again.

At other times, he cut myself as he was slicing the onion into slivers for his breakfast omelet, and his eyes would brim with tears so that it looked like the rivulet of blood, red enough to paint lips or the parting of a bride's head, was drowning the whole world in scarlet.

Then there were cruder nights, nights when he would swallow life whole, like a man ravenous for something so specific, that its dearth had driven him into an astounding and insatiable binge for all else, and in the process, suffocate all agonies in the cacophonies of carousal at the bars and nightclubs of West Hollywood where vulnerability guised itself in arrogance and those that were still foolish enough to hope for a different outcome and linger through the changing guard of youthful faces, had learned how to smile and mask any disenchantment with expertise.

At the end of such nights, he found himself kneeling, not repentant in prayer or ready to take another man into his mouth, but over the cold, porcelain rim of a toilet, regurgitating not only the poisons of life but also the toxicity of what he had thought of as love.

A. changed this. On their last night together, A. reminded him that they had a deal, not so much with words but with that magnificent tilt of his head as he touched his mouth and looked into his eyes with so much pain in his own. It was an impotent gesture, one that could rescind nothing but conceal none of the longing he felt.

He wanted A. to stay as much as he wanted to see him go. If an impending disaster cannot be diverted, then it was better that it came to pass so that he could go about the business of rebuilding. The end was near and he grew anxious more than fearful.

So he responded – with the same tacit though awkward jerking of his head, letting his eyes wander from A. while he was still where he could be seen, touched, felt that – Yes, we had a deal and now you must go to that other desert, one filled with palms and mosques and burning resin instead of ours with the concrete snake and smog and me. You must go to a wife waiting to bear you children so that I can be quickly reassigned to a world of bars and new men and freedom.

You will be grounded by your commitments. I will be suffocated by my freedom. You must go. Look – but only ahead – not at me to change your mind.

But if A. stayed, it had to be his decision. Disowned by kin and country, he would never be able to go back. The land of the free would imprison him for good. Love came at a cost. It was not free and it didn't, contrary to baroque, romantic notions, multiply inherently. It had to be reallocated, detoured, compensated for. No such thing as love without casualties.

He cradled A. into his arms and stayed awake through most of the night, watching him sleep, running his hand over his head, ministering gentle kisses not as a lover would another but as a father would his child. For the last month they had stopped making love, having decided it was better for bodies to be prised apart before the heart would have to follow suite.

Sometime in the night he found himself ensconced by A. and he let himself be sheltered and warmed, terrified of the breadth of the bed, already feeling the space A. would leave behind on it. *Let me know more of this, he thought. Hold on to the way we are before I know anything else.*

Winter had come early and the sky wept, drenching the parched city with its waters and promising to paralyze the runaway and the winged creature that would take A. away to the ends of the earth. They were rooted in the middle of the terminal, surrounded by so much luggage, by A's suspecting friends around whom they could not steal the intimacy that had unfurled between them for a year now. And he thought, *How can they not see? We, our emotions, are like an ancient tree in the midst of all this bustle; our roots thick and gnarled like the legs of a giant wooden spider about to be uprooted. Will the ground not shake? Maybe they will, but like us, they too will hold equilibrium, not speak.*

As he watched the distance between them grow, first as A. walked through the boarding gate as if entering a portal to the afterlife – a life without him – and then, as the plane surmounted nature's wrath and pulled A. into the stony sky, he could think only of life's cruel irony: That somewhere at the end of his lover's journey was someone waiting breathlessly; that a parting must take place at one end so that a welcoming could take place at another. This must be what Becket meant when he talked about the constant quality of tears, how for each one who begins to weep, somewhere else, another stops.

He entered not just a house that screamed its silence at him, but also a life he thought he had deflected.

Glasses waited to be shattered, knives glinted along serrated edges, memories remained trapped and muffled behind glass frames. But now that the one true love of his life had left, he did nothing because no conceivable act could express the gravity of his grief. Nothing could exorcise it. He could not bleed A. out of him like a humor or cut him out from the marrow of his being.

Every act of love and the cruelty inherent in it would remain like the fingerprints on a mirror, imperceptible to most but always there, reminding him of being touched.

He would observe no ritual this time; do nothing to bring closure. Perhaps the world doesn't end cataclysmically, it dies with a whimper.

He would throw himself into life once again, yes, and soon, the features that he had started to see as his own would fade into a sea of other faces unless he looked into old pictures; the sound of that voice too would become warbled by new voices, thank God, so that their promises would no longer even echo in the air around him; and although he would always remember how comforted he felt enveloped in A's arms, surely he would also forget just how warm the skin felt against his own, as if burning from somewhere within.

A was first published in *Love, West Hollywood* (2008) by Alyson.

30735269R10194

Made in the USA
Lexington, KY
17 March 2014